Immurement

Book One

Norma Hinkens

Published by Dunecadia Publishing, California

ISBN 978-0-9966248-0-0 (ebook)
ISBN 978-0-9966248-1-7 (print)

For my children who never stopped believing.

Special thanks to my critique partners Jeanene and Maureen.

Author's Note

Parts of this novel are set in Idaho. I have taken liberties with the geography of that state, including names of places.

Immurement:: the state of being imprisoned, entombed, confined in an enclosed space.

A heavy weight of hours has chained and bowed
One too like thee: tameless and swift and proud.
Percy Bysshe Shelley

Chapter 1

The sun's always two fingerbreadths or higher above the Sawtooth peaks when the Sweepers come. Never at night. I swipe a strand of long hair from my eyes and throw a nervous glance at the horizon. The scrawny cow I'm guarding has all but given up flipping its tail at the droning swarms itching for a carcass. Time to leave it to its fate.

I reach for my hunting pack, and freeze. A muffled crackling sound—too heavy for a rabbit, too light to be the cow keeling over. I hold my breath as I grab my gun and motion to my collie, Tucker, to drop beside me. My heart clatters like a wooden rollercoaster as I pan the charred hillside, my trigger finger tight on the safety. Dead trees poke up like broomsticks all around me. There's nowhere to hide, but I'm troubled by the feeling I'm being watched. I skim the canyon again, my vision blurring in the blinding sun. A flicker of movement to my left. I suck in my breath. For one elasticized moment, I think they've come for me.

"Ba-boom!" My eighteen-year-old brother, Owen, presses a finger to my temple and flops his lanky frame down beside me. He slides his pack from his shoulders and rakes a hand through his wavy, black hair. "You just died, Derry Connolly." His lips curl with satisfaction as he reaches over and scratches Tucker's head.

I take a few uneven breaths, my heartbeat stair-stepping back down from the wild ride it took me on. Ordinarily, I revel in our game of stealth, but this time Owen has unnerved me. Just last week the Sweepers extracted a kid from the camp five miles north of here.

"You zoned out again." Owen throws me the disapproving look he's perfected since Ma died, the one where he flattens his brows and squares his jaw in perfect alignment.

I shrug. "It's not exactly riveting stuff watching zombie horseflies sucking on the last of our steak." I study the stitching on his pack, reluctant to meet his gaze. Everyone's on edge since the last sweep, and I swore I'd stay alert if I took a shift up top.

"This isn't a game, Derry. I was on you before you even flinched. I swear, you turn sixteen and you become some ditzy girl I don't even know. It'll get you killed." Owen knuckles me in the shoulder to get my attention. "Hey! Are you listening to me? They can dart you from five hundred feet and you'll never know what hit you. Like Sam."

I roll my eyes, and jerk my shoulder out from under his expert fist. "Quit acting like my security detail. I can take care of myself."

"None of us can. Not anymore." Owen scowls. "The sweeps are too efficient."

I clench my lips in a tight line. I can't argue with that. The Sweepers' noiseless ships hover over the canyons on some kind of electromagnetic suspension system. Eerily silent. Not even a vibration signals they're coming for you.

In our bunker system deep in the Sawtooth Forest, there are twenty-three of us left, split between eight separate bunkers connected by a shared tunnel—an underground beehive community of sorts. No one ventures up top after dawn unless they're logged out on assignment. And never the clan women, which is why I have no real friends among them. They won't take chances. But, I can't live squirreled beneath the dirt. I need to know the sun still rises. How else can I be sure the world hasn't ended a second time?

Owen pulls out half a fried rabbit from his pack. "Gimme your knife."

"Why? Where's yours at?" I eye him suspiciously. "Have you been gambling again?"

He shrugs. "What's it matter?"

"They'll kick us out if you're caught. They're already looking for any excuse to get rid of Da."

Gambling was outlawed after an Undergrounder was stabbed to death in a fight over a lost wager. Trafficking in weapons is illegal too. The camps all have numerical codes on their possessions now, but stuff still trades hands. And Owen's a master hustler.

He gestures impatiently for my knife. I toss it to him and watch him carve a piece of meat. He's good at it—he can whittle on anything. He's promised to make me an antler handle for my knife, same as his, soon as I spot him a stag. Which could take forever. What's left of the big game has retreated deep into the Wilderness of No Return. There's nothing out here for them to eat. Even the grass is down to a fried stubble.

"You should be sleeping," Owen says, through a mouthful of rabbit. "You're on watch tonight."

"Waste of time." I arch my brows at him. "When do Sweepers ever come after sundown? Prat just makes stuff up for us to do so we don't go rabid down under."

Owen lets out a satisfying snort of laughter, and I allow myself a smug grin. We share a warranted disdain for all things Prat a.k.a. Prentice Carter. We call him Prent to his face, but Prat behind his back. I don't feel too bad about it. I'd take either one over Prentice. Prat only made bunker chief because he said he knew how to manage people. Turns out he spent a summer stocking shelves for his parents—wealthy entrepreneurs who were overseas when the earth's core overheated. I think Owen should run the bunker, but his pedigree isn't up to par, our father being the camp drunk and all.

Tucker licks his lips and whines for a piece of rabbit. I ruffle the back of his neck to let him know I'm on it. "I couldn't sleep in the bunker anyway," I say with an exaggerated sigh. "Da was singing again."

"So?" Owen stops chewing and throws me an incredulous look. "You've been falling asleep to drunken karaoke your whole life."

I laugh. "Not my whole life." I swipe the rabbit from his hand and tear off a chunk for Tucker. Owen's strong, with a grip of steel, but I've always been quicker on the draw. "Ma used to sing to us," I remind him. I swallow and stare out over the disfigured hills, pine branches radiating out from stumps like fried arteries. It's been six years. Some days I forget what she looked like, but I can still hear the lilt in her voice when she sang.

She died the day the earth's core overheated, or the *meltdown* as we call it nowadays. Me, Da, and Owen were fishing up at Steelhead Lake—Da was mostly popping beer cans—when the water began to heave. A tidal wave built in the lurching lake, and we scrambled to higher ground and huddled together, watching helplessly as a fireball the size of a football field ripped through Shoshane City. Molten rock pushed miles of asphalt sky-high forming blacktop mache mountains. Strip malls exploded like piñatas, buildings shot hundreds of feet into the air like gigantic stomp rockets. Da says toxic ash clouds took out the survivors. All hell broke loose after a ring of volcanos around the globe erupted and the sovereign leader issued a thermal radiation warning. That was the last we heard from him. And Ma. I miss her gentle spirit. There's nothing gentle about the world anymore.

I liked how she used to pull my hair back from my forehead with her soft hands. "Makes your green eyes stand out," she'd say, tilting her head to one side. "Now everyone can see those butterfly leg lashes resting on that milky skin."

Half the time I live in my memories. What we're doing now isn't really living.

"Your hair needs cutting," Owen grumbles. "You look like a matted mountain goat."

I jolt upright and glare at him. "Jakob likes it long," I say, shoving what remains of my loosened braid inside my collar.

Owen slings his arm around my shoulder and leans his forehead against mine. "Somebody got a bunker boyfriend?"

I dig an elbow in his ribs and he makes a clumsy move to pin my arms. I grab him by the neck and topple him, and we roll around, jostling for control, until we're too weak from laughing to go at it anymore. I like it when he's just being my brother, but for the most part he's forgotten how.

If it weren't for Jakob Miller, life in the bunkers would be unbearable. I can talk to him about anything and everything, even Ma dying, and he doesn't tell me dumb stuff like *Ma's in a better place*, or *we're the lucky ones.* For that, I can forgive him the goofy overalls and trucker cap he walks around in. Not a hot look, even by bunker standards, but he makes me feel safe, and maybe that's more important now than anything else.

It's against the rules of Jakob's clan for women to cut their hair. His family are Septite homesteaders who moved off grid decades ago when the world government came into existence and the first sovereign leader was elected. As far as the Septites are concerned, the tribulation has begun. Which is odd because they still spend their days making furniture that will outlast any of us. They call themselves Separatists, but the rest of us shortened it to Septites, which bugs them no end.

Jakob hasn't told them we hang out. He says it would be one woe too many for them right now, whatever that means, so we meet in secret in an alcove at the far end of the main connecter tunnel, well beyond the last bunker—too dark and damp for prying eyes to bother us. Mostly we do battle over pawns and castles on a chipped chess set in the tawny glow of a flashlight jammed upright in the hard-packed dirt floor. *Mostly.* I can't say we've never held each other close, hearts beating as one, or that our lips haven't brushed a time or two in the dark. Jakob says if his father ever happens upon us there together, we'd be wishing a Sweeper found us instead.

I toss Owen the half-eaten rabbit. "Do you think we could catch one?"

"What? Another rabbit to fatten up your bony butt?"

I wipe my hands on my shirt. "A Sweeper."

He shoots me a warning look. "Don't go getting any stupid ideas."

I fiddle with the rear sight on my Remington. I know he's trying to protect me because Ma would want him to, but it feels like he's always bullying me into submission since she died. "It's not stupid to want to know what we're hiding from."

Owen frowns as he chooses his words. "Predators. That's all you need to know."

"I don't want to live in a gopher hole the rest of my life. Don't you want to be free again? We should quit running and fight back."

Owen widens his eyes at me and swallows a bite of rabbit. He wipes the back of his hand across his mouth as if he's processing the thought. "They never get out of their ships."

"They must sometimes."

"Forget it, Derry."

"There has to be a way to—"

"There isn't." He chucks a bone at Tucker who snaps it out of the air in one fluid streak of fur. "Let it go."

I stare at Owen defiantly. "You think I'm a hazard up top, but Sam asked for it. He was goofing off, skimming rocks. They sucked him right in before he—"

Owen turns toward me, his dark eyes murky like stagnant pools. "How do *you* know that?"

I study him for an agonizing moment, regretting my decision before the words leave my lips. "Because, I was there."

Chapter 2

Owen grabs me by the collar of my jacket and yanks me toward him. "Are you messing with me, or is this for real?"

I blink, calculating the risks of coming clean. I've never seen my brother's eyes flash like this before. Tucker gets up and pads around, sniffing the air like he does when he detects uncertainty.

My pulse thuds in the back of my throat. If I lie to Owen now, I'll never get the answers I want—like what he was doing with Sam that day, and why he's been sneaking off to other camps. I've had enough of his secrets. I want to know what's going on. "I followed you," I say in a choked whisper. Tucker brushes up against me and I sink my trembling fingers into the thick fur on the back of his neck.

Owen stares at me for the longest time. "You shouldn't have done that."

I fold my arms in front of me, bolstered by Tucker's protective stance. "*You* shouldn't have snuck off without me."

He hesitates. "Did you ... see everything?"

I give a somber nod, the full significance of my admission not lost on me. No one has ever witnessed a sweep, and lived to tell about it, that is.

"What happened?" Owen's voice is thick with emotion.

I take a deep breath to calm my racing heartbeat. If I can make him understand what I saw, maybe I can persuade him to do something. "I was staked out near some rocks, not far from Sam. There was this whooshing sound, and all of a sudden Sam keeled over. I jumped up and spun around and that's when I saw the Sweeper ship. Next thing I know, this telescopic tube thing shoots out and suctions onto him."

Owen rubs a hand over his taut jaw and waits for me to continue.

"It swings back for me, so I duck down and take cover. The tube rams into the boulder I'm hiding behind—makes this high-pitched grinding sound. Then all of a sudden it goes limp and the ship takes off."

Owen looks across the canyon, the violet shadows beneath his eyes illuminated in the sun. "I saw the ship leave the canyon. I didn't know they had Sam."

I grab Owen's sleeve. "Don't you see what this means? The Sweepers aren't invincible. They make mistakes."

He ignores my brilliant insight, kicks at a clod of dirt. "Did you get a look inside?"

I shake my head. "Tinted glass. All I caught was *TerraTechno* on the side of the tube. But I found a dart they fired at me buried in my pack." I pull it out and hold it up, but he turns away, balling his hands into fists. He's smoldering mad at me for taking such a huge risk. But I'm ticked at him too. I survived a sweep and he won't even give me credit for pulling off what no one else has ever done before. I suck on my bottom lip for a minute, stoking my frustration. "Prat needs to know about this. He could rally the Undergrounders, come up with a plan. Seeing *you* won't."

Owen narrows his eyes at me. "Don't be ridiculous! Prat wouldn't know what to do. He's got us all plucking chickens and filtering water, like we're knucklehead Girl Scouts on a camping trip." He scrubs his hands over his face. "You're right about one thing. We'll never be free until we find a way to stop the extractions. But you need to be patient."

He stands, slings his gun over his shoulder, and looks out over the canyon awash in half-shadows. "It'll take more than just us. The camps have to unite. The Undergrounders need a real leader. One who's not afraid to do what needs to be done."

I pat Tucker on the head and get up, an uneasy feeling creeping up my spine. I thought all that sneaking out had something to do with a girl. But now, I'm not so sure.

Back in our bunker, I heat up last night's rabbit stew on our wood stove. I add some dehydrated potato slices and carrots, and give the stew a hearty stirring. I miss Ma's cooking. Our food unit is chock-full with five years' worth of dehydrated supplies in sealed plastic tubs, but most of it tastes like chalk. Prat's supplies are a whole lot better—some highfalutin' NASA MREs, but he'd rather hoard them than share with us.

We're an odd bunch, the ones who made it. Preppers stockpiling for Doomsday, mountain men with beards like rugs, Prat, our wuss bunker chief, who grew up rich, but he's not anymore I suppose, unless you count his twelve-hundred-square-foot custom-built steel bunker with solar-powered lighting. His parents even sprang for the two-hundred-year warranty, for what that's worth now.

Mason says he's a Marine, although I'm not so sure. He's a newcomer to our camp and nothing about him adds up. Then there's us of course, the Connellys, garden-variety suburbanites, grateful our neighbor took us fishing up here and gave us a tour of his bunker. He never showed up after the meltdown. Da says he'd have wanted us to have the place, but I think he'd hate nothing more than to see us holed up here scabbing off all of his hard work. He only brought us here to stick it to us. He wasn't the sharing type either.

My mouth waters as the aroma of real meat fills our-eight-by-forty-foot recycled shipping container. I glance across at Da slouched in a chair, eyelids drooped, clutching a sock in one hand. A halfhearted gesture at getting dressed. He's wearing the same stained sweats he's slept in for months, snoring like a woodpecker. Of course there's a fresh batch of beer fermenting in the corner. Apparently he hasn't been sleeping all day.

For the most part, Da's always too drunk to care where we're at. Drinking's all he's really cared about since Ma died. Jakob told me the other Undergrounders are secretly hoping the Sweepers extract him before he does something to endanger the entire camp. Which seems harsh for Septites, although I kinda get it. The greater good principle and all that. But Da will never get picked up. The Sweepers only come for the young.

Owen sets out spoons and plastic tumblers of water on our camping table and I fill two bowls of stew.

Owen slurps a spoonful of broth. "What did the Sweeper ship look like up close?"

"Long, gunmetal gray body, shaped like a bullet. Like I said, I couldn't see in. The glass looked weird, like it would glow in the dark."

"Mason says it's to absorb radiation."

I throw Owen a disgruntled look. "How would *he* know that?"

"He knows a lot about military stuff. He taught us how to defend the bunkers properly, didn't he? How to secure an area, identify escape routes, assess a threatening situation. He knows what he's talking about."

I roll my eyes. "I think he makes half of it up." I study a piece of carrot in my bowl, my insides working their way into a familiar jealous knot. Owen and I grew close after Ma died—Da being mostly out of it and all. Until Mason came along.

"How old do you think he is?" I ask.

Owen shrugs. "Dunno. Twentyish. He doesn't talk much about himself."

I chase the last piece of rabbit around my bowl. Mason's tight-lipped about most everything, including his large stash of weapons. Which is why I'm suspicious of him—ripped like no man I know, surly, with dark, brooding brows and the biggest feet I've ever seen. I'm sure they never made shoes that size before the meltdown. I don't trust him, or his wife, Kat. When they first arrived, I tried to befriend her, but her glassy eyes look right through me like one of us isn't there, and it gives me the creeps.

I take a swig of water. I hope I'm wrong about Mason. Maybe he *was* in the Marines. How else would he know the windows in the Sweeper ships are designed to absorb radiation?

Inside Prat's spacious bunker Jakob pats a spot on a metal bunk beside him. A fluttery feeling races through my ribcage as his steel blue eyes appraise me, unsmiling tonight. Even Big Ed looks unusually somber. He nods at me as I pass him, his cowboy hat with the snakeskin band crammed on his head, balancing out the grizzled beard that sprawls from his jaw.

Big Ed's the oldest person in our camp, and the wisest. Kind of like having a live encyclopedia around when you need to know something. He was living off-grid for decades before the meltdown. Like a lot of Preppers, who became suspicious of the sovereign leader and one world government, supposedly formed to tackle global warming.

Next to Jakob, Big Ed's my closest friend. He listens to what I have to say like it's important, which is more than Owen does. His left hand is all messed up and Da says it's an old bullet wound. He's convinced Big Ed's on the run. Not that it matters anymore. We're all running now.

I glance around the room and frown when I see Frank, the bunker chief from Sam's camp. "What's Frank doing here?" I whisper to Jakob as I slide onto the metal seat next to him.

"Must be about the sweep," he says, fiddling with the trucker cap in his lap. His parents stare with drooped lips at us from across the room and we instinctively edge an inch or two away from each other.

Prat barely acknowledges us with a curt nod before he calls the meeting to order. "Frank Packer has joined us tonight," he announces. His pale, protruding eyes scan the room as the Undergrounders murmur a greeting. "As you all know, Sam was extracted a week ago." Prat runs a finger around the inside of his collar. "Frank thinks one of us had a hand in it."

The collective hiss of breath around the room sends a shiver down my spine. For months now, there have been rumors of Sweeper snitches in the camps. It's ludicrous of course. Why would anyone help the Sweepers?

Frank slides forward in his chair, arms barred across his chest. "Tell 'em straight, Prentice."

Prat rubs his hands down his shirt. His eyes flick nervously around the bunker. "They've seen more ships. Frank thinks one of us is a snitch."

I look around at the stunned faces, lips slung wide in silent protest.

"This is baloney!" I say, jumping to my feet. "How dare you accuse anyone in this camp of being a snitch if you can't prove it!"

Frank leans over and rummages around in his pack. He pulls something out and tosses it onto the table. "We found this close to where Sam was extracted. Zero-two-five on the handle."

My insides turn to ice. It's a hunting knife with our bunker code on it.

Frank peers around the room, slit-eyed. "Belongs to someone in this room."

Mason snatches up the knife and holds it under the light. There's an uncomfortable moment of silence, then everyone is talking at once, shouting at Frank, arguing with one another, faces twisting like ghouls in the subterranean light. Mason spins the blade back across the table to Frank, his dark, canopied brows drawn tight. I bite down on my bottom lip. There's no mistaking the curved antler handle on the knife. I sneak a glance at Owen. He gives a subtle shake of his head. When I look away, Kat's glassy eyes lock with mine.

Chapter 3

"Dang knife means squat." Mason slams his fist hard on the steel side of the bunker. "Sam could have helped himself to it—he hung out here plenty."

"The kid weren't no criminal," Frank growls. "It's folks from this camp what can't be trusted." He takes a step in Mason's direction. "Strangers what have no business being here."

Prat runs the tip of his tongue over his colorless lips, throws a skittish glance around. The clan women shrink back, eyes wide with fear. For once, I'm with them. The stale air in the bunker reeks of mutiny. I can hear my heartbeat ringing inside my chest like a fire alarm.

"The knife's mine," Owen says, breaking the white-knuckle silence.

I gasp, vaguely aware of my nails slicing into flesh. Jakob lets out a muffled yelp. "Sorry!" I mouth to him.

Frank turns to Owen, a vein bulging in his temple. "So you're the scumbag got him extracted."

Owen pumps his fists at his sides, and I sense what's coming. I slide forward on the bunk so I can grab him before he takes a swing and starts a war.

"Sam was Owen's friend," I say. "He would never betray him."

"Sam and I went hunting together last week," Owen says, after a long pause. "He lifted my knife on accident."

"Well whadda ya know, Frank?" Mason bars his arms across his chest, a smug expression on his face. "There's a simple explanation after all. Looks like you owe us all an apology, you two-faced snake!"

I can almost hear the charged air snap. Frank wheels and reaches for Mason's throat. The muscles in Mason's arm inflate and his meaty fist connects with a crack. Blood spatters from Frank's face over his shirt. He moans and staggers backward clutching his nose. Undergrounders scramble left and right. Jakob's mother lets out an ear-piercing scream, sending the rest of the clan women into a frenzy.

Prat yanks open a drawer and fishes out a ratty towel. "You'd best get going now," he says, tossing it to Frank.

Frank presses the towel to his nose, his eyes flickering with rage. "This ain't over, not by a long shot. Someone's gonna pay for what happened to Sam." He hurls the bloody rag across the room at Prat, and then reaches for the ladder leading up to the entry hatch.

He's halfway up the first rung when Mason pounces on him, slams him up against the bunker wall like a bear with a kill. The clan women scream again in unison. Mason leans into Frank's twitching face. "Threaten me or anyone in this bunker ever again, and I'll rip you limb from limb and feed you to the Sweepers."

"Let him go, Mason," Owen says, laying a hand on his shoulder. "If we turn on one another now, we lose everything we've built. The entire Undergrounder network."

Frank glares at him. "You've already lost it."

"Don't do this, Frank. We're not the enemy," I plead.

"Long as you keep a Sweeper snitch in your camp, you are." Frank shoves past me and throws Owen a jagged look. He adjusts his pack over his shoulder and quickly disappears up the ladder. A moment later, I hear the hiss of the pneumatic lift strut as the hatch opens and then closes.

Mason scowls across at Prat. "You shouldn't have let him spring that on us."

Prat slams the drawer shut. "A man from his camp was extracted. He wanted answers, and he's entitled to them."

"Just remember who calls the shots around here," Owen replies.

Prat squints in Owen's direction, a wary look on his face.

Owen turns to Mason. "Frank's camp will be up in arms now that you've rearranged his face for him. There's no telling what he'll say happened. One of us will have to go up there and reassure them we had nothing to do with Sam's extraction."

"I'll go." The words are out of my mouth before it registers that my lips have moved.

Jakob turns to me, a startled look on his face. "It's too dangerous," he whispers. I know what's going through his mind. It's going through mine too. *The Sweeper ships.*

I take a deep breath and remind myself that there are worse things than dying, like living in the dirt for the rest of my life. "I'll take my chances," I say, fighting the quiver in my voice.

"You can't go with her," Mason says to Owen. "If Frank's camp is after blood, they'll start with yours."

I flash my brother an awkward grin. I'm trying not to gloat, but this is my chance to show him he's not the only one who isn't afraid to do what needs to be done.

Big Ed winks at me. "No better woman for the job. Count me in."

I smile back at him. It's just the kind of thing he would say because he's Big Ed. We both know Owen should be going. If things turn ugly, he'll know what to do. I'll be learning on the fly, but no one else seems inclined to step up.

Kat dissects me with that laser beam look of hers, and I realize my hands are burrowed into Jakob's. I hurriedly untangle my fingers, thankful his father is too busy calming the clan women down to notice the sacrilegious bodily contact. I throw Kat a curious glance. Was she trying to save my skin? Or just staring?

"I'll go with Big Ed," Mason says. "And Prat needs to man up and help sort this mess out too. We don't need Derry along."

"She's a better shot than any of you," Owen says. "She'll have your back."

Mason throws me a dark look as he reaches for his gun.

I bite down on a smile. Whatever sway Mason has over Owen, he hasn't totally torn us apart.

Jakob leans over and whispers in my ear. "Be careful out there. No one else plays a mean enough game of chess to take me on."

I arch my brows. "That's generous, considering you checked me in four moves last night."

"Calls for a rematch at an undisclosed location," he says, a smile tugging at his lips that doesn't quite reach his eyes as he puts his trucker cap back on.

"Sweep Intelligence is adjourned," Prat announces. "We leave in one hour."

"I need to run something by Mason," Owen says, as soon as we exit Prat's bunker. "Be right back." He whips off down the tunnel before I can stop him.

I wait for a minute or two, then follow him into the darkness. Whatever he meant about Prat not calling the shots, it felt like a loaded statement. Ever since he started mixing it up with Mason, he's been hiding things from me. It's time I got to the bottom of whatever it is they're up to, especially now I'm going to be heading out on a mission with Mason. I don't trust him.

I creep steadily along the tunnel, feeling my way along the damp, earthy walls with my fingertips. When I hear voices, I slow my pace and mold myself against the wall to listen.

Mason's voice is low and strained. "You can't charge up there until we know what's going on."

"If they've spotted ships, the camp's already in trouble," Owen says.

"We need to alert the Council before we make a move," Mason says.

"If we wait any longer, we might be too late to help them."

"Keep your voice down. I'm done arguing with you. I'll find out what the Council knows about the ships. Now get out of here before someone sees you."

I turn and leg it back down the tunnel to our bunker.

Inside, I pull my rucksack off the top bunk and assess the contents: compass, knives, fishing gear, whistle, ammo, water bottle, and jerky. Tucker plods over and lays a questioning paw on my arm.

"Not this time, buddy," I say, scratching him behind the ears. "I'll be back before you know it." I zip up the smaller outer pockets on my pack, and stash my tactical knife and flashlight in my jacket pocket in case I get separated from my gear, just like Big Ed taught me.

A few minutes later, Owen returns and I hear him rustling around in the food unit. I sneak up behind him, and dig my fingers into his arm. "What's this Council all about?"

He stops shoving dehydrated food into his pack and turns around, a guarded look in his eyes.

I cross my arms. "I heard you and Mason arguing."

"I've told you before not to follow me. There's things you've no business knowing."

"Whatever you're doing is my business. *I'm* your family, not some shifty stranger who shows up at the bunker out of the blue and starts throwing his weight around. I'm the one who always has your back."

Owen stares at me for the longest time. "All right," he says, resignedly. "But keep your mouth shut. If Prat gets wind of it, he'll make a stink, blow the whole deal."

I give a fervent nod, giddy from my unexpected success in cracking the code on Owen and Mason's secret society.

Owen cinches the strap on his pack. "The Council coordinates efforts between the camps."

I fight back a wave of disappointment. "That's it? What does that even mean? Are we talking community vegetable gardens, or what?"

Owen throws me a withering look. "We're planning an attack on the Sweepers."

My fingers go limp. I stop patting Tucker's head and stare at my brother in disbelief. *This* is what Owen's been hiding from me. My heart's thumping so hard it hurts. It explains a lot, like why Owen's always disappearing, and why Mason has a large stash of weapons and a tightlipped wife. A ripple of excitement goes through me.

I inhale a deep breath. "I want in."

Owen looks at me with an amused expression. "Tonight's not about the Council's plans. I have my own reasons for heading up to Frank's camp."

"Like what?"

Owen rubs his jaw and studies me for a moment. "You really like Jakob Miller, don't you?"

My face flushes. I throw Owen an irritated look. "What's that got to do with anything?"

He leans down and closes the flap on his fluorescent orange pack. "Would you wait 'til morning if you thought he was in danger?"

I catch a sudden whiff of Jakob's sawdust-and-worn-leather scent, and my chest heaves up and down. He's been my safe haven since the first day we met in the bunker. I made up my mind a long time ago that I would lay down my life for him, if it ever comes to that, seeing as, being a Septite, he mightn't see fit to defend himself.

Owen straightens up and swings his pack over his shoulder. I pick up his rifle and hold it out to him like a peace pipe. "So this is about a girl?"

He chuckles and reaches for his gun. He's halfway up the metal ladder to the entry hatch when he stops and turns back around. He pulls out a dog-eared photo and hands it to me. "She was only twelve then, but it's all she had to give me."

"What's her name?" I ask, studying the picture of a young girl sitting cross-legged on a beach. She's laughing at something, head thrown back, blond hair tousled, her teeth startlingly white against her tanned skin.

"Her name's Nikki." Owen snatches the photo back out of my hands. "Now quit following me."

I stand there, jaw askew, listening to the whoosh of air as the pneumatic entry hatch above me closes. My instincts about Owen's mysterious jaunts were halfway right. Now my curiosity is really piqued. Maybe I'll get to meet this Nikki tonight. I might even make a friend. We have Owen in common, if nothing else.

I turn and tread softly back to the kitchen area. Da belches and reaches for his beer. "Where you off to now?"

I shrug. "Night watch."

He swishes around a mouthful of beer. "*Night* watch. What you watching anyway?" He cuts loose with a laugh. "Go on, git."

My heart pounds so hard it hurts as I make my way along the main tunnel, but it's a good kind of hurt, a feeling of being fully alive—my first official mission up top that doesn't involve cowsitting. A chance to prove I'm Owen's equal, and nowhere near as useless to the camp as Da.

To my surprise, Jakob's waiting for me at the main hatch. "I wanted to see you off," he says, a shy smile pulling at his lips.

"I'll be back before you know it." I stick my thumbs in the straps of my rucksack so there's no danger of him trying to hug me good-bye. I don't want to feel his warmth pressing up against me right now, weakening my resolve, and I most definitely don't want him to know how much I'm trembling.

Jakob heads off down the tunnel, turning to wave briefly, just as Big Ed rounds the corner decked out in his standard checked shirt, Wranglers jeans, suspenders, and tactical boots. He tilts his hat at me and reaches for his custom stock rifle with the silver stag inlay. He makes for an imposing figure. I don't pay heed to most of what Da rambles on about anymore, but he could be right about the mountain men being fugitives.

It takes all of our concentration to move in the darkness at a steady pace through the dense undergrowth of bristly-tipped, swordtail ferns and tree roots braided across the trail. Prat's heavy breathing adds to my unease. Mason barely exchanges a word with Big Ed or me as we traipse along to the beat of the trills and caws radiating through the firs My senses are hardwired to the forest's every whisper, the threat of Sweepers front and center in my mind, even though it's still too dark out for their ships. The Sweepers may have habits, but, as Big Ed likes to remind me, predators adapt to the patterns of their prey.

We reach the perimeter of Frank's camp shortly before midnight and hunker down behind a cluster of ponderosa pines to watch for any sign of movement around the camouflaged entry hatch. A pair of red squirrels tear up and down a nearby tree trunk, jabbering a protest at our presence, before they disappear. I throw another glance around to make sure we're alone. There's no sign of Owen anywhere, so I figure he's already inside the bunker. Prat's going to go ballistic when he finds out Owen beat us to it.

After a few minutes, Mason waves us forward. We close in and carefully remove the brush and rotting logs that conceal the bunker entry. I hold a flashlight for Prat as he jiggles the hatch, his face glistening in the yellow halo of light.

"Hey! Over here," Big Ed yells, a ragged edge to his voice.

I turn and point the light in his direction.

He peers into a thicket, muttering under his breath, and then reaches down and grabs what looks like an old boot. He grunts, then pulls on it, slowly easing a body out of the brush.

Chapter 4

Prat moans in my ear when I shine the light on Frank's bloody face. My skin erupts with fear.

Big Ed drops the boot, stumbles backward, and cocks his gun.

Mason crouches down and pans the area, before moving off silently into the brush. I throw a panicked glance after him, and then grab the pistol grip of my rifle and whip it off my shoulder. It hadn't even occurred to me that whoever did this might still be lurking around. I'm kidding myself to think I know what I'm doing out here. Maybe the clan women have more sense than I give them credit for.

I swivel on my heels, eying the warped shadows beneath the ghostly moon. My heart clatters against my ribs. I was up for surveillance for Sweepers. I never imagined things taking a turn like this.

Prat kneels down beside Frank and checks for a pulse. "He's dead," he says, choking out the words.

I shine my flashlight over Frank's chest, half-expecting to see a Sweeper dart, but instead there's a red sinkhole and a glob of pine needles stuck to it. A tremor runs through me. I don't get queasy hunting, but Frank's eyes are open and staring, flickering in the moonlight like haunted orbs.

"Do you think it was Sweepers?" Prat asks.

"Sweepers don't leave bodies, they're snatchers." I swallow hard as a dreadful thought creeps into my mind. Could Owen have had something to do with this?

Prat glances nervously over his shoulder in the direction of the entry hatch, almost jumping out of his skin when a field mouse scurries over his foot. "What about someone from Frank's camp?"

I shrug, unwilling to voice my suspicions about Owen.

"All clear," Mason says, coming up behind us. "There's a trail headed south, several hours old. Whoever did this is long gone."

Big Ed squats beside us and removes his hat. "Rogues I reckon. Likely ambushed Frank on his return."

Prat drops the flashlight. A sheen of sweat glistens on his upper lip.

I look back and forth in confusion between Big Ed and Prat. "What are you … what's he talking about?"

Big Ed stands stiffly and puts his cowboy hat back on. "Tell her. Girl has a right to know what's out there."

Prat blinks, fumbles around for the flashlight.

Mason kicks it toward him. "The Rogues are a gang of escaped subversives from the maximum security reeducation center. They must have made a run for it when the fireball hit."

My eyes widen. The reeducation centers were instituted by the sovereign leader to contain anyone deemed subversive or a threat to world unity. The only way out was in a body bag. Until now.

"They've attacked the Undergrounder network down south," Big Ed says. "They're well-armed with M16s. By all accounts they're killing machines."

I peer over his shoulder into the gloom and shiver at the spooky clacking of a screech owl. Would a killing machine even make a sound? Frank never had a chance. My pulse ratchets up a click. What if the Rogues found Owen too?

Prat gets to his feet and throws his pack over his shoulder. "We need to get out of here."

"Wait!" A sickening bubble forms in my windpipe. "We can't just leave Frank lying here on a pile of roots. We have to bury him."

Prat shrugs. "We don't have shovels."

"We'll come back later and lay him to rest," Big Ed says, pushing up the brim of his hat. "Do it right. Dust to dust, ashes to ashes, and all that."

We settle on pushing Frank's body back into the thicket and covering it up with some broken boughs as best we can. I'm not optimistic he'll be there later for his own funeral, but it's a chance we'll have to take. I know what a pack of wolves can do to a grown man. Big Ed said they never used to bother mountain folk before the meltdown, but wild game's scarcer now, and the wolves have become man-eaters.

"Mason and I will take a quick look inside the bunker," Big Ed says. "Derry, you and Prat keep watch up top for a few minutes. I'll holler if it's safe."

Prat fidgets nervously at my side while Mason and Big Ed hoist open the hatch and climb down into the bunker.

"Chill, Prent," I say, with a smug grin. "I got your back."

He casts a skeptical eye over me, then jumps up and hurries after the others, leaving me alone in the moonlight.

All around, moss rises in thick folds over mysterious shapes. I catch my breath at the sudden whoop-whoop-whoop of a grouse in the brush. I'm not feeling as brave now that I'm alone out here. All I can think about are *the killing machines*. I wipe the sweat off my forehead, and start cranking my flashlight.

Five, ten minutes go by, and there's no sign of the others returning. I take a deep breath to steady my nerves, then make my way over to the main entry hatch and quietly descend the ladder.

Clutching my flashlight, I tread softly along the tunnel, following the faint blotch of yellow bobbing in front of me. When I reach the first bunker, I stash my flashlight and squint through the four-foot-square opening.

I stifle a gasp.

Prat, Big Ed, and Mason are huddled together in the middle of the room, hands bound in front of them. Judging by the stricken look on Prat's face, someone's pointing a weapon at them. *Owen?* No, that doesn't make sense. My heart races. Could it be the Rogues?

Trembling, I pull my head back into the shadows. This has all gone horribly wrong. Apart from me, everyone's either dead, missing or captured. And I'm supposed to figure this out. My breath burns hot as a geyser on my lips when I remember to breathe again. I press myself against the dirt wall of the tunnel and listen, but the only thing I can hear is my heart galloping in my chest. I reach into a side pocket on my pack and pull my flashlight back out.

A circle of cold steel presses into the back of my skull. The muscles in my neck tighten like a screw.

"Hands above your head."

I drop my flashlight and slowly raise my arms as my rifle is jerked from my shoulder.

"What are you doing here?" a rough voice asks.

I know that voice.

I make a halfhearted attempt to turn around. "Reid? Is that you?"

The pressure on the back of my head eases up a notch.

"It's Derry Connolly, from Prentice Carter's camp."

"They never said you was with them," Reid says, gruffly.

"What's going on?"

"Shut up and move." Reid shoves me forward and jams the butt of the rifle into my back.

I wince, my brain whirring. *Did Reid kill Frank? Where's the rest of the camp?*

When we reach the main bunker, Reid grabs me by the collar. "Don't try anything stupid. Sit down and keep your mouth shut."

Mason's jaw doesn't even flinch in acknowledgement when our eyes meet. Big of him not to mention I was with them, but I've blown it now anyway. I glance around the bunker and spot a greasy-haired woman I've never seen before leaning against the wall in the corner, pointing a rifle in my direction.

"Kid's with them, Becca," Reid says.

Becca shakes her lank hair out of her face and lowers her rifle. She takes a couple of unsteady steps forward, and then sinks into a white plastic chair. Reid gives me another shove and gestures to the chair next to her. I sit down and smother a gasp when I notice the ugly, festering wound above her ankle.

"Will someone please tell me what's going on?" I glance from Prat to Reid.

Mason juts out his jaw. "Reid here has cooked up a crazy story about how he went off hunting and came back to find the camp upped and gone, and Frank dead in the bushes."

I watch the hard cords in Mason's neck pulsate as he talks. Every time he opens his mouth things heat up. I wish he hadn't come. He leans forward conspiratorially. "Did you kill Frank, Reid?"

Reid lunges at Mason and swings the butt of his rifle around, but Mason's ready for him. He grabs the gun and cracks Reid on the side of the head with it. Reid falls to the ground, wailing.

"Drop it or I'll shoot!" Becca's back on her feet, rifle aimed at Big Ed, her closest target.

Mason faces her, Reid's gun clamped awkwardly in his bound hands, eyes flashing. I know that look. He won't back down now. Prat's fish eyes latch onto me like a distress beacon. He's so white he looks like he might throw up. I know he's wishing it was Owen sitting here, but all he's got is me. I can't let him down.

I press my elbow lightly to my side and feel the outline of the spring-assisted blade in my jacket pocket. Sucking a cold breath between my teeth, I study the wound on Becca's leg. My fingers slowly slide with a life of their own into my pocket.

As I lunge, I shove the barrel of Becca's gun upward with my left hand, driving my knife into the seeping wound on her leg. She crumples, howling, and I seize her gun and face off against everyone in the room.

Mason gives me a barely perceptible nod of approval. He rolls Reid over with one foot. "Get up. On the chair."

I cut the ties on Mason's wrists and give him the knife to free the others. Big Ed walks over to a folding table at the back of the room and retrieves our weapons.

Becca hasn't stopped screaming since I stabbed her. It makes my skin crawl to hear her but it's better than listening to Big Ed's dying gurgle, which is what I'd be hearing if she'd taken that shot.

"You okay, Derry?" Big Ed lays a hand on my shoulder.

I drop my gaze and shrug. "I didn't want to have to do that. But, when I saw it was you she was aiming at—"

His hand grips my shoulder like a vice. "You did good."

Becca's screams drop a few octaves to a low moaning. Her eyes are glassy when they flutter open.

"Who is she anyway?" I ask.

Reid scowls. "I met her out hunting," he says, holding his hand to the side of his head.

I stare at him for a minute, but he doesn't elaborate. He's hiding something. No one brings strangers back to their bunker. Mason lets out a dismissive snort and hands my gun to me. "If Reid's lips are moving, he's lying." He chambers a round and walks across the room to Reid. "Why'd you kill Frank?"

"I found him with a bullet in his chest," Reid growls. "Looks to me like you boneheads might've killed him."

"It was Rogues," Big Ed says, quietly. He pulls a spent cartridge from his pocket and holds it out. "I found it near the body. It's from an assault rifle."

Prat wipes a shaking palm across his forehead. "It's not safe here. We should go."

"He's right," Reid says. "We need to get out of here." He turns and reaches for the ladder.

I slowly raise my rifle and aim it at a spot above Reid's head. "No one's going anywhere, not until we find Owen."

Chapter 5

Prat stares at me, eyes like marshmallows. "What are you talking about?"

I lower the rifle. "Owen came up here after the meeting. He was worried we would be too late to help the camp by the time we arrived."

Mason gives a grunt. "Seems he was right, seeing Reid here's the only one left standing."

Reid glowers at him.

"We're not hanging around to look for Owen," Prat says.

"The Rogues might have him," I say.

Prat shrugs. "His problem. He broke the rules."

"Forget your stupid rules!" I slam the rifle across his chest and shove him backward. "The rules have changed now that Frank's dead. We need to get on that trail and find Owen before it's too late."

Mason grabs me by the arm and pulls me away from Prat.

I push in vain against his bulk. He might as well be welded to the floor. "Easy, Derry," he says. "I'll go with you to look for Owen."

"That makes three of us," Big Ed says.

"You're all crazy!" Prat yells. "I won't be a part of this, risking people's lives chasing down *her* bullheaded brother." He picks up his rucksack and rams his arms through the shoulder straps. "Just remember, Connolly. If anyone gets hurt, it's on you. And don't bother coming back if you don't want to abide by bunker law anymore."

I watch him disappear up the ladder and out through the hatch, a sinking feeling in my gut. I've set something in motion that will unravel the camp if I can't contain it.

Bunker politics will have to wait. For now I need to focus on finding Owen. I glance over at Reid, watching us with a shadowy look. Becca stares at the floor, angry and sullen. Taking them with us would only complicate things. I don't trust either one of them. On the other hand, we'll have more fire power if we do run into Rogues.

Big Ed removes his hat and rubs the slick, bald spot at the top of his head. "It's too dark to pick up the trail before morning."

I look around at the others. "We can rest here for a few hours. I'll take the first shift. We'll sleep with our weapons, except for Reid and Becca."

Mason frowns. "Be a rookie mistake not to tie those goons up. They'll hightail it out of here first chance they get."

I glare back at him. Like he knows anything. "Not if we post an armed watch."

For a moment, Mason wrestles with some emotion, and then his face relaxes. "Okay, it's your brother out there, we'll do it your way. I'll take the second shift."

Relief leaks through my veins. Mason's letting me call the shots, at least for now. Less chance of a fistfight between him and Reid if it stays that way. And I could use them both if the Rogues have Owen.

I drag a plastic chair over to the bottom of the ladder and sink down in it. Big Ed pulls a chair up beside me and adjusts the brim of his hat so he can see me. "You doing okay?"

I shrug. "Do you think we'll find Owen?"

He adjusts the brim of his hat so he can see me. "Only takes courage to do most anything."

I give him a lopsided smile. "I don't know if I have what it takes. Maybe if I were more like Owen."

Big Ed pauses and scratches the back of his neck. "There's a bird I read about called the Australian lyrebird that can mimic any sound around it—critters, other bird's chatter, a rushing stream. Problem is, soon enough no one knows it by its own sound anymore." He peers at me in-tently through

IMMUREMENT

his glasses. "It's time to make your own mark, Derry. Lead like you did today when you followed your gut and saved my life."

"Owen should lead the Undergrounders. He's not afraid of anything."

He gives a dismissive grunt. "You're afraid because you have no idea yet who you could become. It's time to find your courage and act anyway."

I look over at his leathered face. "What kind of man did you imagine becoming?"

A sad smile deepens the hollows of his cheeks. "A better one." He pats my knee with his mangled hand and yawns. "Time for me to lie down."

I watch him pad over to his pack and curl up on the floor beside it. Something happened with Big Ed a long time ago, something he regrets. But, mountain men and fugitives don't often share their secrets. I check my gun, then slide further down in the hard plastic chair, my thoughts drifting to Jakob.

"Derry!" I jolt upright, disoriented. Big Ed looms over me, his rimmed glasses glinting in the light he's shining in my face. "Those jugheads are gone."

"What? Who?" I rub my eyes trying to remember where I am.

"You fell asleep. Reid and Becca took their guns and left."

I sit up slowly and process the information. *A rookie mistake.* Mason was right.

"Where's Mason?" I ask, raking my fingers briskly over my scalp to wake myself up.

Big Ed gestures at the hatch. "Out searching for them."

Up top the murky darkness is melting into dawn, but the forest is still sheathed in frost. I rub my knuckles together and blow hot breath onto my fingers. A moment later, Mason breaks into the clearing, his rifle swinging from his shoulder. "They're headed south."

I clamp my fingers tightly around my gun. "Any sign of Owen?"

Mason rubs a hand over his jaw. "There's only one trail. Either he's on it too, or he's—" He tightens his lips and looks off into the forest.

—or he's dead, like Frank.

29

Our mood is somber by the time we've buried Frank and covered up the gravesite. We march in silence in the half-shadows, brushing up against flaky-barked tree trunks as we thread our way through the dense woods. In the distance, a thin river of morning fog weaves its way past the moon over the snow-tipped Sawtooth Peaks that straddle the horizon. The sun will soon be up, and even though we're safer here than in the open canyons, we're taking a huge risk traveling at dawn.

We hike south for close to three hours before Mason hesitates at a fork in the trail. Big Ed silently takes the lead, and no one questions him. This is a world he knows best.

You can only see what's in front of you, Derry, but you can hear in all directions.

I step over a granite knob and stiffen, one foot poised in midair.

A rattler shakes its hollow scales in warning. A cold sweat wraps around my neck. I take a deep breath and close my eyes to focus. The clicking is insistent, louder to my right. *Three o'clock. Ten feet.*

I edge slowly left, melting with relief as the rattling fades. When I look up, I'm startled to see Mason staring down the barrel of his gun at the brush the snake retreated into. He straightens up and slides a furtive glance in my direction. "Just a precaution. Big Ed taught you well."

I give him a double-edged smile, the kind that expresses gratitude, but hints at disapproval. The last thing I need is Mason acting like my security detail in Owen's absence.

Suddenly Big Ed whistles a wood thrush warning, flutelike and clear. We drop to the ground and ready our weapons.

"See anything?" I whisper to Mason.

He swishes with his hand for me to be silent and points off to the left.

I peer over a vast umbrella of ferns. Thirty feet away, on an exposed embankment, Becca is slumped with her back up against a splintered stump, her head drooping into her chest. There's no way to tell from here if she's sleeping or dead.

Big Ed makes his way back to us, his face puckered. "I don't like the look of this. No sign of Reid anywhere."

Mason gestures up the hill. "I'll check her out. She could be booby-trapped."

I watch with trepidation as he approaches the tree stump and moves cautiously around, searching the ground for wires or traps. After a few minutes, he kneels down and studies something on Becca's leg. He grabs a fistful of her hair, and pulls her head back just long enough to flash the yawning, ragged slit across her throat. I press a hand to my mouth.

"Bled out," Mason confirms when we reach the tree stump.

My skin crawls. It would have been a death wish to go after Owen on my own. I'm rapidly developing an appreciation for Mason's military expertise after all.

A twig snaps like a firecracker to our left. Big Ed swings his rifle and trains it on a clump of ferns twenty feet away. I hunker down behind a cluster of trees, heart thumping, as the unmistakable sound of someone crashing through the brush grows louder.

Chapter 6

A streak of fur charges straight toward me. My gun goes slack in my hands. "Don't shoot!" I yell to the others as Tucker pins me to the ground. He heaves hot breaths like a steam engine braking hard, and I bury myself in the salted butter scent of his sweaty fur. For a moment I'm heartened by his boisterous greeting, and then a foreboding feeling overtakes me. *What is he doing here?*

Seconds later, Jakob bursts through the brush and comes to a halt in the middle of the clearing. He grips his shotgun with both hands, sweating and flushed, his eyes snapping left and right. He's missing his trucker cap, and his white blond hair sticks up in random tufts, like he's crawled through the undergrowth to get here. He staggers a few steps toward us. Big Ed reaches for him by the shoulders and props him up against a tree. I run to him and he clutches me to his chest with one hand, trying to catch a breath. The familiar scent of sawdust and worn leather fills my nostrils.

"I couldn't … let you go without me," he gasps.

I pull out my canteen and hold it to his lips. "Here, take a drink."

He takes an obligatory sip, before slumping backward.

I unwind my bandana from around my neck, pour some water on it, and press it to his forehead.

"I can't go back now," he says, fumbling with his rifle. His eyes meet mine, and I realize what he's saying. The clan will shun him for this single act of disobedience. He's chosen me over them. It's a sacrifice that's become more dangerous than he realizes.

"We need to get going," Mason says, throwing Jakob a disgruntled look. "You can brief him on the way if he insists on tagging along."

"He's already made his decision," I say. "He's coming with us."

The sun blazes like an angry eye above the muscled peaks of the mountains. We march in silence for the most part, scouring the horizon for any hint of threat, until a deep rumbling fills our ears. For the next half a mile it grows louder until there's no mistaking the boom of water crashing from a great height.

"Elk Creek Rapids," Big Ed shouts over his shoulder.

I make my way over to the edge of the trail and stretch out my neck to take a look. Jakob comes up behind me and hooks a protective arm around my waist. I stiffen, until I remember that his parents are a long way from here. We're both on our own now.

Fifty feet below us, white foam breaks like liquid crystal over the top of half-submerged granite boulders in the churning water.

I retreat a few feet, shaken by the brute power of the water. Big Ed waves us forward and points at a log cabin up ahead. "That's the old Brody place. Follow me. We'll fan out around the building, make sure the Rogues aren't holed up inside before we cross the river."

The hairs on the back of my neck prickle as I edge forward and scan the perimeter. Jakob takes off to the left of the building and I veer right. A stubby-legged toad shuffle-jumps up to me and studies me with lidded, glassy eyes. I'm beginning to wish I hadn't listened to so many of Big Ed's ghost stories about bear grease and moonshine and buckets of fingers cut off at the knuckles. This old cabin has the feel of a place that's swarming with ghosts.

I take a couple of tentative steps closer to the boarded-up cabin.

"Behind you," a voice whispers in my ear.

I swing my rifle around, ready to unload a round.

"Easy! It's me, Mason!"

"Idiot!" I hiss back angrily.

Mason clamps a giant paw over my mouth. He gestures in the direction of the shack.

I stay close behind him as we edge our way around the log exterior to the front porch. He scrapes up against the siding and I grope at a sheet of cobweb that cascades down behind him. I spit a clump of sticky web silk off my tongue, hoping there isn't an irate black widow crawling over me. I'd sooner skin a rabbit than handle anything with more than four legs.

Mason jerks his thumb forward several times, then reaches for the elk-antler door handle, and raises the iron latch above it. He pushes against the wooden door with his hip. It gives easily—too easily for a log door swollen shut from disuse.

I follow him in, gun cocked and ready. Dust itches the lining of my nostrils. For an agonizing moment, I wrestle with a sneeze, before I manage to contain it.

Mason stands rooted in place, his broad back blocking my immediate view of the cabin's interior. I follow the thin beam of his flashlight as he arcs it around, tracing the warped trusses above. I step to the side and flinch when something taps me on the back. When I swing around to take a look, a boot socks me in the mouth. I shriek and stagger backward.

I grip my gun and stare up in horror at a shadow dangling from the rafters. My knees almost buckle beneath me. *It's Reid!* A handwritten sign strung from his neck reads: "Sweeper Snitch."

Jakob and Big Ed come rushing through the door and freeze at the sight of Reid's body still swaying to and fro. I clamp my jaw shut and steady myself on an old, wooden table, my fingers sinking deep into the mantle of dust coating it.

Big Ed rubs a hand over his brow. "This weren't no random killing. That sign's around Reid's neck for a reason."

Sweeper Snitch. I think back to the angry exchange at our bunker the night before Frank died. Was the traitor Reid all along?

"Do you think Rogues did this?" I ask.

Big Ed runs a hand across his forehead. "Ain't no Undergrounder kind of killing."

Mason's features are creased in concentration. He grabs Reid's right ankle, spins it a few degrees as if he's studying something, and then lets go with a grunt. He strides past us to the door, his face unreadable.

Big Ed gestures up at the rafters. "Do you want to bury him?"

I swallow back my discomfort and hoist my pack back on. "Not now. We need to find Owen."

Big Ed stares at me, owl-eyed behind his tiny glasses. He wants me to get out of the shadows and lead, but now that I'm beginning to sound calloused, I don't think he likes it.

Twenty minutes in, the trail curves down a narrow, rocky slope and begins to wind in a series of vicious switchbacks along the lip of a steep drop-off. We spread out, single file, Big Ed leading, Jakob taking up the rear. The lodgepole pines give way to an assortment of sagebrush and wild grasses worming their way through cracked granite boulders. Below, I can hear the crunch of rocks grinding each other into submission in the constant rush of the water. I concentrate on digging in my heels to keep from sliding on the slippery shale. Halfway down the trail, a chilling scream almost rips the hair off the back of my neck.

Tucker bolts into the forest and disappears. I turn in time to catch the glint of an articulated steel tube thrashing backward through the undergrowth.

Mason's strapping forearm scoops me up from behind and we dive beneath a canopy of ferns. I lay there beside him, shaking like a dried-out sack of bones. The ferns part and Big Ed rolls heavily in beside us. "Sweepers," he mutters.

I sit up and rock gently back and forth. "That was Jakob screaming," I say in a far-flung voice I barely recognize as my own.

"Where's Tucker?" Big Ed asks.

I make an incoherent sound at the back of my throat. "He bolted." I clamp my hand over my mouth, half-afraid I might start sobbing and never stop.

Big Ed rubs my arm gently. "Tucker will be all right. He'll head back to the bunker."

"I don't understand how they penetrated the forest," Mason says. "They need clearance to hover."

The knob in my throat shifts up and down. I blink, trying desperately to hold back my tears. How does he know that? *Mason knows a lot about military stuff. Mason says it's to absorb radiation.* Somehow he's connected to this. I've felt it all along. I just can't figure out how exactly. I wipe my eyes and fix a steely gaze on him. "How do you know so much about the ships?"

His features harden. "Educated guess. Hoverships need space to hover."

"Maybe they're using longer tubes," Big Ed says, frowning. "That way they could be operating from outside the timberline."

"We have to look for Jakob," I say, scrambling to my feet. "He might still be out there." I duck back out from underneath the ferns and begin making my way up the hill, shouting his name intermittently, swatting at the brush as I go by. Big Ed and Mason follow me, whistling on and off for Tucker. My vision blurs as my eyes fill with tears again. There's no sign of either one of them.

"Take cover!" Mason yells up to me.

My heart jolts in my chest. I dive and roll beneath the brush, then watch with horror as a Sweeper ship glides overhead. After a few minutes, the leaves part and Mason and Big Ed throw their packs down beside me.

"You okay?" Big Ed asks.

I nod, glumly.

"They must have extracted him," Mason says, frowning. "They wouldn't have left otherwise."

I chew on my bottom lip to keep from crying. "We need to figure out where they're taking him."

Big Ed shoots me a pitying glance. "How?"

"There must be a way," I say. "How did Reid contact the Sweepers?"

"You don't find the Sweepers, they find you," Mason murmurs.

I kick at a clump of rotting wood in frustration. "Like you know what you're talking about." I jump to my feet and gulp down a sob. "I'm going after Jakob."

An iron grip bores into my shoulder and spins me around. Mason stares at me, a flicker of something disturbing in his eyes. I tense my body, half-expecting his fist to explode into my cheekbone. Instead, he shoves me into the embankment and glares at me. "You've got it all wrong." He reaches for his shotgun and loads a round into the chamber. Blood curdles in my veins.

Slowly, Mason brings his gun up and points the muzzle at the horizon before swinging around to face me.

"Reid didn't contact the Sweepers. The Sweepers planted him in Frank's camp."

Chapter 7

My heart pounds so hard it feels like a steel boot kicking my ribs. How could Mason possibly know that? Unless he's one of them. I scoot backward without taking my eyes off him. Every suspicion I've ever had about him converges like a giant avalanche in my brain.

Big Ed slumps to one side, his jaw slack. He looks like he might be having a heart attack, but then I've never seen anyone having a heart attack so how would I know? All at once I realize he's reaching for his knife, his shrewd gray eyes alert as a hawk beneath the brim of his hat. "Easy, Mason," he says. "Let's talk this over like reasonable men."

Mason stares at him, expressionless. If he unloads a round into Big Ed first, I'll have only a few seconds to grab my gun. I wish Tucker were here to set on him. I inch my way into a crouch, ready to dive and tackle him if I have to.

Mason's eyes settle on me. A shade of a grin comes over his face. "I'm not one of them, if that's what you're thinking."

I hold my position. That's *exactly* what I'm thinking. I always knew he wasn't who he claimed to be.

Big Ed removes his hat and runs his hand over his head. "You've been hiding something ever since you rolled into camp. If you've got something to say, now would be the time."

Mason shrugs, leans his shotgun up against the dirt embankment and hunkers down, elbows resting on his knees.

"How much do you really know about the Sweepers?" I ask.

Mason flinches, his eyes boring into me like bullets.

I move back a little so I'm out of range of any sudden blows. His brows shift together in a heavy frown. "I know everything there is to know about them."

In a flash, Big Ed wedges his burly body between us, his hunting blade glinting in the sunlight, pressed tight to Mason's neck. "Dang, boy, who are you anyway?" He tightens his grip on the handle of his knife, forcing Mason's head back. "I swear I'll skin your hide right now if you don't spill whatever it is you're hiding."

"I hate them as much as you do." Mason's eyes flick to me and then back to Big Ed. "I was their prisoner."

I eye him warily, my brain fogged with confusion. No one escapes from the Sweepers. "I don't believe you."

Big Ed sheaths his knife. "Let's hear him out. If he's telling the truth, he might be the only hope we have of saving Jakob."

I stare at Mason, my head spinning. He's a wall of muscle, stronger than seems humanly possible. *Strong enough to break a Sweeper's neck.* If he did escape, I'm going to need his help to find Jakob, no matter how much the idea repulses me.

Big Ed nods at Mason. "Explain yourself."

Mason wipes a hand across his creased brow. "The Sweepers, as you call them, are scientists who've been working for decades in an underground government facility called the Craniopolis. It's run by a man named Dr. Lyong."

I stare at Mason in disbelief. The trembling whistle of a screech owl cuts through the evening air and I shiver. There's been plenty of speculation in the bunkers about the origin of the Sweepers, but nothing even close to this.

Big Ed scratches the back of his neck. "I don't get it. *You're* a scientist?"

Mason forces a grim laugh. "Like I told you, I'm not one of them." He turns aside and chucks a ball of spit into the dirt. "I'm their experiment."

A clammy sensation fingers its way up my spine. I run my eyes over

Mason's thick jaw and bulging muscles, my mind racing. What does he mean by experiment?

Mason reaches for a sapling and begins stripping the bark from it. "The world government publicly denounced human cloning, but the truth is, they've been in a race to perfect the technique. Their goal was to rejuvenate declining populations by cloning the highly gifted for specific traits and purposes. They collected tissue and blood samples through mandatory universal healthcare examinations."

"You mean ... you're a ..." My voice trails off.

Mason nods. "A clone."

Big Ed lets out a long, whistling breath through his teeth.

I slowly rub my temples in tiny circles. The grumping sound of bullfrogs reverberates between my ears as I try to make sense of what Mason is saying. It all seems so implausible. I start with the part that bothers me most. "So ... you weren't born?"

"Not like you were."

I furrow my brow. "Are you some kind of machine?"

"Don't be stupid. Do I look like a machine?"

I shrug. He feels like a slab of granite when you run into him. I've no idea what being a clone means. It's unnatural.

"Reid and Becca were clones too," Mason continues. "The scientists cryptogram our ankles; it's like a branding tattoo that denotes the sector you were cloned for." He reaches over and yanks up the leg of his khaki pants. Above his right ankle is a deeply incised charcoal circle with "M-041" in the center. "Military, placement 041," he says, matter-of-factly.

Big Ed removes his spectacles and rubs his eyes. In the dim light of the rising moon, his face looks as old as corrugated tree bark.

"So if you're military, what were Reid and Becca?" I ask.

"They were bootlegged clones. Not on the official roster."

I wrinkle my brow. "What does that mean?"

"The scientists aren't supposed to conduct any personal cloning of their own DNA, but they all do it. Bootlegging they call it. The official samples for the project are ... were ... extracted from selected specimens in various fields and industries."

"So why did the Sweepers plant Reid in Frank's camp?" Big Ed asks.

"To document survivors of the meltdown. The Sweepers need the breakdown and locations of all the camps in order to collect specimens for cloning. Bootlegged clones are good moles because they don't have any extraordinary skills or abilities that make people suspicious."

I run a hand over my brow. "I don't understand. If they already have DNA why are they going after us?"

"Their DNA is contaminated. When the underground radiation alarms were triggered in the meltdown, Dr. Lyong used a compound vaccine on everyone in the Craniopolis." Mason hesitates. "On the people, not the clones. We already have enhanced immune systems to counteract chemical contamination and airborne radiation. Turns out the vaccine was tainted with a pathogen. It caused a host of medical problems, including genetic mutations."

"What kind of mutations?" Big Ed asks.

"Reject clones." Mason creases his brow. "Deviations they call them. That's why the Sweepers are extracting unvaccinated survivors. They need their pure DNA. Without it, the cloning project dies, and with it, their system of replenishing humankind."

For a few minutes, we sit in stunned silence. I take some comfort from knowing the Sweepers are human at least. It bears some of the rumors going around. "So, they won't kill Jakob?" I ask, my heart racing.

Mason grimaces. "Not if he cooperates. Otherwise he's ... well, let's just say he's spare parts as far as they're concerned."

A shiver runs down my spine. I can't imagine Jakob doing anything other than resisting being cloned. "How do we find him?"

Mason tosses his stick and runs his fingers the length of his jaw. "That's the easy part. It's getting into the Craniopolis undetected that's the problem."

"There must be a way," I say, rubbing my brow. "If the Sweepers had extracted me, Jakob would stop at nothing to get inside."

Mason squares his shoulders. "There aren't enough of us to overpower the security guards."

I pick up Mason's stick and trace a large question mark in the dirt with it. "There is one option worth considering."

Mason frowns. "What's that?"

"We enlist the killing machines to help."

Chapter 8

"Ask the *Rogues* to help?" Mason stares at me as if I'm foaming at the mouth.

Big Ed shakes his head. "You saw what they did to Reid and Becca."

"Because Reid and Becca were ratting them out," I say. "The Rogues want to find a way to end the extractions as much as we do. With Mason's help, we can lead them to the Craniopolis and let them do what they do best."

Mason studies me, his eyes signaling something that tells me he thinks it's possible.

"It all hinges on you convincing them of your story," I say. "They already hate the world government. What you tell them will be more than enough to clinch the deal."

Mason nods. "It's worth a try."

An eerie silence falls over us, broken only by the mellow whoo-whoo of an owl as it veers over us.

Mason pulls some jerky out of his pack and offers it around. I cram several chunks into my mouth and suck greedily on the beef flavor flooding my taste buds.

Big Ed looks at Mason curiously. "So how'd you escape?"

"I stowed away on a Sweeper ship—a Hovermedes."

"Hover *what*?" I rumple my brow.

"Hovermedes. They're named in honor of Archimedes, Dr. Lyong's favorite engineer of old."

"Never heard of him—Archimedes, I mean." I dab my sleeve at some jerky juice on my lips.

Mason raises his brows. "Archimedes was a Greek physicist and inventor in the third century, considered by some to be the greatest mathematician of all time."

"It's not like we have school in the bunkers," I say, defensively.

"Where is this ship you stowed away on?" Big Ed asks.

"It's hidden in the brush a few miles east of our bunker."

Big Ed combs his fingers through his beard and scrutinizes Mason. "It's been there this whole time?"

My pulse races as the import of his words sinks in. If Mason had told us about the ship, we could have used it to fight the extractions. Jakob might still be here. Owen too. "You traitor!" I yell. "You said you hated the Sweepers, but all this time you had that ship hidden and you did *nothing* to help us."

I breathe slowly in and out, long shallow breaths that do nothing to satisfy me. I'm sick to my stomach. Mason passed himself off as one of us, ate our food, slept in our bunkers. All the while he knew exactly who the Sweepers were, what they wanted, and where to find them.

I curl my fingernails into my palms until my skin is throbbing. Every fiber of me longs to throw myself at Mason and tear his eyes out. I clench my fists tighter. First, I need him to take me to the Sweepers. And then I'll have my revenge.

I scramble to my feet and reach for my pack. "We can still catch the Rogues if we hurry. If Mason can convince them to come with us, we'll go back for the Hovermedes." I narrow my eyes at Mason, daring him to challenge me. If he dies trying to reason with those butchers, it will be one less problem for me to deal with later.

"Aren't the Sweepers searching for you?" Big Ed asks, as he gets to his feet.

Mason shakes his head. "According to their records, my expiration date's already come and gone."

Big Ed frowns. "What's that?"

"Lifespan is one element of the cloning process Lyong hasn't mastered yet." Mason lets out a heavy sigh. "Clones don't live past twenty-five units. They simply keel over and expire. I faked my expiration, and a friend who works at the crematorium filed the report." He sifts some pine needles through his fingers. "As far as the Sweepers are concerned I'm already a pile of ash."

I stare at Mason, trying to mask the horror I'm sure is plastered all over my face. I've always guessed him to be in his early twenties, which puts him at death's door in clone years. Ahead of Big Ed. But I want to know for sure. "How old are you?"

"They don't let us access our inception records. Some things are best kept even from ourselves." He flings the pine needles over our heads into the brush and stands. "We need to get across that river."

I stare at Mason for another long moment, then reach for my rifle and swing my pack over my shoulder. Inception. Expiration. It's like he's a product with a shelf life. The whole thing sounds crazy, but there's no time to second-guess his story if we have any hope of saving Owen and Jakob. For now, we'll have to take our chances and trust that he's not leading us to the Sweepers for all the wrong reasons.

Mason steps back out on the trail and begins winding his way down the root-ridden path. Big Ed follows, and I fall in step behind them. Sweat beads on my forehead. Partly from the exertion, partly from the heart stopping thought that something unimaginable has happened to Jakob and Owen, and maybe even Tucker. I can't imagine how Da is coping without us, but I can't worry about him now too. I have to believe the Septites won't let him starve.

Big Ed turns his head and eases up. "Doing okay?"

"Do you believe him?" I ask.

He works his jerky around his mouth for a minute. "There's always been plenty done in secret by the sovereign leader."

"So you really think Mason's a clone?"

He lets out a snort. "Beats anything I ever seen or heard. Messing with

45

God's creatures."

"Clones are hardly God's creatures. It's creepy." I flip my disheveled braid over my shoulder. "Tucker knew something was up. I don't think clones have a scent he can pick up on."

Big Ed takes off his spectacles and rubs the lenses on the end of his fleece shirt. "They ain't just oil and spare parts."

I twist my lips. "Might as well be if they're all like Mason. He's cold as steel."

Big Ed's face clouds over. "He's one of God's creatures until I know different."

He turns around and stomps off after Mason. I step over a pile of elk droppings and follow them down the trail, trying to sort through my tangled thoughts. I don't care what Mason is, I hate him. He deceived us all. I blame him for what happened to Jakob, and he deserves to pay. I can't help thinking about the hunting knife Big Ed pinned to Mason's throat earlier. Everyone has a breaking point. It's only a question of who reaches it first.

I scramble and slip my way down the last few hundred feet, coming to an abrupt halt on a narrow ledge. Big Ed shines his flashlight around. "Trail's washed out from here on down."

I slide my pack off my aching shoulders and elbow past Big Ed and Mason. Cautiously, I peer down at the snarling river beneath us.

"Which way did the Rogues go?" I ask.

"Must have gone across the catwalk." Big Ed flicks his jaundiced light onto the face of a granite cliff forty feet above the torrent. A series of long poles, lashed together with wire, extend some sixty feet across the bare wall to the other side of the river.

"Mountain men put this contraption up years ago, so they could cross the river all year round." He shines the light farther up the rock face. "They drilled pegs into the rock as anchor points to support the poles, and there's a hand cable up above."

I stretch my neck out and study the steel cable looped between the pegs in the slick, jagged wall, scraped clean of vegetation. The gooseflesh inverts on my skin. The only way across is to shuffle sideways on the poles, clinging to the cable, forty feet above the treacherous spray. One misstep, and we'll splatter on the rocks like overripe watermelons.

Mason pushes past me and stares, bug-eyed, at the poles lashed together like cooked spaghetti across the wet granite. A nerve twitches in his cheek. I've never known him to be afraid of anything, but I swear it's fear I see now in his taut features.

"What are you waiting for?" I prod him in the spine.

He swings around and glares at me. "I hate heights."

"Sucks for you." I brush past him, oddly charged by his admission, and make my way out to the edge of the ledge.

Big Ed lays a restraining hand on my shoulder. "I'll go first. Trust the tension in the hand cable, 'cause it's gonna feel like you're tumbling backward with your pack ripping out your shoulder blades. I watched a man fall from here once. River washed him away like fish guts."

I shudder.

"Ready?" Big Ed looks pointedly at Mason.

He scowls. "After you old timer."

I reach for the strap of Mason's pack and yank it hard. "Show some respect, *traitor*."

A dark look flits across Mason's face. He may be built like a bison, but I'm convinced his heart's hollow.

"Keep at least five feet apart," Big Ed shouts over his shoulder. "If one of us goes in, we don't want the next one getting pulled down too." He reaches above his head, grabs the cable, and steps carefully onto the poles. He adjusts his stance and the tension in the cable tightens. He edges farther out onto the poles, his leather gloves clinging to the cable above him in a death grip.

Mason watches intently, arms barred across his chest as Big Ed inches his way along. When he's close to five feet across, he yells at me to go next. I shift my pack and glance hesitantly at the ramshackle pole bridge. The slightest shift of the load on my back could send me hurtling into the foaming whirlpools below. I take a steadying breath and reach out to grab the cable. An icy mist sprays my face and I shiver. I slide my feet across the poles and keep my eyes firmly fixed on Big Ed. When I'm far enough out, Big Ed gestures at Mason to follow me.

Mason clenches his jaw and reaches for the hand cable. He moves tentatively onto the pole bridge, dragging each leg awkwardly behind him. I glance back and realize immediately he's in trouble. Only the toes of his enormous boots fit on the poles as he scrapes along, like a bear trying to balance on a clothesline. I hold my breath and watch for a few minutes as he struggles to shuffle across.

"Keep moving!" he barks. "Weren't you listening to old man Ed?"

"Quit calling him that," I shout back over the roar of the water. "He's got a whole lot longer to live than you."

Mason narrows his eyes at me, his fists bulging on the steel cable.

I look away, masking a grin. I've found an entry point of pain beneath his armor. *He doesn't want to die.* I can taunt him all I want up here. There's nothing he can do to me now, hampered by his hulking frame, and cursed by his odd fear of heights—apparently *not* something the cloning process took care of. There's something intensely satisfying about this shift in the balance of power that stirs a twisted longing inside me for revenge. After what he did, endangering all of our lives with his lies, he doesn't deserve my sympathy. He's not one of us.

I stare at him until he feels my eyes boring into him, and directs his gaze toward me.

"Face it, Mason, if you're really a clone you could expire at any minute." I give a hollow laugh I barely recognize as my own. "Do us all a favor, why don't you?"

His eyes flash a strange sequence of emotions like a train signal switching tracks.

I throw him a contemptuous grin that melts from my face when he pushes out from the rock face with his steel-toed boots and freefalls backward into the yawning watery darkness below.

Chapter 9

A yell rips up my throat but never makes it through my lips. I shoot my right hand out to grab him, but not quickly enough. My footing slips and I dangle from the cable, one-handed. My left hand fuses with the cable in one pulsating cramp. The roar of the water pounds in my ears. I struggle to drag myself back onto the pole bridge, my fingers flapping in vain for something to latch onto. My pack inches sideways and the muscles in my back scream for release as I try to pivot in toward the rock face. Panic rises up inside me. I know I can't hold on much longer. The straps on my pack dig deep into my shoulders, cauterizing my nerves until I want nothing more than deliverance from the all-consuming pain.

A jaw-like grip on my right forearm yanks me upright and pins me against the granite wall. Big Ed's wiry beard scuffs the back of my neck as he leans over me, heaving for breath. My right hand searches out the steel cable and locks onto it, my whole body shaking with terror and relief. I press my forehead against the cold, wet stone. For a moment, neither of us speaks. All I can think about are Mason's flat eyes staring at me, like rocks lodged into his skull.

"You okay?" Big Ed gasps.

I shake my head, not trusting myself to speak.

He tightens his grip on me. "What happened?"

"He … I tried to save him."

"Dumb idea. He could have dragged you down with him."

I glance beneath us at the rapids, shaken by a nightmarish image of Mason's body thrashing around in the frenzied whirlpool.

Big Ed releases me and shuffles sideways a few steps. "We need to get off this bridge."

Knees knocking, I drag myself mechanically along the poles after him. Mason's stony stare drills further into my conscience with each step. What have I done? I wish Tucker were here so I could wrap my arms around him and know that in his eyes I can do no wrong.

Big Ed's face relaxes when I finally step onto the trail on the other side of the gorge. He reaches out a hand to steady me, but I plough past him and dive into the brush, just in time to hurl the contents of my stomach.

He comes up behind me and squeezes my shoulder. "I'm sorry. It must have been rough for you watching him fall."

Straightening up, I wipe the sleeve of my shirt across my mouth. I wish that were all I was struggling with. How can I tell him it was my fault?

"We need to find cover. It's too exposed out here." Big Ed turns and wades off into the undergrowth. I stumble after him, numb from what I've set in motion. I've blown the only real hope we had of rescuing Owen and Jakob. Without Mason to back us up, the Rogues will never believe our story. And none of us know how to fly a Hovermedes, so even finding the ship won't help.

Big Ed's silhouette melts into the distance and I break into a jog to catch up. The trail is trenched from snowmelt trickling down from the craggy peaks, heightening the risk of skidding on the slippery shale underfoot and hurtling downhill. My legs ache and I'm soaked through from the bone-chilling spray of the rapids.

I slow my pace once I spot Big Ed again, not wanting to give him the opportunity to prod me with any more questions. Guilt stabs at me razor-edged and deep. I wanted revenge, but not like this. What kind of monster am I? The briny tang of tears burns my eyeballs. I desperately need someone to tell me everything's going to be all right, but the truth is, it's not. It's never going to be all right again. My stupidity might just have cost the lives of those I care for most.

After a mile or so, Big Ed veers off the trail and begins bushwhacking his way through dense alder thickets. I drag myself after him, barely able to keep up the pace, even though he's doing all the work. Hopefully he's looking for a place to make camp. I can't go much farther.

The moss-mantled ground beneath my boots squishes like an old mattress. Up ahead, Big Ed pauses at a blackened tree trunk. He ducks his head and disappears beneath the hollowed-out root system. When I catch up with him, he's already undone his pack and pulled out his sleeping bag. My body sags with relief.

"We'll rest here for a few hours," he says, throwing me a concerned look.

I nod, breaking eye contact as I slide my pack from my throbbing shoulders. "I'll look for some firewood." I walk off before he can object.

I gather the driest pieces of wood I can find, then pull some dead bark for tinder and head back to the hollow where Big Ed has already fashioned a couple of brush beds over the pine needles and spread out our sleeping bags. He watches me intently while I place several small boulders in a circle and assemble the tinder and wood in the center. Big Ed can read anything from a moody sky to a guilty conscience. He's biding his time, but I know he's gonna hit me up again about what happened. And part of me wants him to.

He takes out his magnesium fire starter and scrapes it with the blade of his knife over the bark until the sparks take hold. "That should do her." He rubs his hands together, his silver-framed glasses glinting in the glow of the quivering flames. "Got any water left?"

I shake my canteen. "Half full."

He nods. "We can boil more for tomorrow. I'll look for a stream in a bit."

I rub my hands over my face and scoot back from the fire that's getting hotter. Or maybe it's just me burning up from shame.

"Do you want to talk about what happened to Mason?" he asks, after a few uncomfortable minutes of silence.

There's no condemnation in his tone, but I still blink guiltily. "There's not much to talk about. He … slipped." My face flushes and I'm thankful for the shadows.

"You gotta let it go, Derry. There was nothing you could have done." He leans forward and stokes the fire with a stick. "Mason knew the crossing was risky."

I press my thumbs hard into my aching temples. The kindness in his voice only makes the guilt worse.

"He was scared of heights," I stammer. "But I said it anyway."

Big Ed frowns. "Said what?"

"I told him to drop dead." Tears slide silently down my cheeks. "Then he jumped."

Big Ed's eyes grow wide. "*Jumped?*"

I give a glum nod. "He let go of the cable and pushed himself backward."

Big Ed rams his stick into the embers and it snaps, the sound ricocheting around us.

"It was my fault," I say, my insides numbing over. "I was taunting him to do it."

Big Ed frowns at me, his ordinarily rheumy eyes hard like steel. "Whatever you're guilty of in your own heart, that sucker killed himself."

He reaches for his hat and gets to his feet with a grunt. "I'm going to set some snares. With a bit of luck, we'll have fresh meat by morning. Get some rest."

I pull off my boots and crawl into my sleeping bag, peering out at Big Ed's silhouette as he disappears into the trees. He can try all he wants to make me feel better, but what I did to Mason was unforgivable. So far I don't much like the person I'm becoming. I close my eyelids and immediately begin to drift, marinating in the scent of burning wood.

"Derry! Wake up!"

I spring into a sitting position, my arms still tucked inside my sleeping bag. My nose twitches at the tantalizing aroma of cooked meat.

"There's a storm brewing," Big Ed says. "We need to get moving." He takes a mouthful of water from his canteen, rinses and spits in the dirt. "The Rogues are camped up ahead."

My chest heaves like it's set in cement and straining to break free. "Did you see Owen?" I hurriedly slide my legs out of the sleeping bag and fumble around for my boots.

"No, just a couple of Rogues on patrol."

I cram my sleeping bag into my stuff sack, cinch the straps on my backpack, and zip the mesh pocket closed.

"Here." Big Ed hands me a bowl of rabbit stew. "Eat this while I bury the fire."

I slop the food into my mouth and swallow as much as I can without chewing. My stomach recoils, but I force myself to chug it down. I need the energy for what's to come. Big Ed pulls apart our brush beds and scatters fistfuls of pine needles around the hollow.

Five minutes later, we're underway. The thin slit of morning that appeared between the tips of the trees and the horizon has disappeared, and the sky is caked with clouds the color of bruises. A horsefly buzzes past my ear and I swat and holler at it.

Big Ed turns around and motions at me to be quiet.

"Sorry," I mumble, as the first drop of rain splatters on my head.

Within minutes, the sky's unloading everything it's got on us. I trudge forward, head down, focusing on Big Ed's muddy footprints. Soon the wind kicks up, vicious and high-pitched, slapping around everything in its path. The trail quickly turns to mush. As we veer downward into the valley, rain slices sideways at my face. I squelch my way forward, barely able to make out Big Ed's outline bobbing up ahead.

He halts at a stump and signals for me to find cover. Another patrol? I duck silently into a clump of trees and press myself against a towering trunk, listening to the sound of my own breathing, and the pummel of raindrops on the leaves around me. I wait for his wood thrush whistle, but instead he appears behind me, silent as a ghost.

"All clear. Their camp is just over that ridge." He tilts his head in the direction he came from. "I reckon they're making their way south to Lewis Falls."

He moves forward again in a half-crouch and motions for me to do the same.

The ground churns beneath my feet, mud oozing over the top of my boots like treacle. I have a bad feeling about how quickly the trail washed out. This could turn into a raging flash floods in minutes. Another limb of lightning lights up the sky, and I tense as I wait for the inevitable crack of thunder. Each step is slower and heavier as I flounder after Big Ed through ankle-deep water, rain sheeting down on me.

He turns around and yells something at me, but it's swallowed up in another thunderous bellow. He clambers onto a tree stump and gestures upward. *Climb!*

I turn and plunge through the goo, now reaching to my knees. I make for the nearest pine and grab onto one of the thick boughs, grunting as I swing myself up. I claw my way up higher, my soaked pack hampering my movements. Exhausted, I flatten myself against the trunk and cast a wary glance at the writhing mud bath below.

A dull terrifying rumble fills the valley. A moment later a wall of nut-brown water, studded with tree limbs and rocks, razes the stump where Big Ed had stood.

Chapter 10

My arms are stiff and useless when I finally unwrap them from the tree trunk I've been cradling. It's eerily silent beneath me, quiet as an ocean graveyard. The flood retreated as suddenly as it surfaced, leaving a trail of forest guts in its wake.

"Big Ed! *Big Ed!*"

I call out his name several more times before I shinny down from my perch. My boots sink all the way into the silt left behind. Shivering, I begin ploughing through the mud toward the ridge. After fifty feet or so, I throw off my pack and lean forward on my thighs to catch my breath.

Something flaps in the brush. I reach over to grab it, and my heart stalls.

It's a cowboy hat, caked in mud, the snakeskin band dangling from it like entrails.

A wave of panic curls around my gut. "Big Ed! Where are you?" I yell until my throat is raw, and then sink to my knees, sobbing silently. I crumple the snakeskin in my fist, and double over with grief.

A foot slams into my stomach and I fall onto my side, sucking for air.

"On your feet!" A bone-crushing hand latches onto me and hauls me upright. "Who are you?"

"Derry Connolly. Don't hurt me, please," I gasp, holding my stomach with one hand. I tilt my chin up and squint at my attacker. Dark eyes in a shaved skull, flay me like razorblades. A ragged scar gouges its way from the left corner of the man's lip to a half-missing brow. Both sides of his long, corded neck are tattooed with lightning bolts and a pair of crossed cleavers. My mind floods with fear.

A Rogue.

"Who's Big Ed?" The man's voice cracks like a whip.

I flinch. "My … my dog. The thunder scared him. He … he took off."

"What are you doin' out here?"

I squeeze my brows together in what I hope is a forlorn expression. "Sweepers—they found our camp."

The Rogue studies my face for a minute, and then pats me down. I grimace, violated as much by his lecherous grin as his roving hands. My heart sinks when he pulls my gun from my backpack. He removes the magazine and empties the chamber in one seamless move.

"What's your name?" I ask, trying to weigh up how much immediate danger I'm in.

The skinhead's cold, flat eyes meet mine. "They call me Blade."

He glowers at me, forcing the metal piercings in his brow into a menacing "V." The jagged scar channels deeper into his cheek.

I take a step backward. I think I know why he goes by Blade, but I don't ask for confirmation.

"Get your pack on. We're moving."

"Where are we going?"

He shoves me in front of him by way of response.

My fear explodes. I'm guessing he's taking me to his camp. My legs shake with every step. If the rest of the Rogues are anything like him, they'll show no mercy. Tears prickle my eyes. I force them back, determined not to show weakness.

We trudge for a mile or so beyond the ridge before I hear voices. Blade halts and whistles loudly, and after waiting for three short whistles in response, he marches me forward again. My breath sticks in my throat when several shadowy figures with Glocks and M16s close in behind.

Rigid with fear, I walk mechanically, avoiding eye contact. After a few minutes I chance a glance around. I'm relieved to see a couple of women in the group, although they're tatted up too, and almost as menacing looking as the men. Most of them have dark beanies pulled down low over their eyes, but I'm guessing they're skinheads like Blade.

We reach a clearing and I spot the camp tucked up to the left of the path the flash flood has gouged out to the river.

I cast another glance around. Big Ed's nowhere in sight. I hope he managed to evade the patrol—if he's still alive.

A tall, thin-lipped man with a graffitied, cleft chin and a tight mustache approaches. He jerks his head in a questioning way.

Blade scowls at me. "Says she was looking for her mutt."

The thin-lipped man flashes me a cold smile and then yanks my rucksack off my back. He empties the contents onto the ground and kicks at the pile with his steel-toed boot. Blade reaches into the mesh side pocket of my pack and grabs Big Ed's cowboy hat. I try to snatch it from him, but he tightens his spring-loaded grip on my arm until I writhe in agony.

"Get a load of this, Rummy." Blade tosses the hat to the thin-lipped man. "Kid was holding it when I found her."

Rummy walks over to me, and snaps the brim taut in front of my face. "This yours, Butterface?" He cocks his head expectantly, but I take too long to answer. He drops the hat onto my head where it promptly slips over my eyes. I push the brim up with one finger and flinch at Rummy's steely expression. His thin lips curve into a sneer. "Must be *the dawg's*, eh?" He throws back his head and howls with laughter. Blade lets out a snort, watching me through narrowed slits.

"Tie her up," Rummy says. "She ain't alone. We'll double the patrols." He snaps his fingers at Blade and walks off.

Blade kicks aside my rucksack and marches me past several tents before motioning for me to sit down by a smoldering fire pit. He secures my ankles and wrists, and then sits back and stokes the embers. I throw a furtive glance over at him and scoot closer to the fire. If I'm going to learn anything about the Rogues, Blade's probably my best shot. I clear my throat nervously. "Rummy's not much of a talker, is he?"

Blade flicks a dispassionate gaze over me. "How'd you spring the sweep?"

I raise my brows. "What?"

"You said Sweepers found your camp." Blade sneers at me. "Greener like you couldn't bust her way outta a sweep."

I eye him warily. "I jammed the tube with a boulder."

Blade's face goes slack. He stares at me for a moment and then jumps to his feet. "Don't even think about trying to make a run for it. Remember, I'm strapped up and you ain't." He slaps his holstered gun by way of demonstration and strides off in the direction of the tents.

I stare into the shadows after him. Have I just signed my death warrant? Or is this going to work in my favor? After all, the Rogues have got to be as desperate as we are to find a way to stop the extractions.

I straighten up and check out my surroundings. I need to have the area mapped in my brain in case there's any chance of escape. I'm only twenty feet from the tree line, but even if I could make a run for it, I'd have to navigate a belt of jagged boulders left behind by the flash flood. I shiver. The Rogues won't hesitate to slit me ear to ear if they catch me trying to escape.

I wonder what they're planning to do with me. If they're recruiting Undergrounders, I'll have no choice but to play along. I wince when I think of the tattoos on the women's faces. Maybe they'll ink me as part of the initiation. Ma would roll over in her grave. If she had one, that is. I choke back a sob. I wish I could feel her comforting arm around my shoulders right now.

A few minutes later Blade and Rummy come back into view. Rummy cracks his neck from side to side and stares intently at me. My blood runs cold. I'm not sure if he's telegraphing a desire to snap my neck, or if it's just some kind of tic he's developed to intimidate his victims. He walks over and hunkers down in front of me. I let my gaze travel down to his tattooed fingers, relieved to see he's not wearing brass knuckles.

He rubs his eyebrow back and forth, rippling the skin above his piercings.

"How'd you know to jam the tube with a boulder?"

I throw a sidelong glance at Blade. He passes his grubby hand over his shaved head, and my own scalp prickles.

I shrug. "Lucky guess."

Rummy crunches forward, almost as if he doesn't want Blade eavesdropping on us. He wrinkles his brow, and I stare, creeped out and fascinated, as the tattoos on his forehead fold into a murky kaleidoscope.

"Thing is, snitch, I know you're lying."

Snitch? Reid's lifeless body flashes to mind. My palms sweat profusely behind my back. If that's what Rummy thinks I am, it's over. My only hope is to convince him I'm more valuable to him alive than dead, that I know something about the sweeps he doesn't.

"You've never dodged a sweep?" I feign a laugh.

Rummy tightens his lips in a thin cord of disapproval.

I fix a bemused look on him, blood pounding in my swollen wrists. "You look like the kind of guy would have figured out—"

Suddenly a searing pain hits and my jaw swivels sideways. Two displaced Rummies dance before me, then the salty taste of blood fills my mouth.

Rummy clasps my throbbing jaw and squeezes it between his fingers like I'm a zit he's trying to pop. "Lemme show you what happens to suckers what diss me." He snaps his fingers and Blade slices the cord around my wrists and ankles in a lightning fast move with a knife that suddenly appears like an extension of his arm. He grabs me and hauls me to my feet.

Rummy strides off, Blade half-dragging me after him.

"Please don't hurt me!" I beg. "I was just trying to help."

We stop outside a small two-man tent and Blade shoves me to my knees. My throat constricts with fear. He reaches for the nylon door flap, folds it back, and forces my head inside. "Welcome to the hole."

I sway back and forth, disoriented and dizzy from the blow to my jaw. The stench of sweat permeates the space. I blink to accustom my eyes to the darkness. There's a body, gagged and bound, lying at the back of the tent. A corpse? Someone kicks me from behind. Tentatively, I crawl forward. The man's eyes are swollen shut like two purple grapes. His head is shaved, but it's hard to tell if he's tattooed because his bruised skin is so mottled. A dry web of blood laces his face, crusting on his bulging nose and smashed right ear. His chest moves up and down, but I'm guessing by his uneven breathing that some of his ribs are broken. My heart races. *Lemme show you what happens to suckers what diss me.* I back slowly out of the tent on clammy palms.

That's when I see the grimy orange backpack stashed in the corner.

Chapter 11

I press my knuckles to my lips. Fragments of rational thought explode in my head. *Owen!* I wheeze like I'm dying, unable to catch a breath, vaguely aware that Blade is stringing syllables into unintelligible words. I collapse in the dirt, silently screaming my brother's name.

"Git up!" Blade yells. He tucks the toe of his steel-toed boot beneath my torso and flips me onto my back. Blood trickles into my throat and I sit up and spit out another mouthful of gunk. My face pulsates with pain.

Rummy rolls up some kind of cigarette and lights it, watching me with half-lidded eyes. I rock forward, violent chills running through my limbs. I can't let them know they have my brother. They'll use it against us.

Rummy takes a drag of his cigarette. "That sucker told me the same boulder wack you did. Blowing smoke 'bout 'scaping from Sweepers."

I gingerly touch the back of my hand to my swollen lips. "It's true."

"Prove it." Blade leans in close. "Prove you're not just a filthy Sweeper snitch."

I rack my brains for something to tell him. Something that will give these thugs no option but to keep me alive. One thing comes to mind, but it's a huge gamble. I fix my gaze on Blade. "I can take you to a Sweeper ship."

He raises his brows and glances at Rummy before turning his attention back to me. Rummy tosses his cigarette on the ground, grinds it beneath his boot, and heads my way, his face expressionless.

"It crashed," I stammer, as Rummy gets closer. "I can show you—"

He lunges for my throat and squeezes hard, cutting off my air supply. "I swear I'll pop your eyeballs out of their sorry sockets if you're jerkin' my chain." He shakes me loose and hovers over me while I writhe around and catch my breath. "Where's this ship at?"

I make a gurgling sound. My throat feels like it's been cinched tighter than a bronc's saddle. I might just have made the biggest mistake of my life. What if there is no Hovermedes? If Mason was lying about the abandoned ship, Owen and I are as good as dead. But I'm committed now. If the Hovermedes exists, I have to find it. I take a shallow breath. "A few miles east of my bunker."

"Ain't that convenient?" Rummy juts his chin at me, his features hard and impenetrable. "How'd it get there, Butterface?"

I hesitate, toying with several plausible answers. None that involve Mason. I'm reluctant to give him everything I know in case I need information to barter with later on. The Rogues will only keep me alive as long as I'm useful to them.

"We dragged it out of the river," I say.

Rummy narrows his eyes at me until I feel my pupils dilate. I'm so tired I could collapse right now and sleep in the dirt, but I will myself to stare him down.

He rewards me with a stinging slap across the jaw. "You mad dogging me or what?"

I shake my head fervently, eyes now firmly planted on the ground. My jaw pulsates with pain. I'm learning the hard way not to challenge him in any way.

"Put her in the hole with the meathead," Rummy says over his shoulder to Blade. He turns back to me, his pierced brow glinting menacingly. "You even think about tryin' to bust outta here, Butterface, and I'll tattoo your wuss-white cheeks with my switchblade."

Blade motions at me to get back inside the tent.

I crawl inside on all fours, my heart pounding with a mixture of fear and relief.

I stretch my throbbing body out alongside Owen. Up close, the grotesque proportions of his swollen face are even more shocking. But, at least he's still breathing. I lay perfectly still, straining to listen in on Rummy and Blade's conversation.

"… let Diesel hear what she has to say."

"I ain't down for taking them to Diesel."

"You ain't in charge! We're rollin' out at midnight."

I awaken to Owen's moans. I blink and bolt up into a sitting position. He twists from side to side, groaning like a wounded animal.

"Owen! It's me, Derry," I whisper into his feverish ear.

His body responds with a couple of spastic jerks, and then his cracked lips open and close. I dive for his pack and rummage around for water. I cradle his clammy head in my arms and hold his canteen to his lips. The first mouthful spills down his chin as he struggles to swallow. I lift him a little higher and try again, this time allowing only a few drops at a time to trickle into his mouth.

His throat spasms, a loud, uncomfortable gulching that makes me shudder.

"Owen!" I lean over his face. "Nod, if you know it's me."

His neck muscles twitch in the palm of my hand. "What … are you doing … here?"

"We followed the Rogues' trail."

"Frank's … camp?" His voice rasps like sandpaper. "Did you find them?"

I hesitate. If I tell him what happened to Reid he might lose all hope. "Not yet."

"They're not here." Owen lets out a heavy sigh as if the few words he's spoken have exhausted him.

I offer him another sip of water, but he flops sideways, eyes scrunched shut.

I lay his head down carefully and screw the cap back on the remaining water. I'm tempted to take a swig, but there's no guarantee Blade or

Rummy will replenish our supply any time soon.

I lie back down and carefully shift my jaw from side to side. It's stiff and it aches, but as far as I can tell it's not broken. That's about all that's still intact. In the space of a few short hours I've lost Jakob, Mason, Big Ed, my dog, and even my pack. I blow out a long, despairing breath. I can't lose Owen too.

My thoughts return to Jakob. I press my knuckles to my temples and work them around in circles to ease the pressure building inside. Do the Sweepers even have him? Maybe he fell from the trail into the river trying to get away from them. My stomach twists. I can't allow myself to go there. I have to believe he's alive, for now.

I close my eyes and start to drift off again when I hear Blade's voice. He yanks the flap on the tent aside. I shield my eyes with the back of my hand when a blinding beam searches out my face.

"On your feet," he barks. "We're movin' out."

"What about him?" I motion to Owen.

"Shut up and get out!" Blade yells, making a fist.

I scramble past him, averting my eyes. I've no desire to invite another sucker punch.

He tosses me Owen's pack. "Put this on."

I adjust the straps and load it on my back without a word.

A few minutes later, two skinheads appear, carrying what looks like a combat stretcher between them. I watch, sick to my stomach, as they drag Owen feet first out of the tent and toss him onto the stretcher like he's nothing more than a rotting corpse.

Rummy appears with several more Rogues. "You take the rear," he says to Blade. "Keep a close eye on the girl."

We walk for miles, stepping over downed trees, following the cottony beams of half-charged flashlights beneath a chalky moon, until the first rays of dawn spill over the mountains. Blade is never more than two feet from me, but I constantly scan the braided undergrowth in the vain hope there might be an opportunity to escape. Not that I could leave Owen behind.

"Where are we going?" I ask Blade.

He stares back at me, a wooden expression on his face.

"South? Lewis Falls?"

He grunts, and shoves me forward with the barrel of his gun just as a nine-point buck trots out of the brush. Spooked, it bolts into a nearby grove and threads seamlessly into the forest. That's when I hear the long, flute-like trill of a wood thrush.

Chapter 12

The shadowy forest freezes in time like a giant leafy still life. My ears ring with the familiar coded call of a creature I know has neither wings nor feathers. I trudge forward, my body twitching, alternating between shock and relief. *Big Ed's alive!*

I peer frantically into every fern-draped nook we pass, trying to gauge how far away the whistle was. I'm not even sure if it came from behind or up ahead. I throw a wary glance over my shoulder at Blade. His eyes are glazed over, shoulders sagging as he marches, lost in the steady pace Rummy has set.

I listen for another trill, but it doesn't come. Maybe we've already passed Big Ed's hiding spot. A wave of panic grips me. What if he was trying to signal to me and I missed it? Or what if he's injured and needs my help? Blade tosses a bone he's been gnawing on into the foliage, and I glance despairingly at the mud-caked brush where it lands.

Eyes like a flounder camouflaged into its green surroundings blink silently at me from inside a thicket. I suck in a frozen breath and quickly turn my head forward. The hairs on the back of my neck tense in anticipation of Blade's suspicion. Did I stare too long at the ferns? I keep moving, spastic steps on jellied legs. Blood pounds in my temples.

"Step on it!" Rummy yells over his shoulder. Blade prods me in the back and I trot forward on cue.

We descend for a couple more hours, the lukewarm morning sun massaging my stiff limbs. The sun-washed pines give way to thickets of willows and leafy bluebells. All I want to do is collapse somewhere and sleep. I'm beginning to think I mistook the whistle, even the watchful eyes in the brush. Maybe it was an animal of some kind.

I'm close to passing out from hunger when we finally break stride and crash by a shaded stream garbling its way down to the river. I watch out of the corner of my eye as the Rogues toss Owen down beneath a tree. They glug heartily from their canteens, but don't offer him anything.

"Here." Blade tosses me some jerky. "That's it 'til we get to camp."

"How much farther?" I ask, tearing off a hunk of dried rabbit.

Blade chews on one side of his mouth and looks past me as if he's concentrating on something. After a minute, he grimaces and presses the palm of his hand into his cheek.

"Toothache?" I raise my brows.

He lets loose a string of profanities and nurses the side of his face, rocking back and forth.

"Is there a doctor in your camp?"

Blade pokes tentatively at his cheek. "Doc got done in."

There's an edge to his tone, almost as if he's daring me to ask what happened. I'm not sure I want to know, but it's another opportunity to learn something.

"Sweepers get him?" I ask, opting for our common enemy.

Blade slides a discreet glance in Rummy's direction. "Doc got killed in the center, 'long with the guards."

My eyes flick over the tattoos writhing up the sides of Blade's neck. *Gang tattoos.* A hot flush creeps over me. The reeducation center was due south of Shoshane City. Only three miles from our house. Blade might know if the south side of the city is still intact. I avert my eyes for a minute, digesting the idea. I don't really believe Ma's alive, but it's hard not to harbor a kernel of hope.

My pulse quickens. I wonder how far I can press him for more information before he clams up again. "So you were in the maximum security reeducation center?"

"Eleven years."

"How'd you get out?"

Blade leans back on the grass and stretches out his legs. "It was every dawg for himself when the power went down. If you weren't part of a gang, you didn't get far." His eyes flash as if he's recollecting the carnage. "Reds went down first though. That were only right."

"Reds?"

"Reeducation guards. Everyone wanted their weapons."

I gesture at his M16. "Reeducation guards don't carry weapons like that, do they?"

Blade leers at me. "Smart little sucker, ain't you? We found these ladies at a deserted air force base. Free for the taking now we don't got no military."

I avert my eyes, wondering what else they might have taken from the base. Fuel? Vehicles? We could use it all to take down the Sweepers.

I look up at the sound of footsteps. Rummy strides over, eying Blade with an air of mistrust. "Time to move out."

Blade scowls and stands. I sense a loaded animosity between them. If I'm careful not to push too fast too soon, Blade will talk again. If only to defy Rummy.

We gather up our packs, and the two Rogues who were carrying Owen walk back over to the stretcher and hoist it up between them.

"Leave the meathead." Rummy gives a dismissive wave of his hand. "He ain't come round by now, he ain't coming round."

"Wait!" I yell, before I can stop myself. I stumble forward, Owen's pack half-slipping from my shoulders. "He was conscious last night."

Rummy lets out a snort. "What do you care?"

I shrug, scrambling to cover my slip-up. "Just saying, he talked, so he's not dead."

"Ain't that somethin'?" Rummy twitches his lips in a fleeting smile and then snaps his fingers. "Let's go, homies."

I grab his sleeve, and then gasp when he spins around in a lightning move and slams his fist into my stomach.

"Don't *ever* touch me!"

I try to say something, but I'm too busy fighting for breath.

"Move it! Or I'll tie you to that piece of road kill over there and you can join the maggot fest."

I back away from Rummy, jagged waves of pain radiating through me. Blade grabs my elbow and shoves me forward. These Rogues are sick and twisted. For all I know, being captured by them may turn out to be a worse fate than extraction.

I throw one last glance over my shoulder at Owen, a bundle of rags in the moss, oblivious to the flies already landing on him. My stomach twists. It's killing me to leave him, but if I let Rummy know that, he'll finish him off anyway. I have to believe Big Ed's alive and following us, for Owen's sake. He's our only hope.

Eyes to the ground, I plod forward in a trance, tormented by thoughts of Owen being eaten alive by whatever descends on him first. When I lift my head again, the rest of the Rogues are already out of view. And somewhere along the line, Blade quit prodding me forward with the tip of his rifle. Big of him, but out of character.

I glance behind, and then pull up mid-stride in disbelief. Blade is nowhere in sight. I quickly scan the brush on both sides of me to see if he's stepped off the trail to relieve himself. I glance up ahead to make sure there's no one watching, and then silently slip into the brush. I might have only seconds before one of the other Rogues realizes we've fallen behind. I backtrack through the brush as silently as I can, listening for any sound of movement.

A rough hand clamps over my mouth. I stiffen.

"Shhh!" Big Ed's voice vibrates in my ear.

My muscles turn to mush and I sink down in the undergrowth. He kneels beside me and grips my shoulders. "You okay?"

My jaw shudders with relief. "I thought you were dead!"

"Hard to kill a mountain man." His leathery cheeks crease into a grin.

"Did you find Owen?"

Big Ed grimaces. "He's conscious."

I bite my bottom lip. "Where's the skinhead who was behind me?"

"I knocked him out. He'll live."

I scramble to my feet and adjust my pack. "We've got to get out of here. You were right. The Rogues are escaped subversives from the reeducation center, part of a gang."

He nods thoughtfully. "Figured those were gang tats." He turns and motions for me to follow him.

When we reach the stream, I spot Blade first, bound and squirming, beneath a tree. I rush past him to Owen's side. His eyes look like they're fused shut, and he doesn't respond when I try to wake him. "He's unconscious. We're going to have to carry him out."

"We can use my tent as a makeshift stretcher," Big Ed says. "I'll take a quick scout around first and make sure we're clear."

I lean over my brother and shake him gently. "Owen! Can you hear me?"

Sweat beads on my forehead as minutes tick by and he doesn't respond.

I prod him gently, blinking back tears. He's got to live—I can't lose anyone else. Finally, he groans and his eyes flutter open.

"Owen, it's me. It's going to be all right," I whisper, trying to keep my voice steady as I stare down at his mangled face.

He gives me a weak grin with swollen lips that barely stretch.

"Big Ed's here too," I reassure him, as footsteps crunch through the pinecones behind me.

Chapter 13

"Ugly looking pug—that Big Ed."

My blood chills at the familiar, steely voice. I turn my neck slowly like I'm roasting on a spit. Rummy hovers over me, black eyes smoldering with rage. Twenty feet away, two Rogues hold a gagged and bound Big Ed between them. He looks older, and smaller somehow, his bulk shrunk like a deflated balloon. I gulp to stem the fear clawing its way up my throat.

"I had a feeling you was playing head games with me," Rummy says, with a twisted grin, his tone way too casual to be trusted. "Big Dawg Ed. That's bad. Way bad."

He rolls another cigarette and takes a drag, watching intently as one of his men unties Blade and pulls the gag from his mouth.

"Who jumped you?" Rummy calls over to him. "Butterface? Or the old geezer?" The other Rogues snicker.

Blade gets to his feet, grunting. He glares at Rummy, then jabs an accusatory finger at Big Ed. "Dirtbag whacked me on the back of the head with his gun."

"Looks like we got ourselves a gun-toting trio: Butterface, Big Dog, and Road Kill over there." Rummy turns back to me and flicks the ash from his cigarette onto my boots. "Big Dog Ed's been tracking us the whole time. Who else you got out there?"

I throw a darting glance over at Big Ed. Knowing him, he's stayed tightlipped.

"No one. I met Big Ed on the trail, couple of days ago." I gesture at Owen. "I don't know who he is."

Rummy lets out a snort of disgust. "Throw the meathead back on the stretcher," he says to the other Rogues. "We'll take them all to Diesel. If they're snitches, he'll get it outta them."

The sun is hung high above the distant granite peaks by the time we reach the outskirts of Lewis Falls. Big Ed was right about where the Rogues set up base. It's the perfect hideout, a remote river rafting outpost edged up against the Wilderness of No Return, sandwiched between the Salmon River and the towering Sawtooth Mountains.

We march silently into town, single file. I glance around at the forlorn scattering of small, wooden cabins winding downhill, spaced a few feet apart. The place looks deserted, not even a scrawny cat or dog loping down the dirt streets. Just enough wind to stir up a little dirt and shake a board here and there. My heart pounds like a sledgehammer at the thought of meeting the notorious Diesel.

Rummy holds up his hand to halt the group. "Where's the lookout?"

My eyes dart over the rooftops, but I can't spot anyone wedged in position, watching our approach.

"Hammered, I'll bet." Blade sneers.

Rummy grunts and motions us forward with his gun.

"Diesel?" Rummy yells when we're thirty feet from the first cabin. "Where you at?"

A stocky man with jowls like a bulldog sticks his head out the door of a boarded-up cabin on our left. He glances up and down the street, and then waves us over impatiently.

Rummy quickens his pace, his face strained. Something's amiss in Lewis Falls. Whatever it is, I only hope it works in our favor.

Inside the dark cabin, eight young skinheads cluster around on benches. They stare at us with hard, jagged eyes hooded by lightning bolts and double-edged daggers.

Diesel watches us intently as we crowd onto the remaining bench, his thick, muscular forearms crossed in front of him like crowbars—thickly sleeved in tattoos. Even Big Ed has his sprawling beard to cover up with. I feel naked in comparison. I can already feel the skinheads' eyes crawling all over me.

My heart quakes. There's only one person I can imagine taking these Rogues on, and he's dead. Drowned, or smashed on the rocks. A horrible death I egged him into for no good reason. I'd give anything to take back what I said and have Mason here with me right now.

Rummy, Blade, and the other Rogues place their weapons by the door. I get the feeling Diesel doesn't trust his own people. His nostrils twitch constantly, as if he's sniffing out the scent of betrayal. He looks about thirty, a good bit older than the rest of them. He flicks his eyes over me and then studies Big Ed for a moment longer. "Where'd you find 'em?" he asks Rummy.

"Spying on us, upriver." Rummy frowns at Diesel. "Where's Ulrich?"

Diesel spins a chair around and slams a boot down on the seat. Black, cowhide, standard eight-inch height. Military. Probably from the base they raided.

Diesel cracks his knuckles and pans the room. "Some thug broke into our weapons stash last night. Busted nine of our M16's outta there, took a buncha ammo. Ulrich was on lookout. He's gone. One of these goons here must know something. I'm gonna busta cap in the lot of them if someone don't come clean."

Rummy narrows his eyes. He strides over to me and grabs me by the throat. "You sure there's no one else with you?"

I shake my head, flinching when I feel his hot, foul breath steam my face.

He shoves me backward and then turns to Diesel. "Says her camp was raided by Sweepers."

Diesel swipes his thumb across the tip of his nose and stares at me. "Lotta raiding goin' on all of a sudden. How do I know you weren't in on lifting my stash?"

I make a show of rubbing my bound wrists. If Diesel has bigger issues than me to deal with right now, maybe I can use it to my advantage. "Untie me and I'll tell you what I know."

Diesel jerks his chin in Blade's direction. Blade pulls out his knife and slices the ties on my wrist.

I flex my arms. "First we need food, water, and a medic."

Diesel lets out a snort. "You trading now? Got something worth smoking?" Or maybe you're offering something a little more … personal. The skinheads glance at Diesel, hike their lips up, like they're afraid to laugh, afraid not to.

"How about a Sweeper ship?" I say.

No one speaks, but I catch a flash of curiosity in Diesel's eye. He moves his jaw slowly side to side.

"Where is this shhhhip?" He drags the word out until it sounds like a threat.

I steady my voice and tell him what I told Rummy about finding the Hovermedes. And then I add to the lie. "It still runs. Just needs a few minor repairs. We're going to use it to attack the Sweepers' base."

Diesel and Rummy exchange dubious looks. I hope I haven't stretched it too far, but it's going to take a doggone good reason for Diesel to keep us alive.

I gesture over at Owen lying in the corner where the Rogues unloaded him. "He's a mechanic. He can get the Hovermedes running."

Blade narrows his eyes at me. "Thought you said you didn't know him."

I throw him a scathing look. "Like I told you, *bozo*, he talked in the tent last night."

The veins in Blade's neck bulge, but I detect a faint smile on Diesel's lips. He rubs the piercing above his eye in a leisurely fashion, as if he's weighing my usefulness. "Sweeper raids still don't explain my missing weapons. Them dawgs got all they need." He takes a step toward me. "But Undergrounders need weapons."

I shake my head in a show of disbelief. "Do we look like we're capable of raiding anything?" I peer up at him through a few matted strands of hair.

Diesel's face creases into mottled folds. "I gotta boatload of missing ammo and weapons right about the time you show up. That don't add up in my book." He walks over to Big Ed and yanks the gag from his mouth. "Your turn to talk, old man."

Big Ed brushes the back of his bound hands over his mouth and adjusts his glasses.

"How'd an old fart like you make it through the meltdown anyway?" Diesel traces his fingers across the skull on his chin. "You one of those crazy draft dodgers was living up in the mountains running traps and skinning rattlers?"

The furrow in Big Ed's forehead deepens.

"I could use a mountain man's skills around here," Diesel adds. "My homeboys are fit for fighting, and not much else." He sniffs long and hard. "We got rafts here, but no one to run them at night when the Sweepers ain't out prowling." He moves his pierced face inches from Big Ed's silver-rimmed glasses, and grins. "I reckon you could run the river in the dark. Bet you know every rock like the back of yer knotty ole hand."

Big Ed stares at him, unflinching.

Diesel takes a step back and throws an arm over my shoulder without breaking Big Ed's gaze. "Tell you what. You sign on with me, old man, and I'll let your little girl live."

I gasp when he twists me into a headlock and blocks my windpipe with his forearm. I grapple in vain to move the wall of muscle from my neck, my knuckles close to exploding from the effort. The room spins, tattooed faces swirling around me. I'm close to blacking out when Big Ed speaks.

"Where to?"

"Down river, clear to the coast. We'll pick up the Sweeper ship on the way."

"Turn her loose," Big Ed says, a vibrato edge in his voice. "I'll take you as far as the rafts can go."

"Now we're dealin', Santa Claus." Diesel laughs and flings me across the room. I fall to my knees beside Owen, shuddering as my lungs gorge on the sudden intake of air.

Diesel turns to Rummy. "These dimwits didn't come alone. We got company out there. Set up a lookout."

Rummy retrieves his gun from the stacked pile. "Stinks of an inside job to me."

Diesel paces back and forth, scanning the taut faces around him. "Last chance. Any you boys got somethin' you wanna tell me?" The tension in the room heightens, but no one speaks.

I glance down at Owen. He blinks once, twice, deliberate, measured motions. I lean over him. Is he trying to tell me something? His eyelids flicker again, rapidly, and this time he doesn't stop. A wave of panic courses through me. Is this some kind of seizure? Suddenly, his eyelids stop fluttering and he stares, transfixed by something above us. I throw a discreet look in Diesel's direction. He's deep in conversation with his men.

Cautiously, I tilt my head back and scan the rafters. The hairs on the back of my neck prickle. At first, I don't trust what I see, but then my brain whirs in comprehension.

Chapter 14

Lodged in the trusses like a giant bat, a shadowy hooded figure aims an M16 at the black shamrock tattoo on Diesel's bald head. I drop my gaze. Is this the missing lookout? No wonder Diesel's watching his men—and his back. There's some kind of mutiny afoot. I glance over at Owen and he mouths a single word to me.

Mason?

A wave of guilt hits me. I've been dreading telling Owen. "He's dead!" I blurt out.

Diesel spins around, his jowls twitching

I gesture helplessly at Owen. "*Half* dead. But he won't make it if you don't get a medic in here."

"Tie her back up." Diesel curls his lip at me in disgust and then turns to the Rogues. "Rummy, take your homeboys and scout the perimeter."

He strides over to the door and halts, his shadow falling over Owen huddled on the stretcher. "And get some food and bandages in here for this meathead." He pins me with an acid stare. "I could use a mechanic."

My lips quiver, but I hold his gaze. I've bought Owen some time, but if he recovers too quickly, I might just have dug his grave a foot deeper. He can't even figure out the filter system in our bunker.

The skinheads tromp out and my eyes go straight to the rafters. The hooded figure puts a finger to his lips. I give a shaky nod. What was the lookout called? Albrecht? Ulbrecht? Something like that.

Moments later a tall, gaunt woman appears with a metal first aid kit that looks like it's been ripped from a wall.

She flips the latch open, rummages around, and tosses me a half-full tube of antibiotic ointment, a wad of gauze and some tape. "Ha-have at it, k-k-kid." She clears her throat, her eyes never quite meeting mine, then perches on the edge of a bench. She's barely old enough to be calling me kid. And what's with the stutter? Her tattoos look fresh. I wonder if she's an escaped subversive too, or if the Rogues took her from a bunker.

I glance up as a pudgy Rogue walks in with a pot and a ladle, and a half-gallon plastic jug of water.

"Leftovers. Compliments o' Diesel, wants his guests to keep up their strength for our river rafting adventure together." He splits his lips in a silent laugh and a gold tooth glitters at me. His gaze flits around the room.

Heart pounding, I rack my brains for a way to distract him before he spots the figure in the rafters. "Why's he called Diesel?"

To my relief, the Rogue pulls out a stool and sets the pot down in front of me. He wags his finger in my face. "Dumb folk always ask that. And he'll show you. Ain't that right, Lipsy?"

The gaunt woman shifts uncomfortably.

"She ain't been right in the head since Diesel got done with her." The pudgy Rogue pulls out an old cigarette lighter and flicks the spark wheel. My eyes widen at the flame. I haven't seen one of those in forever—Da used to have one. I wince at the blistering heat when he waves the lighter under my jaw.

"Likes to light 'em up, don't he?" The pudgy Rogue pockets the cigarette lighter and flashes his gold tooth again. "Doused a man and took a blowtorch to him once."

The lid on the metal first aid box slams shut like a kill switch on the disturbing image. The gaunt-looking woman stands and tucks the box under her arm. "We g-gotta go."

The pudgy Rogue scowls. "What's your problem, Lipsy? Kid asked for a bedtime story." He lifts the lid off the pot and gives the stew a vigorous stirring before turning to leave.

He follows Lipsy out of the cabin and slams the log door shut. I listen for a key to turn, but apparently, there is none. Maybe they posted a guard outside. Their footsteps fade away in the direction of the lodge. I count to fifty and then make my way across the room and peer cautiously through a crack in the boarded-up window by the door. There's no one outside. I take one last look around, and then peer into the rafters and give a tentative thumbs up. To my relief the dark figure lowers his gun. He slips off his hood and our eyes lock.

My heart jolts like a freight train shuddering to a stop.

"What the—?" Big Ed's voice wafts across the room, thin and uncertain. An icy chill grips me. Are we *both* seeing a ghost?

The figure swings from a rafter and jumps down to the floor in a crouch. I stare at the huge feet and shrink back, my spine tingling. *No! It can't be!* My head spins as I take him in. Thick, muscular and ruddy. Hardly a bloodless apparition.

I watch, dumbstruck, as Mason's double makes his way over to Owen. He mutters something under his breath and balls his giant hands into fists. "Who did this to you?"

Owen swallows. "Rummy."

I scoot back another few inches, my heart catapulting wildly in my chest. Confusion floods my brain. My bound hands shake between my knees.

Big Ed gets to his feet. "We thought ... Derry said you ..." He frowns, throws me a perplexed look.

Owen tries to lift his head, and then groans before flopping back down. "Rummy ... thought I was a snitch tracking them." He sighs deeply and closes his eyes.

"He did his best to beat it out of you," Mason says with a grimace.

I stare at him in disbelief. Same thick, brooding brows, taut jaw, even the voice is right. But Mason's dead, isn't he?

"How?" I squeak out. "No one could survive that fall. It isn't possible."

Mason's eyes snap briefly in my direction. "Neither are clones, far as the rest of the world knows." He peers into the pot between us, as if to evade my manic stare.

"I washed ashore a mile or so downstream," he says. "Maybe I can't die before my time after all."

Big Ed holds out his bound hands to Mason. "You knew before you jumped you wouldn't die, didn't you?"

Mason pulls out his pocketknife and slashes the ties on Big Ed's wrists. "Like I told you, I was cloned for an elite military. Our bodies are virtually indestructible. The proteins in our cells are engineered with a tensile strength equivalent to steel." He pauses and gives a rueful grin. "First time I put it to the test though."

He gestures to me with the knife.

I stand and hold out my trembling hands. I'm still trying to wrap my head around the notion that it's really Mason in front of me.

"What's tensile strength?" Big Ed asks.

Mason plunks down and tosses his knife on the floor beside him. "Clones can deform elastically, like spider silk, when force is applied. It's not magic, just bioengineering."

Big Ed rubs his misshapen hand over his head.

"You're freaking them out, Mason." Owen laughs softly.

I suck in my breath. *Owen knew?* My mind races, trying to piece together the clues I missed. I watch out of the corner of my eye as Big Ed cradles Owen's head in his lap, and spoons some stew into his mouth.

"So why did you jump?" I ask, eying Mason's burly frame.

"Did you a favor, didn't I?"

A pang of guilt hits and I bite down on my lip. "I was mad at you for lying to us. I didn't mean what I said. It was a stupid, reckless thing to say. I'm really sorry."

Mason studies me for a minute. His expression slackens. "I had to jump to prove to you who I really was. You had no reason to trust me. But, I came back for you, didn't I?"

I nod, but with some reluctance.

"You're going to have to trust me now. The only way we're getting out of this alive is if we have each other's backs. The Rogues know they have an intruder. If they find me they'll kill me."

I furrow my brow. "*You* took their weapons?"

Mason grins. "Hid them, just in case we need to persuade them to cooperate."

"They have their own agenda," I say. "They're not going to help us."

"You heard them. They want that Hovermedes."

I rub my wrists distractedly. "So let's say we take them to it. Then what?"

"We promise them the ship if they agree to help us penetrate the Craniopolis. Once we're in, we lose them. I have clones on the inside I can trust. We'll find Jakob and fly the Hovermedes back out."

"What happens to the Rogues?"

Mason tightens his lips. "Our mission is to get Jakob out."

He stares dispassionately at me. Evidently, he has no qualms about ditching the Rogues. I probably shouldn't care what becomes of them either. After all, Blade didn't flinch when he told me about the guards they butchered when they fled the reeducation center.

I peer over at Mason, my heart pounding. I can't shake the feeling we'll be selling a piece of our souls if we lead the Rogues into a trap. Shouldn't they at least have a fighting chance against the Sweepers? They're human beings too, after all.

"So, what's your plan?" Big Ed asks Mason.

"First, we eat." He grabs a ladleful of stew and wolfs it down before handing the dripping ladle to me. "And then, we turn up the heat around here."

I swallow a mouthful of lukewarm stew with a hunk of trout in it. Some kind of peppery seasoning explodes in my mouth. I lick my lips and hand the ladle back to Mason. "What does that mean?"

"I'm gonna give them someone to pin the weapons theft on. Doctor the crime scene—make it look like it was an inside job. Diesel's already suspicious of his people. Let's see if he lives up to his fire-breathing reputation."

He walks over to the crack in the boarded-up window and peers through it. "Wildlife's asleep." He throws his hood over his head and treads across to the door. "Time to plant some ammo." His eyes slide over to Owen, propped up in Big Ed's arms.

"On someone who has it coming to him."

Chapter 15

I rub my eyes to make sure I'm not dreaming. Did Mason really just fall from the rafters and walk out the door? How many lives does a clone have anyway? With an expiration report already on file at the Sweeper crematorium, this makes the second time he's faked his death.

Big Ed gestures impatiently at the gauze and ointment lying on the floor. "Grab that stuff and let's get Owen fixed up." He reaches for his backpack and pulls out a clean bandana. "And pass me some water."

I gather up the scattered medical supplies and the half-gallon jug, and kneel at Owen's side. "Does it hurt?"

"Lot worse than wrestling with you." He gives a weak grin. "Nothing broken far as I can tell."

"What were the Rogues doing so far north?" Big Ed asks, as he dampens the bandana.

"They suspected someone from Frank's camp was ratting them out to the Sweepers. They've lost sixteen men in the past three months, extracted when they were out hunting, or scouting." Owen shifts his weight onto his elbows and winces. "Rummy planned to take out the entire camp, but when they got there, the camp had already fled. They tracked down Reid and Becca though."

Owen flinches when Big Ed applies ointment to the lacerations on his face.

"Reid and Becca were—" I break off, unsure of how to explain exactly what they were.

Owen exhales softly. "I know about the bootlegged clones. Mason told me everything."

My jaw drops. "So you've known for months Mason's a clone."

"And Kat."

I gasp and look over at Big Ed. The furrow of confusion between his eyes tells me he's as shocked as I am. Slow-moving, lizard-eyed Kat is a *clone?*

"Something went wrong with her," Owen says. "The cloning process is fraught with problems. Mason's seen some horrific things."

"What do you mean?"

Owen hesitates. "Deviations. Worse than Kat."

Worse than those eyes, boring into me like empty husks? My skin crawls. I can't imagine what he means. Half-human forms? Or something worse?

Big Ed takes off his glasses and rubs them with the edge of the bandana. "How did Kat get out of the Craniopolis?"

"Mason's friend in the crematorium is Kat's brother," Owen replies. "He asked Mason to smuggle her out on the Hovermedes. She'd failed the screening tests. The Sweepers were about to submit her to the laboratory for experimentation."

My spine stiffens. *Cloning material and spare parts.* So that's what Mason was hinting at. No wonder Kat's brother was desperate to get her out. Kat may have failed the Sweeper's tests, but she's not stupid. Somehow, her intelligence is locked inside her like a seed waiting to sprout. It scares me though, even more than Mason's superhuman strength, the way her eyes flick through me like she can read my mind.

"You shouldn't have come after me." Owen wets his cracked lips. I reach for the water, but he shakes his head. "The camp needs you now more than you realize."

I stare at him for a moment, the pain of everything I've lost radiating through me like a powerful, mind-altering drug. My voice cracks. "The Sweepers extracted Jakob."

Owen groans, scrunches his eyes shut. "I'm sorry."

"We're going to attempt a rescue, if Mason can get us to the Hovermedes."

"You have to trust him," Owen says. He twists his mouth in pain as Big Ed tapes a square of gauze beneath his chin. "He's your only hope of finding Jakob before it's too late."

"Your brother needs some rest now." Big Ed screws the top back on the tube of antibiotic cream. He pulls his jacket from his pack and fluffs it up under Owen's head.

I take the pot of cold stew to a bench by the back wall of the cabin and sit down. "What is this anyway?" Big Ed asks, sniffing the pot warily when he joins me.

"Some kind of fish," I say. "Tastes great."

He raises the ladle to his puckered lips and sucks at the congealed broth. "Not half bad. For cold stew."

I lean back against the wall, shattered from the rollercoaster of emotions I've been through in the last few days. "Do you think Mason's okay?"

Big Ed looks at me sideways. "Seems to have a few lives up his sleeve. I wouldn't worry about him."

"He's setting Rummy up, isn't he?"

"Wouldn't you?"

I drop my gaze. I'd like to give Rummy a piece of what he did to my brother and me, but kill him? That's what Diesel will do to him if he thinks Rummy's double-crossing him. I pick at a shred of fish wedged in my teeth. I've learned firsthand that revenge is hard to live with. "You're okay with Mason doing our dirty work for us?"

Big Ed runs his fingers slowly over his mangled hand. "We're all in this together. No one's hands are clean, Derry. Never forget that."

I shiver. How can I ever forget? *Do us all a favor, Mason, why don't you?*

I gesture at his hand. "What happened to you? You never talk about it."

"It's a long story."

"We've got time."

He grunts and appraises me for a moment. "Time and regret. Funny how those two go hand in hand." He lets out a heavy sigh. "I worked for a rancher named Wild Gulch when I was 'bout your age. He was uglier than a rattler on steroids when he hit the bottle. One night, when I'd been there a year or so, he caught a ranch hand stealing liquor from him." Big Ed shudders, as if a blast of cold air just went through the cabin. "Marched that ranch hand right out to the woodshed and shot him square in the chest. I was sleeping in the back, saw it all go down."

I widen my eyes and wait for him to continue. I don't want to appear over eager now that he's ready to talk.

"I popped right up and told him I was going into town to fetch the sheriff. Gulch just stood there, hands on his hips and smiled wide at me. Then all of a sudden, he grabbed a pitchfork from a rack, and pinned my hand to the wall with it. Told me I weren't going no place ever again if I didn't swear we was hiding in the wood shed, fearing for our lives when that drunken ranch hand doggone attacked us."

My eyes dart to his mangled hand. I shudder at the thought of how much he must have suffered.

"Gulch told everyone he killed the ranch hand in self-defense. I backed him up that night, never said nothin' to nobody 'bout it after that. But I knew then what he was capable of and I kept my distance." He breaks off and stares at the floor.

I lean in toward him. "What is it? Did something else happen after that?"

He throws me a startled look, scrubs his hand over his face. "Couple years go by and Gulch marries a young woman named Kitty March from the town o' Riggins. Kindest-hearted woman I ever knowed. From the get go he beat on her something awful. I saw her face all swelled up big as a melon, more than once." He pauses for a moment before he straightens up and continues. "One night, I heard a noise in the barn and when I went back to check on the horses, there she was with a rope hooked up 'round her neck, 'bout ready to jump off a stool." His voice catches. "I talked her down off it, and I promised I would fix it so Gulch would never hurt her again."

"What did you do?"

Big Ed scratches hard at his cheekbone. "Snuck in while he was sleeping."

I wait, averting my gaze when he wipes a finger along the underside of one eye. Minutes go by and he sinks into himself, trancelike.

"And … so you shot him?" I prompt.

He turns and fixes me with a piercing stare. "Took off his head with an axe."

Chapter 16

My breath scrapes up my throat. I grip the bench tightly with both hands.

I can't connect the Big Ed I know to the story he's telling me. It sounds like something Diesel would be capable of. But not the gentle, mountain man who's become one of my closest friends. Seems we're all only as good as the secrets we keep. I don't even trust my own heart anymore.

"How could you do something like that?" I ask.

Big Ed bows his head, the brim of his cowboy hat hiding what his eyes are saying. He lets out a heavy sigh. "I'm not proud of what I did. Back then, I had only my anger to tell me a thing was right or wrong. I thought it was my job to save her." He blinks up at me, owl-like.

I stare back at him, my ragged breathing resonating in my head. "So you went on the run?"

"It's hard to find a quiet place in your soul when you've killed a man. Moving off grid was the easy way out." He strokes his beard absentmindedly.

I shift uncomfortably in the silence that follows.

I get why he ran, but the fact is he never paid for murdering Wild Gulch. And now that the world's fallen apart, he probably never will. I'm not sure how I feel about that.

The door of the cabin grates open. I stiffen. Big Ed scrambles to his feet.

"It's me," Mason whispers, closing the door behind him. He strides over to us, leans his M16 against the bench, and lifts the lid from the pot.

"You can have the rest," I say, pushing the stew toward him.

He shovels it down without stopping between mouthfuls.

"What's happening out there?" Big Ed asks.

"Nothing, yet. Rummy's still out scouting." Mason grins. "I hid the missing ammo in his room at the lodge."

I frown. "What if Rummy finds it first?"

"Diesel's men already found it." Mason wipes the back of his hand across his mouth. "They about tore that room apart trying to catch the skunk I let loose in there."

Big Ed laughs deep in his throat.

"Rummy's men will side with him," Mason says, "so be prepared for a shoot-out."

"Might be our chance to escape," I say.

Mason gestures at Owen. "He's in no shape. Best just hunker down and wait for me." Mason stands and slams the lid back on the empty pot. "I'll let you know when it's safe." He throws his hood up, gives me a two-fingered salute, and slips through the door.

"Don't worry. He'll be back," Big Ed says. "He's like some kind of phoenix, always reappearing from the ashes."

I nod, unconvinced. One way or another, Mason's days are numbered. But it's not just him I'm worried about. It's finding Jakob before it's too late.

Owen lets out a soft moan. I grab my water bottle and hurry over to him.

He pushes the bottle away. "Help me up."

I grab him under the armpits and drag him into a sitting position. His head flops forward. "Dizzy."

Big Ed helps me prop him against the bench.

I swig back a mouthful of water and settle down beside him. To my relief, the swelling on his face has gone down some already.

A sudden burst of gunfire hits my eardrums like a jackhammer splitting rocks. I shove Owen back down and squeeze myself between him and the bench. I throw a darting glance around the room. Big Ed is sprawled prostrate a few feet from us. "Stay low," he says.

"What's happening?" Owen asks.

"Shoot-out between the Rogues." I inch a little closer. "Mason planted the missing ammo on Rummy."

A volley of bullets pelts the cabin, followed by a heavy thud as if someone's fallen against the door.

I turn to Big Ed. "What if it's Mason? He could be hurt."

"I'll check it out. Stay with Owen."

Before I can stop him, he slithers across the floor on his belly. He crouches on his haunches, pushes down on the iron lever and yanks open the log door. I smother a scream when a body topples inside.

Big Ed gets to his feet and hauls the man by the shoulders over to the corner where Owen and I are huddled together.

My eyes widen. It's the pudgy Rogue with the gold tooth who brought us the food.

I quickly pat him down for weapons. "He's clean. Must have dropped his gun when he was hit."

"Is he alive?" Owen asks.

Big Ed kneels and shakes the man gently. "Can you hear me?"

The Rogue's eyes fly open and he stares at the ceiling. He groans from some place deep inside. I glance down at the ruby-red stain glistening like a silk sash over his belly. I grab the jacket Owen was using as a pillow and press it to the Rogue's stomach. "You're going to be fine. Just hang in there." I throw Big Ed a helpless look. We've nothing but a near empty tube of antibiotic cream and a strip of leftover gauze to patch him up with.

The Rogue tilts his chin up and swallows, his neck twitching as he gulps for air. "Smoke, pl—*ease*."

At first, I think he's joking, but then I see the desperate look in his eyes. I lean over and pat the dying man's pockets.

He grimaces, his gold tooth winking in the dimly lit cabin. His inked face contorts like a crumpled newspaper. A moment later, his limbs go slack.

I pull the bloody jacket over the Rogue's face. My eyes meet Big Ed's and I see the flicker of fear in his. Then he blinks and it's gone. But it's enough to make me realize he's old and tired, and I can't lean on him forever. I need to find my own courage and take control of the situation.

"There's no knowing how this bloodbath's going to end," I say. "We should make a plan in case Mason doesn't come back."

Big Ed nods. "I'd put my money on him, if I had any, but we'd best prepare for the worst."

"We'll have to jump whoever comes through the door and use them to negotiate our way out of here."

Big Ed looks unconvinced. "How are we supposed to ambush a Rogue without a weapon?"

I hike my lip up in a smart-alecky grin and grope around in my pocket. "With the knife I always carry in my jacket, like you taught me."

Big Ed raises his brows admiringly. "I should follow my own advice more often."

"Do you still have snare wire?"

He fumbles with the straps on his rucksack. "One of the Rogues went through this, I'm not sure what they took out."

He rummages around and pulls out some fishing line and a toothbrush. "Took the wire, but they missed the nylon. This stuff will sever an artery." He runs his finger along the green, plastic handle of the toothbrush, and then tosses it to me. "We can sharpen this too. We could use another blade."

"It may not come to that," I say. "We only need to surprise whoever comes through the door long enough to grab his gun."

"I wish I could be more help," Owen says, struggling to sit up.

I catch his elbow and help him into a more comfortable position.

"Here," I say, handing him the knife and toothbrush. "This is your specialty. Carve something dangerous." I don't tell him his life might depend on it. Right now, I don't want to think about that possibility.

I turn back to Big Ed. "You take the fishing line. If there's a second Rogue, you'll have to noose him."

I glance down at the small pile of green plastic curls in Owen's lap. He whittles, head bent over the disfigured toothbrush, one eye opened enough to see by. He has to know this is a long shot. He's not strong enough to gut a fish.

A feeling of sadness comes over me like a dark, charged cloud. Whatever I do next, I'll have to live with my decision, just like Big Ed. I test my blade against the tip of my finger and square my shoulders. I can't let anyone get past me. No matter what I have to do. Owen's life is in my hands. And maybe Jakob's too.

Minutes go by, ten, fifteen, interspersed with rapid streams of gunfire. Sweat beads in droplets along my eyebrows, the salt half-blinding me when it trickles into my eyes. If a Rogue bursts through the door right now, I won't even be able to see who I'm stabbing at.

Big Ed stirs in his spot behind the door. "Been quiet out there an awful long time."

I nod and lean back against the wall.

Voices drift to the door. Every muscle in my body tenses. Heavy footsteps approach. The voices are louder now, but I still can't make out what they're saying. The conversation ends abruptly. One set of footsteps fades away. I signal to Big Ed and flatten myself against the wall.

The door grates open. A Rogue steps through, head bent low to miss the lintel.

I leap toward him, faster than a bobcat on a squirrel. The vein in his neck twitches under the pressure of my blade. His dark eyes latch onto mine. A flicker of confusion crosses his face. I feel him breathe, a shallow, uncertain breath that tells me he knows it could be his last. A tremor crosses his graffitied chin. My blade glistens, and I sense how easy it would be to slice him open and have my revenge. The drum roll in my head grows louder.

"Derry!" Big Ed yanks the gun from Rummy's shoulder and slams the door behind him, jolting me back from the edge. My heartbeat booms in my ears, but the will to do the deed has left me. Slowly, I release the pressure on the blade and take a step backward.

I stare for a long moment at Rummy, my skin tingling all over, blade poised and ready to slice him if he makes any sudden moves. Big Ed takes aim with the gun.

Rummy shifts his attention to him. "You wanna piece of me, ol' timer?"

My muscles tense. "I killed the last man called him that." The steel tip of the blade in my hand glints enticingly.

Rummy turns his head slowly toward me, his thin lips twisted. In a lightning move, he lashes out and knocks the knife from my hand. It clatters across the floor and slams to an abrupt halt in the corner. In the instant his eyes flick to it, I grab the gun from Big Ed and take aim at Rummy's chest.

He takes a couple of unsteady steps backward. "Ea—sy, Butterface."

I gesture with the gun at a bench on the back wall. "Shut up and sit down."

Hands raised, Rummy treads cautiously across the cabin. "Now what? You gonna blaze a trail outta here with Santa Claus and the cripple?"

"Did you kill Diesel?"

"You ain't gonna pull that trigger." He parks himself on a bench and taps one knee up and down.

I blow a strand of damp hair out of my face. "I'll do what I have to."

Rummy lets out a snort. "You ain't got what it takes. Killing's an intimate thing." He sniffs as if to let the impact of his words settle with me. "Knife to the neck, gun to the chest. Gets real close and personal when you hear a man suckin' for air." His mouth splits in a sneer. "How many bleedin' hearts you watched wallow in their own blood, beggin' for their lives?"

"Ask me another question and I'll blow your kneecap out." I blink, jarred at the sound of my own voice carrying across the room in a way it never has before.

Rummy's tight mustache twitches a couple of times.

I glower at him over the sight on the gun. "You're going to take me over to the lodge and tell your men to surrender."

Rummy laughs. "My homeboys will die before that happens."

"No, *you'll* die." I take a step backward and flick the coat off the dead

Rogue with the toe of my boot. "Like that sucker before you."

Rummy's eyes bulge. The sneer washes from his face.

"Now move it." I motion with the barrel of the gun in the direction of the door. "Keep your hands in the air."

"Stay with Owen," I say to Big Ed. "I'll bring the stretcher back with me."

He grabs my jacket and leans in close. "Watch your back. Remember, you can hear in all directions."

I pick up my knife and pass it to him. "Just in case."

He nods, and pockets it.

I march Rummy out into the early morning chill. My heartbeat ratchets up a level. I've no idea how many Rogues survived the gunfight, or if any of Diesel's men are still alive. If they spot Rummy, they'll shoot to kill and likely take us both out. It's a risk I'll have to take.

I follow Rummy around the side of the cabin and into the street. Gravel crunches beneath our feet, broadcasting our every step. My throat constricts with fear. "Keep moving," I say, leveling the muzzle at the back of his head. "If they shoot, you die with me."

I scout left and right, checking the rooftops for a hooded figure. No sign of Mason anywhere, dead or alive.

When we reach the far side of town, Rummy turns to me. "You're making a big mistake."

"I told you to keep moving." I prod him in the back with the barrel of the gun.

He scowls, hands held high above his head, and then stomps heavily up the front steps of the lodge. I follow a few feet behind, keeping an eye out over my shoulder.

"Homeboys! It's Rummy!" He reaches for the handle, then drops to the ground in front of me. "Shoot!" he bellows.

I drop too, my skin prickling, but no one fires. My heartbeat clatters in my chest. I should have known he'd try something once we reached the lodge. I breathe hard, trying to gauge the situation. Either his men aren't here, or they're afraid to show their faces. I grit my teeth and scramble to my feet.

The hairs in my ears tingle. A barely perceptible whooshing.

Remember, you can hear in all directions.

Chapter 17

In my mind I'm already running, but instead my limbs go slack with fear. The Sweeper tube lashes out like an articulated whip. Rummy crashes to the floor, his body vacuumed tight to the scaly pipe that slithers out of sight before I can reach him.

I jump up and stagger backward, shooting savagely in every direction. The blasts echo inside my skull until my magazine clicks empty.

My ears are blocked and ringing, but in the background I hear muffled sounds. A moment later, strapping hands grip my shoulder and haul me up the front steps and into the lodge. I trip forward and steady myself on the roughhewn reception counter. Heart pounding, I peer warily out from under the slick hair plastered over my face. Five pairs of eyes in shaved skulls flicker back at me. With a jolt, I recognize Blade's icy stare beneath his half-missing brow. Instinctively, my fingers reach inside my jacket for my knife. My stomach plummets when I remember I've left it with Big Ed.

"Sweepers," I whisper.

Lipsy steps forward. "We kn-kn-know."

I throw her a grateful look and carefully lay Rummy's gun down on the counter. "Rummy dropped this." I steal a glance in Blade's direction. He knows better than to trust me. He cracks his knuckles, eyes boring into me. My skin crawls. If he's in charge now that Rummy's gone, my luck just ran out. "I tried to save him," I say.

A dark look flickers across his face.

I rub my arms nervously. "So you're the new alpha dog?"

He frowns distractedly over my shoulder.

"Blade answers to me now."

An electric volt pulses through me at the familiar voice. I spin around as Mason strides into the foyer. He places his assault rifle on the counter beside Rummy's, and folds his tightly muscled arms across his chest.

"How ... did ... ?" I look at Mason in bewilderment, unsure what I'm even asking.

"You mean how'd I inherit these clowns?" Mason laughs. "I saved them from the tube, that's how. They were about to get suctioned up for science."

He gestures at a scowling Blade. "We've come to an understanding. They've agreed to help us infiltrate the Craniopolis. And now that the Sweepers have Rummy, everyone has skin in the game."

Blade sniffs, eyes dark as thunderclouds.

My mind reels. *We lead them to the research facility. Let them do what they do best.*

"Jakob's running out of time," I say. "We need to go."

"Not with Sweepers on the prowl." Mason reaches for his gun. "Big Ed and Owen will have to stay put until tonight. In the meantime, we'll go over our plan to reach the Hovermedes."

"What happened to Diesel?" I ask.

"Unconfirmed." Mason turns abruptly to Blade. "Make yourself useful and drum us up some food."

Blade scowls and turns on his heel. He's following orders, but only just. He's plotting something. I'm sure of it.

Seated around a large trestle table in the lodge's dining hall, we devour platefuls of scrambled eggs and fried fish.

"Cats can cook." Mason smacks his lips together.

"That would be Lipsy." Blade sneers. "She can fry up most anything, but that's about all she's good for, that right homies?"

The room erupts in laughter.

Lipsy raises her head and glances skittishly around.

"Likes to keep on the down low, now she ain't calling the shots no more, ain't that so, Lipsy?" Blade prods.

Lipsy clears her throat, her eyes twitching in my direction like a rabbit in a trap. She opens her mouth as if to say something, but then changes her mind and looks back down at her plate.

"Yup," Blade says. "Lipsy liked to lay down the law at the reeducation center, but we've been showing her who's boss ever since."

My blood chills. Lipsy must have been a reeducation center guard. I feel sick at the delight they take in torturing her now that she's under their control. Maybe I can talk Mason and Big Ed into bringing her with us when we leave the Craniopolis.

"All right, listen up everyone." Mason pushes his plate aside. "We'll leave here at dark. It would take the best part of two nights to hike to the Hovermedes, but if we raft the river back, Big Ed can get us there in a few hours."

Blade scowls. "How do we know the ol' geezer can even see to raft at night?"

"Maybe you're forgetting who *the ol' geezer* ambushed on the trail yesterday," I interject. "You're not exactly Hawkeye, are you?"

Blade bolts out of his seat and lunges toward me, but Mason thrusts out an arm like a steel rod and bars his way. "Big Ed's run that river forty years, day and night. There's no one more fit to man a raft down it. You got a problem with that, you can stay here and wait for the Sweepers to suck on your marrow."

Blade's eyes glower from narrowed slits. The other Rogues shift uneasily. Lipsy reaches for the plates and starts stacking them.

Mason pushes his chair out from the table. "Get the boats inflated and loaded up. We'll need enough supplies for a couple of days. Food and water, shovels, medical necessities, camping gear, guns and ammo."

I stand and turn to follow the Rogues out of the dining hall. Mason grabs my arm. "Leave them to it. We need to talk."

I slump back down at the table. "Did you kill Diesel?"

He throws a discreet glance behind him, and then rubs his hand over his jaw. "He got away. Either legged it into the forest or the Sweepers extracted him."

I groan. "I'm rooting for extraction. I don't want to have to think that he's still out there somewhere." I prop my elbows on the table. "Are you sure about taking the Rogues with us?"

"We need mercenaries." Mason perches on the edge of the table beside me.

"It's risky," I say. "We can't trust them, but we can't watch our backs every second either. And there's more of them."

"They won't be a problem until they get their hands on the Hovermedes." Mason gestures at his M16 leaning up against the table. "We're in charge of the weapons now. That levels the playing field."

"Do they know ... that you're a clone?"

Mason raises amused brows, then shakes his head. "The Rogues are hired thugs. The less they know the better."

He reaches for some leftover scrambled egg and swallows it in one gulp. "We'll stick with the Marine story for now. Once we're safely on the Hovermedes, we can decide how much to tell them." He stands and stretches. "Let's go check on those rafts. We have to get to the Hovermedes before someone else finds it."

"Who? No one else knows about it."

"The Rogues do." His eyes meet mine. "And they're not all accounted for."

I stare at his retreating back, puzzling over his words for a moment. *Diesel!*

Under a pall of darkness, I shove open the door of the cabin I marched Rummy out of twelve hours earlier. Big Ed looms in my face, knife raised in his right hand. He exhales loudly and sinks back against the wall. "I thought you weren't coming back."

My jaw trembles with relief. "I wasn't sure I'd ever see you again either. There were Sweepers on the far side of town."

He folds my switchblade and hands it back to me. "I almost used this."

I slip it into my jacket pocket. "I'm grateful you didn't."

I hurry across the room and kneel at Owen's side.

"You okay?" he asks.

I nod, my throat too tight to speak.

Big Ed walks over, mopping his forehead with the back of his hand.

"What about Mason?" Owen asks.

"He's fine. The Sweepers got Rummy though."

Owen's good eye widens ever so slightly. "Good riddance. They can harvest his organs for all I care."

I squeeze his shoulder gently. "You can't think like that. We're not savages."

Owen's eyes flash between me and Big Ed. "That's all that's left of any of us."

Big Ed grimaces. "No, there's always something more, but you have to hold on to it."

Shortly after eleven o'clock, we cast off our ropes and glide into the river at Black Canyon. The moon is full, flushing the forest on either side with silver light. Towering mountains of angry granite fringe the sky in sinister formation. I shake off a foreboding feeling and remind myself it's too dark out for Sweepers.

The inky water seethes beneath our rafts as we drift downriver. Owen is wedged between the seats behind Mason and me, supply bags packed tightly around him to keep him from slipping out. Lipsy and Blade are parked in the middle section, awkwardly clutching their oars.

No one speaks as we skim forward. Big Ed huddles in a half-crouch at the back of the raft, a steady shine in his eyes as he scours the dark current and directs our paddle strokes, backward and forward. Behind us, the other Rogues mimic our maneuvers as they cut through the water in the second raft loaded with more supplies.

The Rogues don't know it, but Big Ed hasn't run this river at night in years. I hate it when people call him "old man," but he is old, after all, and I'm only just beginning to realize what that means out here when our survival is at stake. He's pitted his skill as an oarsman against this river for decades, but tonight the stakes are higher than they've ever been. I only hope he's up for the challenge.

Before long, I hear something like the rumble of thunder. Big Ed's instructions become increasingly terse and we paddle with a growing sense of unease. Boulders and shrubs zip by as we accelerate. I can feel the power of the water beneath me throbbing like a jet engine about to take off.

One missed stroke is all it will take for the rocky jaws of the rapids to grind our rafts into ribbons. My muscles expand and contract as we race ever closer to the crashing cauldron of water. I paddle like a woman possessed, but we still splash back and forth like a discarded piece of plastic.

"Get ready!" Big Ed yells as he signals to the raft behind us. He maneuvers fiercely with his arms and shoulders to keep the raft parallel with the current, his knuckles gripping the rudder so tightly they look like sausages about to burst their skins. The roar of the rapids is deafening, like a sonic booming against a giant drum.

We round a bend in the river, and for a brief moment we're poised at the top of a liquid rollercoaster, half the length of our raft suspended in mid air. My stomach rockets up into my throat. I picture Jakob one last time, and then we plummet. I gasp as a shivering sheet of aluminum, the size of the sky, breaks over the boat, plunging us into darkness. I slide forward and claw at the safety rope, my life vest tight around my chest in a crushing bear hug. My lungs fill with panic at the sudden downward thrust.

"Owen!" I cry out, my voice muted by the watery avalanche pounding me from every direction.

We freewheel through the icy spray. My limbs lose all sensation, numbed by a deadly concoction of fear and cold. I can't tell if I'm in the raft or free falling in my life vest. My eardrums vibrate with a deafening sound, like clouds bursting apart around me. Or is it my lungs imploding?

My fingers burn, as though the flesh has long since been ripped from them and I'm clinging to the rope by bone alone. I brace for the violence of impact, praying the end will be brief and painless.

Seconds later, the boat shudders, as if absorbing some tremendous force.

My spine compresses. My fingers, still melded to the rope, scream in raw protest. Without warning, the raft pops up like a foaming, half-drowned wildcat, water streaming from it in every direction.

I heave several shaky breaths. It takes a moment to register that we're at the bottom of the falls, and I'm alive.

Blade lets out a string of expletives. Gasping, I look with trepidation over my shoulder to see who else survived. Lipsy stares at me, wide-eyed, like she's seen the ghost of Neptune. By some miracle, Owen's still wedged in the bottom of the raft, draped like a sopping clump of seaweed over what's left of our supplies. Mason clutches his paddle, pokerfaced at the prow of the ship.

A rough jolt startles me back into action. I clench my paddle, blinking to get my bearings. The raft shoots forward over the froth.

"Left back," Big Ed yells. The exhilaration in his voice is all the confirmation I need that somehow we've survived the death plunge.

I paddle hard, half-sobbing with relief when we pop out of the whirlpool and back into the current. I keep up steady strokes, not daring to look downstream yet. After a few minutes, we float into a pool of deep, calm water. A startled beaver does a flip turn and disappears beneath the surface.

We look around, stunned into silence as we contemplate what just happened. I rest my paddle on the edge of the raft, but before I can take a breath, three or four rapid cracks cut across the water.

"Gunfire!" Big Ed turns and scans the cliff tops.

I look up in time to see the second raft toboggan down the rapids. I hold my breath until it leaps out from behind the veil of water and rights itself. It swirls for a few seconds in the stew at the bottom of the rapids before merging with the current. A foreboding feeling grips me as I watch it glide awkwardly toward us, sagging on one side like a punctured tire running on a rim.

Chapter 18

The deflated raft slips into the pool and drifts toward us. Mason waves his flashlight over it.

A spasm of fear goes through me. There's no mistaking the bullet holes in the rear compartment. Blade shoves me aside and reaches for the safety rope. He yanks the punctured raft toward him and peers inside. His face settles in a stiff grimace. "Empty. Even the supplies are gone." He pushes it out of our way and snatches up his paddle.

"Whoa!" Mason reaches for Blade's shoulder. "We're not going to find them alive now, not if they're in the river. And whose to say they didn't ditch us before the rapids?"

"You d-d-don't ... know that," Lipsy protests. I throw her a frustrated look. If she's trying to keep Blade calm, it isn't working.

Blade raises his paddle to take a swing at Mason, but he blocks it with ease and Blade stumbles backward into Owen. Big Ed dives to shield him and throws me a harrowed look. Blade's about to blow a gasket. If I don't defuse the situation, we could all end up in the river.

I whack my paddle across the center seat and gesture at the deflated raft. "Right now, we're someone's target practice. We don't have time for search and rescue. We can look for bodies along the way, but we're not going back. We keep going to the landing point."

Mason rubs the back of his hand across his jaw. "Diesel's gotta be behind this. No one else knows we're out here."

"Ain't Diesel shootin' at us." Blade scowls. "This here's Undergrounders. Hunting us down like they're on safari."

"Whoever it is, we need to get off the river as quickly as possible." I grab my paddle and take my seat at the front of the raft. Blade and Mason exchange festering looks, before resuming their positions.

Within minutes, we've maneuvered out of the pool and back into the current. It's slow going, but no one has the energy left to propel the raft any faster through the water. Instead, we scan the shadows for bodies, randomly poking and slapping at the weeds along the edge of the river with our paddles. A shiver runs across my shoulders. If Diesel's out there, we're sitting ducks in this raft.

My aching arms, limp as noodles, make ever-dwindling paddling motions. Now that my heartbeat has slowed, and the last dregs of adrenaline have leaked from my veins, the cold is creeping into my bones.

Other than an occasional command from Big Ed, no one speaks. We paddle like disembodied rafters, each in his own world. I grimly visualize the next stroke, barely able to raise my arms, let alone think a coherent thought.

"You all right?" Owen asks.

"Yeah, just cold," I lie.

"Me too," Mason interjects. "Time we picked up speed."

I glance over at him, sensing a note of resignation in his voice. "There are no bodies, are there?"

He tightens his jaw. "Not yet, there aren't."

Flushed smudges of dawn are already permeating the darkness by the time we reach the North Fork landing point. We ground the raft in a gravel outwash and reach for our weapons. I'm soaked and cold, but inwardly glowing from the thrill of licking the rapids. At least I feel alive, a gift the bunkers never gave me. But, it's a bitter thrill without Jakob by my side.

Mason slings his gun over his shoulder. "I'll do a quick scout around."

He clambers out and disappears into the forest. I clutch the barrel of my gun and pan the perimeter of trees from the refuge of our raft. Apart from the usual owl tweets and cricket clicks nothing moves or makes a sound.

After a few tense minutes, Mason reappears and gives the all clear. "I'll get Owen. The rest of you can unload."

We wade in silence through the sludge at the river's edge to the gravely shore, and then hand off the backpacks and supplies in a chain up the bank. My heart pounds in my chest. We're almost at the Hovermedes. One step closer to finding Jakob. I've tried not to think too much about him in the past few days. I don't know if he's dead or alive, and it's too painful to imagine a future without him.

I watch as Mason hoists Owen over his shoulder. He ploughs easily through the mud toward the shore on legs of steel. I toss my backpack down and take a quick steadying breath. We're about to cross from what's left of my world into Mason's. I pull my soggy, knotted braid over my shoulder and finger it hesitantly. I have no choice from here on out but to trust my life to a clone. Even Jakob's life is in Mason's hands now, and that disturbs me. But, Mason's the only one who can take me to the Sweepers. I wish I believed in him as much as Owen does.

"Let's move." Mason strides by me without breaking pace.

Big Ed falls in behind him. I gesture with my rifle to Blade and Lipsy to get going, and then cast one last glance around before I hurry after them.

A few feet from the shore, a familiar dense foliage wraps its tentacles around us, lending a greenish hue to the peachy dawn. I duck to avoid a low-hanging limb, crunching over a thick bed of fallen twigs on anemic legs still in recovery mode from our brush with a watery grave. Out front, Mason slashes his way through everything in his path like an excavator. His strength is beyond natural, but I still marvel that he survived the fall from the pole bridge.

We barely cover a quarter mile before Mason pulls up abruptly. He slides Owen down from his shoulders and props him up at the base of a tree. "This is the spot."

I look around, frowning. A sea of ferns and brush stretches in every direction.

A hint of suspicion crosses Blade's face. "Where's the ship at? I don't see nothin'."

Mason wades forward into the undergrowth, drops down several feet into a depression, and reaches for a giant armful of loose brush. He tosses it aside and then digs around some more. "Help me move this stuff."

Blade and Lipsy hustle into the ferns and begin tearing at the brush and hurling it over their shoulders.

I plow through the undergrowth after them, as eager as they are to see a Hovermedes up close.

Mason works methodically, never quite taking his eyes off Blade. I'm sure Blade won't try anything yet, not until he knows the Hovermedes is operational, but Mason's not taking any chances.

"There she is." Mason steps back and looks around at us, a satisfied gleam in his eyes. I throw another armful of twigs aside and gape at the sleek, bus-length gunmetal body, peeking through the brush like a half-surfaced submarine.

For a moment, I'm paralyzed with fear, and then a volt of anger surges through me. Jakob, Sam, so many others, some whose faces are already slipping from my memory, all extracted. It's time to put this diabolical machine to good use and right some wrongs. Like finding Jakob and bringing him home. After that, the Rogues can do with it what they will.

Mason straightens up and looks around. "Let's see if she still flies."

Blade runs his bare hands down the seamless side of the Hovermedes. "Ain't no door on this thing."

Mason bars his arms and stares at him. "First, we need to go over the ground rules."

Blade slams his fist on the side of the Hovermedes. "We ain't got time for no seatbelt demo, you dumb hog. Rummy's in trouble. Now open the bleedin' door!"

Mason widens his stance. "I got all the time in the world."

Lipsy shuffles from one foot to the other, watching from beneath drawn brows.

Blade spits into the dirt. "Okay, soldier boy, I'm listenin'."

Mason gives a guarded smile. "Good, 'cause once we're on board, I'm in charge. No exceptions. No one touches the control panel, or attempts to operate the ship, other than myself."

Blade shrugs. "You wanna drive that badly, have at it."

Mason gives an abrupt nod and turns back to the Hovermedes. He traces his fingers lightly down the side, and then presses firmly on a spot halfway down the cigar-shaped barrel of the ship. I hold my breath waiting for a door to magically appear. Instead, the entire roof of the Hovermedes splits open with a pneumatic hum, and the sides glide apart like an armadillo snapped in half.

"Yikes!" I take a step backward as the ship powers up and a strip of lights flicker on.

Mason chuckles. "There is a retractable side door, but it's easier to open it up all the way when we're loading a group." He turns to the others. "Let's roll. To the rear. Stay behind me."

Before he can take a step, Blade shoves past him, and darts to the back of the ship. He grabs the metal sides of the opening, pulls himself up, and disappears inside.

"Hey!" I yell, panic ballooning up inside me. "What's he doing?" All my hopes of rescuing Jakob lie with this ship. If Blade takes control of it, I might never see Jakob again.

Chapter 19

Mason bolts past me to the rear of the ship just as Blade staggers back out. He wipes his mouth across his sleeve, and glares at Mason, his piercing glinting like a third eye. "Think that's funny, road dog?"

The look on Mason's face tells me he's as perplexed as I am.

"You playin' me for a sucker?" Blade waves his fist at Mason. "You knew that cat gone and croaked in there, didn't you?"

Mason turns to me, his voice low and urgent. "I'll check it out. Keep your gun on him. Might be a ruse."

I clutch my rifle tighter and watch out of the corner of my eye as Mason climbs into the back of the Hovermedes.

"I don't like this," Big Ed says. "Someone beat us here." He adjusts the strap of his gun and peers around the dense undergrowth.

"Hey!" Mason yells. "Grab the feet!"

I race over to the Hovermedes and reach for the boots protruding through the entry. Men's, about Owen's size. I glance up. A black knit cap is pulled down over the face. I shudder and adjust my sweaty grip.

Mason grunts and lifts the arms. "Got him?"

I give a tense nod and pull on the legs. We ease the body out and lay it down in the brush a few feet from the Hovermedes.

"Poor bugger don't smell yet," Big Ed says, coming up behind me. "Can't be dead more than a few hours."

Mason hunkers down and yanks the wool cap off. I gasp and take a step back, a searing pain steaming through my chest. *Prat.*

"You know that sucker?" Blade leers at me.

My chest tightens like it's filling with sand. "He's … he was our bunker chief." I stare down at Prat's pale face, the scant ginger-hued stubble on his chin a sad reminder that he was barely a man. Remorse for all the ugly thoughts I ever had about him washes over me. Prat and I never saw eye to eye, but at the end of the day, he was just another kid trying to do what he could to make a life for us. I'm learning it's not so easy to lead.

Mason smashes the knit cap in his fist, and hurls it into the trees.

I blink rapidly, trying to process my thoughts. *If Prat's dead, what about Da and the others?* My stomach churns. Even if all Da does is drink, I need him just the same. He's the only link I have left to Ma, the only one who can tell me stories about her, at least when he's sober.

Faces gesture in slow motion around me. Everyone's talking at once, arguing over what went down. Blade shoves Big Ed in the chest. He stumbles backward, arms flailing for support. Mason grabs him, and then reaches for Blade and shoves him against the side of the Hovermedes.

"Shut up and listen," Mason yells in his face. "Whoever killed Prat could show up here any minute. That's if the Sweepers don't beat them to it. We need to load up and leave right now."

I glance up at the salmon-tinged sky. "How long will it take to get us airborne?" I ask.

"Not long, if she starts right up. I'll give it my best shot." Mason flexes an uncertain smile, and then climbs on board.

"You're on lookout," I say to Big Ed. "Blade and Lipsy, clear a spot in the brush so we can cover the body."

Blade lets out a snort of disgust. "I ain't no gravedigger. Gimme back my gun and I'll find the hog what did this and blow his brains out."

I level my gaze at him. "If you're not done grave digging by the time Mason's ready to fire up the Hovermedes, you can stay here and fist fight the *hog* who did this."

Blade throws me a dirty look, and then walks off, muttering to himself. Lipsy looks at me uncertainly and then hurries after him. I should try harder to reach out to her. She always looks so scared. And I could use a friend, even one with a stutter.

I sling my gun over my shoulder and make my way over to Owen.

"Do you think our bunker's been outed?" he asks, his good eye misting over.

I squeeze his shoulder gently. "I don't know. Maybe the rest of them got away."

"Even Da?"

"The Septites wouldn't leave him behind."

Owen shakes his head. "If he hadn't already drunk himself to death."

"That's on his head."

A pained look flits across Owen's face. I feel a twinge of remorse for my harsh tone, but I'm done dragging the guilt for Da's choices around with me. Eventually he'll kill himself, if he's not dead already. It's a reality we both need to face.

I tense at the sound of three electronic beeps, followed by a smooth whirring that fills the air with a peculiar energy. The hairs on the back of my neck quiver, even my teeth tingle deep in my jaw.

"Let's go," Mason says, appearing at the rear of the Hovermedes.

"Hey! Wait a minute!" Blade tosses an armful of brush aside. "You want your pal here what got rubbed out to get his final resting place or not?"

I slide my gaze in his direction. "Throw in a grave marker and we'll wait for you." I turn my back on him, and follow Mason to the rear of the Hovermedes. He jumps on board, reaches out a giant hand, and pulls me in.

My jaw drops. Ten egg-shaped, pearlescent-white seats, lined with a matrix-like red cushioning, line both sides of a sleek center aisle. The entire surface area at the front of the ship—walls, floor, ceiling—is covered with a massive array of violet screens, flickering colored lights and electronic gauges. I shake my head in disbelief. "This thing is sick. It's like walking around inside a lava lamp."

Mason grins. "Aerospace technology. These ships were designed for the world government under the guise of a mission-system upgrade. They used commercial space travel as their cover."

I run my hand along the back of the nearest seat. The material feels peculiar, sponge-like almost. Air intake ducts, shaped like rocket boosters, are recessed into the ceiling, and a flashing control panel nests in each armrest. I sink down into the nearest chair and press the button marked *WÄRME*. Warmth radiates through the chair, and the matrix-like material instantly molds itself to my body. Cocooned in the softness, I let out a sigh, and close my eyes.

When I slide up in the seat again, I notice a sign at eye level, *TRICHTER AKTIVIERUNG*. I squint at it, groggy from the comforting heat of my chair. I can't decipher it.

I reach for the cabinet handle below the sign. Behind the small metal door is a red release pull. I pull my hand back and frown at the logo, trying to remember where I've seen *TechnoTerra* before.

It hits me in a flash. *The logo on the tubes.* Trembling, I slam the cabinet door shut. I press the palms of my hands into my eyes, trying to rid my mind of the gruesome image of a retractable metal arm suctioning up Sam.

"Derry!"

I startle at the sound of Mason's voice.

"What are you waiting on? In-flight service? Go out there and round them up."

Owen limps his way to the back of the ship, brushing aside my attempt to help him. I can tell by the way he moves he's in a world of pain, but at least he's on his feet again. After we get him situated in the middle section of the Hovermedes, Big Ed herds Blade and Lipsy inside. Hands bound again behind their backs, they plonk down in a pair of egg-shaped seats, a mixture of apprehension and awe in their faces.

"Everyone in?" Mason calls over his shoulder.

I give him two thumbs up and lean back in my seat. The sides of the Hovermedes come together with a vacuum seal whoosh. I scrutinize the ceiling. It's impossible to tell from here there's an opening anywhere in the body of the ship.

I lean into the aisle and crane my neck around to check on Owen. He's already nodded off again, head flopped forward on his chest.

"Derry, come up here with me!" Mason calls back to me.

Blade jerks his chin at me. "Where you think you're bleedin' goin'?"

I flash him a brassy grin. "Guess I'm your new co-pilot."

His features contort into a plaster cast of rage.

I head up to the front of the ship before he explodes. I know better than to wind him up like that. I'm already a marked woman in his book, but the satisfaction I get from watching him squirm now that he's not calling the shots is worth it.

Mason sits hunched in front of a screen, sketching both forefingers over it in seemingly random circles. I watch him for a moment, frowning. "What are you doing?"

"I just sent an encrypted message to my contact in the Craniopolis." He looks up, a sober expression on his face. "Operation Jakob's officially a go."

I blink, feeling the weight of his words in my bones. There's no turning back now. And, I don't want to. I just hope we don't arrive too late to save Jakob.

"Listen to me carefully." Mason lowers his voice. "The only way to get the Hovermedes up and running is by activating the launch button with a chip."

I glance over the vast array of dials and buttons. "So where's the chip?"

"It's an implant. Every clone is chipped at inception. All I have to do to start the Hovermedes is slide my fingertip into the slot on the launch button."

My eyebrows shoot upward.

Mason rubs a hand over his thickset jaw. "The reason I'm telling you this, is that if anything happens to me, you need to retrieve it." He waves his right index finger in front of my nose.

"What?" I shrink back. "You can't mean for me to cut off your finger?"

"Just slice the tip and look for a silver chip the size of a piece of corn."

I push his meaty finger out of view. "There's no way I'm slicing you open, even if it is just a finger."

I pout my lip at him. "Anything else I should know?"

He motions to the seat beside him. "Yeah. How to fly this baby."

"For real?"

Mason's eyes cloud over. "I'll take us in to the Craniopolis, but there's no guarantee we're all coming back out."

"Time we was flyin'," Blade yells around the back of a chair. "Get this lump o' lead in the air! And have that doggone waitress bring me a cocktail."

Lipsy laughs. "Ma-ma-ma-make that two."

I arch a brow at Mason. "Do we *really* need them?"

Mason throws me a reproving look. "You're balking at slicing a fingertip. Blade could slash throats in his sleep. And Lipsy can handle a gun. So, *yes*, we need them. Now pay attention."

He does have a point. I slide forward in my seat to get a closer look.

"First you need to memorize the takeoff sequence." He demonstrates a series of buttons in front of him. "Got that?"

Before I can reply, I hear a scuffle at the back of the ship. Big Ed bellows out my name. Heart pounding, I race back down the aisle to find him desperately trying to wrestle something from Blade's fingers. "Keep him still!" he grunts.

I grab Blade's wrists and hold them in place.

Big Ed straightens up, clutching his prize. "Stinkin' grave robber!" He holds out his hand. "Get a load of this."

Chapter 20

I blink in confusion. It's a piece of paper—torn from a notebook of some kind—with a single word in Prat's handwriting scrawled across it.

Diesel.

"I heard him telling Lipsy 'bout the stuff he found in Prat's pockets," Big Ed says.

My lungs squeeze together. I lean over Blade's face. "What else did you take?"

Blade's face splits in a broad sneer. "You gonna dance with me 'bout some dead dude's junk?"

Big Ed taps his cheek from behind with the muzzle of his gun. "Answer her."

The tattoos on Blade's neck twitch under the cold steel. He hesitates and then reaches awkwardly beneath his coat and pulls out a small leather sack I recognize as Prat's.

I snatch it from him and tip the contents out on a seat on the opposite side of the aisle. I rake through the miscellaneous items, trying to ignore the guilt I feel for invading Prat's privacy. A watch with a dead battery, a dog-eared photo of Prat and his parents at Disneyland, an insignia pin from a high school debate club—miscellaneous pieces that prove he was once a participant in life. I swallow back a sob. I've often wished I had some of Ma's things to remind me of her.

I crush the paper in my hand and glare at Blade. His eyes flash me a silent message of hate in return. Somewhere along the way, I crossed a line with him. Given half a chance he'd slit my throat, and I'd better not forget that, even for one minute.

"Keep a close eye on him," I say to Big Ed.

I walk back up the aisle and hand the note to Mason. "This was in Prat's coat. He must have figured if he didn't make it, at least we'd know who killed him."

Mason grimaces. "So Diesel made it here before us. We wasted too much time dragging the river for bodies. We should have kept up the pace and got here sooner."

I rub my hands briskly over my face. "We have to make sure the rest of the Undergrounders are okay. Da, and Kat."

"We can't stop at the bunker now," Mason says. "It's light out. Another Hovermedes might spot us."

"That's a risk we'll have to take."

"What about Jakob?" Mason throws me a harried look. "We're running out of time to save him."

A huge sob wells up inside me. The closer I get to seeing him again, the greater the fear of losing him becomes. But Prat's death has me worried for everyone now. "Jakob would want me to make sure his parents were safe," I say, swallowing back my tears. I'm worried about Tucker too. If he did find his way back to the bunker safely, he may not have food or water.

Mason gives me an infuriated look. "Belt up," he says, turning back to the controls.

Without warning, the Hovermedes lurches forward. I roll on my heels before falling clumsily backward into my chair. I fumble around in vain for a seatbelt.

Mason gestures to the armrest. "Control panel."

I tap the seat icon on the screen. Out of nowhere, a harness writhes diagonally across my chest in both directions and plugs into slots in the seams of the chair—slots I swear weren't there a moment ago. Pulse thudding, I sink back against the cushioning as we build up speed.

I'm supposed to be learning how to fly this thing, but Mason appears to have changed his mind about that now that I've diverted the mission. I can't blame him for being upset with me. The last time I ignored his advice, Reid and Becca escaped. And now they're dead. Maybe not a bad thing for us, but they didn't deserve to die the way they did.

Frustrated, I slide down in my seat and study the menu on the screen. I scroll through the choices and click *English on* the languages option. Comfort controls mainly—heat, light and incline—but a few are more obscure. I shrug and select *Periscopic Infrared.*

A clear convex disc the size of a dinner plate descends in front of my face. When my fingers graze the edge, it recoils like a living thing, lights up, and powers on.

My jaw drops. In the disc I can see every magnified inch of the forest terrain we're hovering over. The view and range is unrestricted, almost as if the entire underbelly of the ship is a giant lens. The resolution of the images is remarkable, no blurring or shaking, despite our increasing speed. Through the thick canopy of brush and trees, every bird and animal is captured as an infrared image and analyzed in the bottom left corner; species, weight, height, age, temperature, each flashing onto the disc in quick succession.

I watch, fascinated by the unending stream of data. "Is this how the Hovermedes searches for Undergrounders?" I ask Mason.

He gives a terse nod, but doesn't even look in my direction.

I roll my eyes and turn my attention back to the disc. If the Sweepers are able to scan us and assess all our vitals before they pick us up, it explains how they're able to target the young.

I tap on the image of a deer that flashes onto the screen.

"Might not want to—" Mason sighs. "Too late."

A hologram of a white head with no distinguishable facial features materializes in front of me. I shrink back in horror. For one crazy moment, I think I've conjured up a Sweeper. Lips form like a sand dune in the ghostlike head. An electronic voice fills the cabin.

Funnel activation request. Confirm extraction.

I yank my shaking fingers away from the screen in my armrest and recoil from the freakish image in front of my face. "Help me, Mason! How do I turn this thing off?" I wriggle to slide out of my chair, but my harness tightens like a boa constricting its coils.

The mouth in the head moves like animated clay, lip-syncing to the electronic voice, *Extraction denied.*

The hologram flat lines and fades from sight. I stare at the spot for a moment longer, half-afraid the head might reappear. I swat the space in front of me for good measure.

"I overrode your permissions," Mason says, a grin playing on his lips. "The last thing we need is to bag a deer."

I let out a relieved breath. "Beats hunting with a gun."

"Sweepers don't hunt. Their food is lyopholized."

"Ly—*what?*"

"Dehydrated, macrobiotic nutrients—scientific junk food I call it now that I know better."

I twist my lips in disgust. "Guess we won't be dining out at the Craniopolis."

"Won't be there long enough if everything goes according to plan."

"Speaking of a plan, you're supposed to be teaching me how to fly this thing. I've got a million questions."

"Shoot!"

"You said the ships hover above the ground and draw from the earth's core, but we've got to be close to two hundred feet up in the air right now."

"For short periods of time we can leave the electromagnetic suspension system and fly at a higher altitude on battery packs. Right now I'm taking the quickest route to the bunker, even though it means depleting the batteries."

"Can the tubes extract through trees?" I ask.

Mason shakes his head. "Not without damaging the equipment and potentially killing the target. Which kind of defeats the purpose of an extraction."

I swallow back the bile that rises up my throat. Of course they need to bring their targets in alive. All that talk of body parts and medical experimentation swishes around inside my brain. I can't bear to think of what the Sweepers might end up doing to Jakob if he resists them—pirate his DNA, harvest his organs even. A shiver runs down my back. I can't imagine his heart beating in anyone else's chest. Not after I've felt it beating next to mine.

"That's our camp up ahead." Mason points down into a clearing. I lean forward and furrow my brow. My eyesight's good, but nowhere near as good as his enhanced vision. I can tell by the way his knuckles tighten on the control shift that something's wrong. "What is it?"

"Hatch is open."

I grip the armrests on my chair. The sun's been up for a while. If the hatch is open, either the Undergrounders have abandoned the bunker, or they're all dead.

The Hovermedes slows to a soft whirring and then drops.

A slight vibration goes through my seat as the ship touches down. Mason cuts the engine and presses a sequence of buttons. A sliding panel retracts into itself on the left side of the ship.

I jump up out of my seat and hurry back to Big Ed. He looks up at me from somewhere inside the folds of skin that seem to have mushroomed over his face in the past few days.

"I'll check the bunker," I say. "You got the Rogues under control?"

He nods and pats his gun.

Mason comes up behind me, a taut expression on his face. "Diesel might be down there."

I flick the safety off my gun. "I'm lighter and faster than him."

Before he can talk me out of it, I jump from the Hovermedes and run to the bunker's main entry hatch. I shimmy down quietly and turn on my flashlight, fighting the urge to start yelling for everyone at once. In my head, I repeat everything Mason's taught me. *Assess the situation. Secure the area. Identify escape routes.* My heart thumps methodically as I jog down the main tunnel.

My instinct is to go straight to our bunker and look for Da and Tucker, but Prat's bunker is the muster point. If there are survivors, that's where they'll be.

As I run, my mind flashes back to the circle of cold steel Reid pressed into my skull when he caught me in his bunker unawares. This time I'm not slowing down long enough for anyone to pull a fast one on me. They'll have to shoot at a moving target.

When I get to Prat's bunker, I lean my palms against the tunnel wall, and steady my breathing. What if they're all dead? What if Kat's eyes are open, like Frank's, still watching me with her unsettling stare? I'm not sure I'm ready for this. With a heavy sigh, I straighten up and reach for the access hatch. I can't back away now. I have to find my courage. Whatever's inside has to be faced.

Chapter 21

A loud thumping echoes through the tunnel. I crouch down, the hairs in my ears tingling. *Someone's coming!* A cold sweat erupts across my neck as I cock my gun. I hope I'm ready to do this. I force myself to think of Prat's lifeless body and the name on the note in his pocket.

The pounding gets louder. Breathless, I take aim into the shadows. My trigger finger twitches, then slackens with relief.

Tucker barrels into me, knocks me to the ground, and buries me beneath his thick fur.

"Good boy!" I sob, running my hand over his coat.

When he tires of slobbering all over me, I sit up and hug him tight. His heartbeat hammers against my chest. It's a morsel of hope. If he's okay, maybe the others are too. I pat him on the head. "We gotta find Da and the others." I stand and he follows me over to the hatch. "Are they down here?"

Tucker turns his head aside and waits for me to make a move.

I climb down into the bunker and hurriedly shine my flashlight around.

The place is trashed. Vandalized, except there's no graffiti. Every drawer's been yanked out and emptied, the contents tossed in a pile at the far corner. Tucker huddles against my legs, clearly ill-at-ease.

"Anyone here?" I walk around and peer into Prat's bedroom.

The covers are ripped from his bed, the mattress tipped on end.

I turn on my heel and walk back to the access hatch, a queasy feeling in the pit of my stomach. "Let's go check our bunker, Tuck."

He whines and pads to the far side of the room.

"What is it, old boy?"

Head cocked, he sits down on his haunches beside the pile of debris and splintered cabinetry. My gaze flits over the wreckage and then back to Tucker. A foreboding feeling grips me. I want to say something to reassure him, but my tongue feels numb. I mouth *Good Boy*, but he looks away.

I sniff the air tentatively, willing myself not to detect the odor of death. It's damp and humid in Prat's bunker. I can tell the heater hasn't been run in a couple of days. I stick my flashlight between my teeth and fiddle with the low voltage lamp in the ceiling.

After a few frustrating attempts to coax it to life, a yellowish hue filters reluctantly through the darkness. A soft whir kicks in, and my shoulders sag with relief. At least the generator still works. Tucker gives a sharp bark, directing my attention back to the debris.

He gets up and paws gently at the pile. He's not going to let me leave it undisturbed.

I prop my rifle against the wall, grab a piece of splintered plywood and fling it aside to placate him. That's when I hear a moan.

My brain combusts in panic. It came from somewhere deep inside the pile. Tucker digs frantically now, barking in short, insistent bursts.

I dive in beside him and wrench out armfuls of hunting gear and clothing. In the ghoulish light I spot what looks like an unshaven chin. My heart knocks like a hammer in my chest. I struggle to free my shaking fingers from the fishing net they're entangled in, then scrabble to unearth the half-buried face.

"Hang on!" I say as I heave a broken cabinet aside. Sweat oils my forehead, stings my eyes. The cabinet creaks and rolls onto its side, the plywood flattening like the floor of an imploded building. Another pitiful groan makes my heart gallop faster.

I burrow through shoes and clothing and reach my arm under the man's dust-covered head. He stiffens, as if fearful of my touch. His eyelids flicker open.

"*Da!*"

Confusion floods his face. "D … Derry? Z'at you?"

"Yes! It's me, Da." I adjust my arm to cradle his head more comfortably.

He reaches for me, his eyes clouding over. "Git outta here! It's a trap!"

I shake my head. "I'm not leaving you."

He clutches me to him. "He knew you'd come here when you found Prat's body."

"Who?" My mind races to the note. "Diesel?"

Da blinks in assent. "He wanted us to fire up the Sweeper ship. We told him we didn't know nothin' about it, but he forced Prat out of the bunker at gunpoint."

"Where are the others?"

"They fled before he came back."

"Why are you still here?" I ask, a sob sticking in my throat.

He exhales softly. "I couldn't find Tucker. Wasn't about to leave without your dang dog."

My eyes brim with tears.

"Diesel went ballistic when he realized the camp was gone. Son of a gun swung at me with the butt of his rifle, knocked me out cold."

A balled fist of anger slams my gut. "Let's get you out of here before he comes back."

Da squeezes his eyes shut. "He knows you're here, count on it."

"Can you walk?"

"Aye." Da sits up slowly and groans. "But my bloody nose is broken."

We exit Prat's bunker and make our way along the tunnel to the main access hatch. Tucker stays glued to my heels every step of the way. He's not likely to let me out of his sight again, no matter what command I give him. Da moves like an old man, one arm wrapped around his ribs. I steady him at the foot of the iron ladder. "I'm right behind you."

He hauls himself slowly up onto the first rung. Tucker gives a low growl and I tense.

Pop! Pop! Pop!

My adrenalin spikes. I reach for Da's shirt and yank him back down off the ladder. We drop to the ground and I cover him as best I can. I force air through my lungs, one hand on Tucker's head to keep him calm. My ears tingle in the darkness. Lead on metal. Someone's shooting at the Hovermedes.

"It's him," Da wheezes.

I hunker down, straining to hear what direction the bullets are coming from.

"Wait here," I whisper. "I'll see if I can get a decent shot."

Da grabs my sleeve. "Be careful, me wee girl."

I twist my lips and look away. He hasn't called me that since Ma died. I don't often admit it, but I miss Da too.

I snake my way up the ladder, my tread light as velvet on each metal rung. Tucker sits on his haunches, ears aloft, his soft brown eyes watching my every move.

More gunfire bounces off the Hovermedes. Then silence. When I reach the top of the ladder, I shut my eyes and listen for Big Ed's voice in my head. *You can hear in all directions.* My heart drums in my chest as I catalog the sounds. A Northern water thrush warbles along with the forest vibrations. Strange. The shooting's stopped.

I pop my head up through the opening and peer hesitantly around. A thick arm locks around my neck in a death embrace.

"Make a sound, and you're dead."

Somehow, I contain the gasp that's halfway through my lips. My heart feels as if it's marshmallowed to twice its normal size. I grit my teeth, flailing helplessly against the chokehold Diesel has on me.

"Real slow," Diesel hisses in my ear. "Pass me your gun."

I play the only card I have left and let my weapon slip from my trembling fingers into the shaft. It clatters against the iron rungs as it falls down into the tunnel. I scrunch my eyes shut, hoping it didn't take Da out on the way. At least I had the sense to flip the safety.

Diesel tightens his arm against my windpipe. He grabs my hair with his free hand and drags me out of the tunnel. "On your feet."

I stagger up and splutter. "Can't ... breathe!"

"Move it!" He rams the butt of his M16 into my back. My nerves light up with pain.

"Hands above your head. Walk toward the Hovermedes. Real slow."

I take several unsteady steps forward, sick with fear as I weigh my options. I can't let him use me as bait to take control of the Hovermedes. Whatever Diesel demands, I won't let Mason open that door.

Three feet from the nose of the Hovermedes Diesel grabs my shoulder and wrenches it back. "Hold up!"

Rooted to the spot, I close my eyes and breathe slowly in and out. The only advantage I have in this situation is my speed. If Diesel's distracted for even a second, I could make a run for the bunker hatch. I'm under no illusions what the outcome will be if I make the attempt and fail.

"I know you boneheads are in there," Diesel yells. "Girl's gonna croak out here, unless you open up and drop your bean shooters out the door. Any of you come outta there packing, I'll blast your guts into tomorrow."

I tighten my lips and give a slight shake of my head. I know Big Ed and Mason can see me through the tinted glass. My body tenses as the minutes tick by.

"Be a bum rap to have to shoot the little vixen in her own backyard." The menacing edge in Diesel's voice creeps up another notch. "Already wasted two today."

I lick a salty drop of sweat from my lips. He thinks Da's dead.

Diesel raises the barrel of his gun to the back of my head. "Better get the meat wagon coming for baby girl."

A ball of terror lodges in my throat. There's no chance to run. Maybe I can drop, topple him, and wrestle the gun from his hands. I blow my lank hair out of my eyes, and freeze when I hear a click.

A pneumatic door pops out and glides seamlessly along the body of the Hovermedes.

"No!" I yell.

Diesel positions me in front of his body like a human shield. I watch in disbelief as Mason emerges through the doorway. He lays his rifle on the ground and looks up, hands raised above his head.

"You got what you wanted." Mason's voice is slow, methodical. "Now let her go."

I shift nervously from one foot to the other.

"You know how to fly this ship?" Diesel asks.

Mason moves his jaw side to side. "Fixin' to try."

Diesel draws his studded brows together and jerks his chin at the Hovermedes. "How many you got in there?"

"She's the only one left." Mason motions at me.

Diesel's eyes cut to the Hovermedes and then back to Mason. "Show me."

Mason shrugs. "Knock yourself out."

Diesel jams his gun into my left shoulder blade. I let out a gasp.

"Move!" he shouts, propelling me forward again.

I open my mouth to yell at Mason to get back inside the ship when Da's voice cuts across the clearing, "Drop your weapon, scum."

Diesel hesitates. I lunge, too late. He swivels and shoots. Then, another crack rings out. Diesel sprawls backward, arms flung high above his head in a red-handed reflex that tells me he's been hit. But what about Da?

I'm vaguely aware I'm running madly across the clearing. My thighs burn with adrenalin coursing like acid through my legs.

When I reach the hatch, I crumple to the ground beside Da. A pool of blood is seeping through his shirt.

"Da!" I scream.

A gurgle escapes his lips. He strains to sit up, and I pull him toward me

"It's okay. Keep breathing." I turn and yell over my shoulder to Mason. "Get a medical kit from the Hovermedes."

Da reaches for my collar and draws me close. His eyes flicker in his head like the power's about to go out. "It's all right, darlin'."

"No!" I blink back the tears stinging my eyes. "We need you. *I* need you."

He shuts his eyes and smiles, a vague, distant smile that tells me he's drifting.

"Da!" I shake him softly.

His eyes pop open and he stares past me. "I can see her, Derry."

"See who?" My voice pitches in despair. I throw a harried glance over my shoulder. *What is Mason doing?*

Da's grip on me releases and he sinks back in my arms. "Your Ma. I see your Ma."

Chapter 22

I stare down at Da, slack-jawed and ashen in my arms. A wave of pain sears my gut. Trembling, I shake him again, my grip weakening as the nightmare takes hold. "No!" I scream. "Please, Da! You can't die!" I collapse on his bloody chest, sobs tearing through my throat like razors.

"Derry!" Mason runs up and lifts me off Da's body. I stare in horror at the blood smeared all over me. *No! No! No!*

Mason kneels and checks for a pulse. I watch his face for confirmation of what I already know in my heart. I felt it the moment Da's spirit left his body. A barely perceptible shiver that left me holding him like an empty shell.

Shaking, I wipe my sticky hands on my pants.

Mason stands and takes a step backward. "He saved our lives."

I stare at Da's chest, slick and dark like an oil spill. Eyelids sealed shut, and not in a drunken stupor, for once. An inexplicable calm washes away the sobs still jammed in my throat. He knew what he was doing. It wasn't a mistake, and it wasn't senseless. It was a gift. Maybe he wasn't there for his kids when he should have been, but in the end he got a chance to do something remarkable. Ma would have been proud of him.

A lone tear slides down my face. I crawl forward and lean over Da's lifeless body. "You did it," I whisper in his ear. "You saved us."

Mason takes on the unsavory task of disposing of Diesel's body. When he's done he digs a grave and we bury Da next to a diabetic woman who passed away a few months after we moved into the bunkers. I fashion a twig cross and lay it on Da's chest before we cover him up with dirt. It's too risky to leave a grave marker here, but despite my suspicion that God's forgotten we're here, I can't let Da disappear into the earth without some icon of resurrection.

Tucker circles the proceedings, clearly uneasy. He helped me dig Da out of the bunker an hour earlier and now we're burying him again.

Owen, red-eyed and in shock, says a few quick words, and the rest of us cover the site with dead brush and pinecones. I take some comfort in the fact that it wasn't the drink that took Da in the end. Now it's up to me to make sure he didn't die for nothing.

I climb back into the Hovermedes with Tucker. Despite what happened to Prat and Da, I'm still clinging to the hope that the other Undergrounders made it out safely. A quick search of the bunkers revealed no trace of them, but thankfully no bodies either. For now, I'm spared the task of burying Jakob. I really don't think my heart could take that.

I glance down the aisle at Blade and Lipsy, gagged and bound in the back of the ship.

Big Ed comes up behind me. "Weren't no way I was letting Mason give up his weapons with those two apes on the loose. I'll untie them now."

"I wouldn't mind leaving someone hogtied for the rest of the trip." I say, loud enough for Blade to hear me.

Rage ripples over his face, contorting the crossed cleavers on his neck.

"No one's getting out of the Craniopolis alive unless we go in as a team," Mason says. "We're in this together now. From here on out, our only enemies are the Sweepers." He gestures at the Rogues. "Cut them loose. We're gonna need their help going in."

Big Ed slices the rope around Blade's hands, then frees Lipsy. Blade rubs his wrists, inked knuckles bulging. His lips slit in a grin that I take as more of a threat than a gesture of solidarity. I scrape a hand over my matted hair and look away. Blade's no fool. He'll stick with us until we find Rummy, but after that I'm fair game.

"We'll partner up to go in," Mason says. "Once we're through the access point, each of you is responsible for your partner. Owen, you'll wait in the Hovermedes with Tucker while we locate Jakob and Rummy."

"Derry, you take Lipsy," Mason continues. "Big Ed, you pair up with Blade. I'll float between, coordinate intelligence." He knots his thick arms across his chest, knuckles clenched. "Questions?"

Blade scowls. "I don't do partners."

"Trust me, cowboy, you're gonna need one."

Blade lowers his brows. "Whadda you know? You some kinda hot shot soldier?"

"Something like that."

"U. S. Marine." I pipe up. Until now, we've kept Blade and Lipsy in the dark about the cloning program and Mason's elite military training under the Sweepers. The way things are going, it might be best to keep it that way.

"You're a jarhead, eh? Figures." Blade cracks his knuckles. I was hoping he'd back off if I clued him in to Mason's credentials, but it only seems to have riled him more.

"Who you coordinating with anyway?" Blade fastens a suspicious gaze on Mason.

Mason widens his stance, his commanding physique filling the aisle.

"He has a contact in the Craniopolis," I say.

I can almost hear the hackles rise on the back of Blade's neck. He studies Mason for a moment, the ink curdling on his face. "Ain't *nobody* got contacts in there, but snitches." He gets to his feet, veins straining beneath his skin.

"Watch out!" I yell, sensing what's coming, but Mason's already in motion.

His fist flies forward and connects with Blade's jaw. Blade stumbles backward and sinks to the ground, out cold like a deflated balloon.

Lipsy moans and rocks furiously back and forth.

"Tie him back up." Mason throws me an irritated look, and walks up the aisle to the cockpit.

I grimace. I should never have mentioned the contact. Blade's devious mind jumps on any sliver of information. If he suspects Mason is from the Craniopolis, he's never going to trust us enough to help us.

I reach for the discarded rope lying on the seat beside Lipsy and secure Blade's hands behind his back. "Sure we should still bring him?" I ask Big Ed.

"Blade hates the Sweepers more than he hates us. And he wants to find Rummy. He'll have our backs when it matters."

The door of the Hovermedes seals with a familiar whoosh.

I hurry up the aisle to the cockpit and slide into the seat beside Mason. "So, what happens once we're inside the Craniopolis?"

Mason adjusts the gauges in front of him. "I'll radio in our ETA to my contact, Ramesh. He'll rig the computers to authorize our entry down to the landing dock. Once it's safe to disembark, we'll hide in the supply carts until Ramesh can take us to the crematorium. That'll be our staging area."

"Can you count on Ramesh? What if he turns us in?"

"He won't."

"How can you be sure?"

"He's Kat's brother."

My jaw slackens. "Ramesh faked your expiration report?"

Mason gives a terse nod.

"Is he leaving with us afterward?"

"He can't. Someone's got to stay and authorize our departure from inside the Craniopolis."

A chill goes through me. I can only imagine what the Sweepers will do to Ramesh if they find out he's been smuggling people in and out of the Craniopolis.

"There's another military clone coming out with us," Mason says. "Should have been two, but one of them reached his expiration date yesterday."

I fall silent. This is one topic I want to steer clear of for now.

Within minutes we're back in the air, moving soundlessly above the dense forest. I decide against turning on the Periscopic Infrared again. If I spot Undergrounders from our camp, I'll be torn between stopping to help them and pushing on to the Craniopolis. Right now, I'm still struggling to separate my shattered emotions over Da's death from my resolve to do whatever it takes to bring Jakob home. I glance over at Mason. I wonder if emotions are just as confusing for clones. I'm never really sure what's going on inside Mason's head. At times, I think I see something human in his expression, but then it's gone again, and the clone is back in control.

"Five miles out," Mason calls over his shoulder. "Time to check in with Ramesh. I'll put him on speaker." He dons a headset and adjusts the mouthpiece.

I stare at the contraption on his head. "That doesn't look very hi-tech."

Mason chuckles. "That's 'cause it's not Craniopolis issued. We're on a closed repeater circuit." He flicks several switches and then holds a finger to his lips. "Jailbird, do you read me?"

The line crackles briefly. "Come in Wildhorse, get on twelve."

Mason fiddles with a knob and changes the frequency. "Are we secure?"

"Channel twelve secure."

"Aliens in the space station?"

"Negative. You're cleared to land in ten."

"Roger that."

"What if someone's at the landing dock?" I ask.

"It's all A.I. down there—robotic entities—the only life forms will be us." He turns to me and grins. "That's if you count me."

I frown. "Real funny." I still get uncomfortable every time Mason reminds me we're different. He's enhanced, that's a given, but the real difference between us is what the clones have been robbed of—a decent lifespan.

"Listen up." Mason throws a quick look over his shoulder. "When we touch down on the dock, give Lipsy back her weapon. She bugs out first. You and Big Ed cover her. Head for the supply carts and climb in. Ramesh will take it from there. Once we're safely in the Crematorium, I'll give you the all-clear to come out."

I nod my assent. I can only imagine what lies ahead. We're flying right into the jaws of the predators we've been running from for years. Owen told me to trust Mason, and after everything he's done for me, I think it's finally time.

Mason flicks several switches and the Hovermedes begins a gradual descent. "Go back there and let Big Ed know we're one mile to target."

When I stand, the ship pitches unexpectedly. I grab the back of my chair, grit my teeth, and propel myself down the aisle, lurching from side to side. Big Ed looks up, his features registering confusion, as the Hovermedes veers hard left. The tail of the craft tips up and I slam into the chair behind me as Mason's voice booms down the aisle.

"Bandits in the sky!"

Chapter 23

The staccato sound of gunfire fills my ears. Tucker growls deep in his throat. I dive into the nearest seat and scramble to activate the harness. I've no idea if we've been hit or if Mason's evasive maneuvers are what upended the tail. Lipsy whimpers in the back of the ship like an abandoned puppy.

An iron clamp of despair crushes my heart. We were minutes from infiltrating the Craniopolis—*from finding Jakob*. The Sweepers must have intercepted Mason's signal.

I give up on the harness, drop to all fours, and begin crawling up the aisle to the cockpit. Tucker follows me, alternating between licking my ears and sniffing at me, unsure if this is a new game, or if I'm hurt. I reach up and give his neck a quick rub.

As I inch forward, the tail of the Hovermedes begins to right itself, but I'm not taking any chances. I stay low until I reach Mason. "Is it Sweepers?" I pull myself up and peer through the windscreen.

"Get away from the glass!" Mason hisses.

I promptly flatten myself on my belly. "Are we hit?"

"I think so. A plane came out of nowhere. I banked left, but too late. They had a machine gun on a mount and they were firing at us out of the cabin."

"Plane? You mean—a Hovermedes?"

Mason shakes his head, frowning. "Some kind of modified small aircraft."

I jockey myself into a sitting position so I can breathe more easily. "But no one else has air capability."

"Someone does and they just tried to kill us."

My brain reels. I peer at the screen, scanning the treetops. Rogues? It's possible they found an intact civilian plane, but where did they strip the fuel from? The air force base?

Above Mason's head, a sequence of red and orange lights blinks on and then off again. He mutters under his breath and rams his finger repeatedly on a button. "Everything's frozen. I can't get any relevant flight readings."

"What does that mean?"

"System's shutting down. We're gonna have to land." He braces the controls, his face glistening with sweat.

I stare at him in disbelief. Judging by his grim expression, we have no other options, and this one's precarious at best.

"I'll tell the others." I reach up and give his shoulder a quick squeeze. "You can do this."

He glances across at me, and his taut features soften momentarily. "Take this with you," he says, sliding a slim metal box out from under his seat. "I'll explain later."

I clamber to my feet, tuck the box under my arm, and hurry down the aisle, a conviction growing in my gut. Soul or no soul, Mason has a human heart after all. I can see it in his eyes, and even a clone's eyes don't lie.

"We're hit, aren't we?" Owen asks, when I reach his seat.

"The electronics are fried. We're going to have to make an emergency landing."

Big Ed pulls at his beard. "There'll be a pack of Sweepers waiting on the ground. Could be the end of the road for us."

"It wasn't Sweepers," I say, in as firm a voice as I can muster. I'm on the fence about that, despite what Mason said, but right now Big Ed needs reassuring. "It was a civilian aircraft."

Big Ed draws his brows together and stares at me for a moment. "So they *thought* they were firing on Sweepers."

"That's my hunch."

Behind his glasses, Big Ed's eyes gleam. He shoots a darting glance at Owen. "Could've been the Council."

Owen nods thoughtfully. "Which means they've initiated engagement."

"This is it!" Mason yells down the galley. "Buckle up!"

Lipsy grinds her teeth and pitches forward over her knees as if she's about to hurl. "It's gonna be okay!" I yell back to her. I dive into the seat in front of Owen and manage to trigger the harness by slamming every button on the control panel. I sink back, my mind racing. If the Council is close by, it could change everything.

The Hovermedes veers left again like it's just been shoved by a giant hand. My stomach flutters and I grip the armrests tighter. There's a metallic clicking sound coming from the underbelly of the ship, as if it's about to self-destruct. Tucker sinks down at my feet. I close my eyes and take a deep breath.

"Hang on!" Mason yells.

The Hovermedes sways from side to side like a rollercoaster cart at the mercy of gravity and momentum, and then stalls. We hang, motionless, for an elongated moment, before plummeting toward the ground. My stomach lurches again. Several warning chimes come over the speaker system before the engine shudders back into action. I press myself into my seat, electroplated with fear. A few rows behind me, Lipsy thrashes around like a caged animal in distress. "You'll be all right," I yell, trying again to calm her.

We descend in a series of jerks, swaying first right and then left, inching ever closer to the canyon walls. I feel a bump and grit my teeth. Seconds later, we hit the ground with a hard jolt and skid toward the tree line.

The ship shudders to a stop and tilts sideways, metal creaking like the hull is about to burst open. An aroma like welding fumes fills the cabin. A sour taste prickles the back of my throat. I jump up and stumble down the aisle to the back of the ship.

"We need to get out. Now!" I yell.

Blade stares up at me, eyes bulging, like he's just woken up from a nightmare and has no idea what planet he's on. Lipsy huddles in the next seat, hands clapped over her ears, like she doesn't *want* to know what planet she's on.

I grab the rope around Blade's wrists and untie it. "Let's go!" I turn around and call up to Mason. "Do we have to shoot our way out of here?"

"Hang on," he yells. "There's a manual override for the door."

The side of the Hovermedes retracts into itself and I lock my gaze on the square of forest framed by the doorway. Fern fronds undulate up and down in a light breeze, as if signaling our arrival to an invisible enemy. We're buried deep in the undergrowth. My heart gallops in my chest. We might still have a chance of disappearing before the Sweepers locate us.

"Everybody out!" I yell, and duck though the door opening.

Eyes forward, I run to a clump of pines, Tucker loping at my side. Mason follows, half-carrying Owen. Big Ed brings up the rear, herding Blade and Lipsy in front of him with his M16.

"Will the Sweepers know a ship has gone down?" I ask Mason.

He shakes his head. "No, they don't have access to the closed circuit Ramesh and I were on."

Blade listens intently, but when I catch his eye, he looks away. He's not in any shape to go toe to toe with Mason about any suspicions he has. Still, I'm convinced there's more trouble brewing in that graffitied head of his.

I glance around at the sparse shelter of pines. "We should move deeper into the forest."

Mason frowns. "There's another way in to the Craniopolis."

"What are you talking about?"

"We can go in through the backup air vent."

Blade leans against a pine tree and spits in the dirt. "I ain't going one step farther 'til you meatheads tell me what's going on." He gestures derisively at Mason. "How does this son of a gun knows the joint so well if he ain't one of them."

The swish of a squirrel scampering around our feet is the only sound in the silence that follows. I open my mouth to tell Blade to shut up—the less he knows the better—but Mason gestures to me to be quiet.

"You're right." Mason bars his arms across his chest and pins his gaze on

Blade. "I do know the joint well."

Blade eyes Mason appraisingly.

"I was a prisoner there."

A slow grin spreads across Blade's face. "I knowed somethin' was up with you." He throws Mason a sly look. "How'd you escape?"

Before Mason can reply, a flock of birds startles. I look skyward, expecting a hawk, or even an eagle. Instead, a cigar-shaped shadow approaches from the east. Fear floods my mind. "Sweepers!"

There's a freeze tag moment of disbelief, and then we all take off sprinting through the lodge pole pines. Mason powers past me, Owen slung across his shoulders. Big Ed veers off to my left. Almost immediately, I lose track of the Rogues.

I plow my way over the spongy forest floor. Twigs slap at my face in the ever-thickening undergrowth. I know the tubes can't operate in this dense brush, but I don't stop running. For all I know, the Sweepers may come after us on foot.

My lungs gasp for air. I swallow a bug and stumble onward, choking while it goes down. I can barely see through the hair plastered across my face. Tucker hurtles along to my right, panting hard, but I can't risk taking my eyes off the root-ridden path to check on him.

To my left I hear someone thrashing through the brush about thirty feet behind us. I don't dare call out for fear it's Blade. My breathing grows more labored. I can't keep up this pace much longer. My legs are dissolving like jelly.

Up ahead I spot a hollowed out tree trunk. I slow to a lurching trot. Limbs convulsing, I make my way toward it, squeeze inside, and collapse on a bed of forest litter. Tucker barrels in after me and I place an arm around his heaving belly. We lay in a jumbled, sweaty heap, gasping in the air reeking of decaying wood and damp leaves. I listen for footsteps, but all I can hear is a thrush twittering above us.

After several minutes, I shift my position to relieve my cramped legs. Tucker whimpers softly and licks my face as if to reassure me we're safe. I stretch, then lay back down and curl into the fetal position. Tucker pants hot breath in my face, his tongue dangling through his lips.

When his breathing finally slows to a normal pace, he gets up and sniffs at my pack. "Need some water, old boy?" I lean on one elbow, unscrew my canteen, and pour him a cupful. It's not enough to satisfy him, but it's all I can spare for now. I roll over and peek out through the cracked tree trunk. A splash of sun accents the pea green ferns clustered around. Must be close to noon. *Prime time for Sweepers.* My stomach cramps. Are the others safe?

"We can't stay here, Tucker. We have to find Owen."

He wags his tail and slips out through the opening in the tree trunk. I gulp a few swigs of water and screw the cap back on my canteen. I shove my pack through the trunk and take a deep breath before climbing out after him. I search the patch of sky visible through the soaring pines, but there's no sign of a ship.

Tucker comes tearing back to greet me, happy to be hitting the trail again. I throw a glance around. I'll have to watch my back with Blade and Lipsy on the loose. At least they don't have weapons.

Up ahead, Tucker pauses and sniffs meticulously around a rotten log. I chuckle to myself when a squirrel darts out and spooks him.

Something tickles my ear as it flies by, and I swat at it distractedly. Tucker looks up, ears pricked, and then keels over on the forest floor.

Chapter 24

My head jerks toward the soft thud of Tucker's body hitting the ground. I plunge forward, hollering his name, my cramped legs responding in slow motion. I fix my eyes on the patch of fur thirty feet in front of me and reach down inside myself, summoning every last drop of adrenaline.

But, I'm not fast enough. The Sweepers' tube slithers out of nowhere and fastens itself on Tucker like a shivering viper. In a final burst of speed, I fall on it, heedless of the skin shredding from my fists as I whale on it.

"No! Not Tucker! You monsters!"

The tube retracts like a giant muscle, catapulting me into the brush. I watch, horrified, as it coils upward, dragging a writhing Tucker with it. The breath in my lungs hardens like concrete. My eyes blur with tears as a flash of fur disappears with the retractable arm of chain mail into the underbelly of the Hovermedes.

"No! No! No!" I hurl a fistful of leaves and pinecones into the air, and then sink back down, pounding the dirt with my fists. My mind whites out. I press the palms of my hands into my eye sockets and scream from deep within. My rib cage shudders, and for a moment I think I've been darted too.

"Derry!" Mason reaches for me by the scruff of my neck and drags me deeper into the brush. His eyes flash with annoyance. "Keep your voice down."

I sit up, and wipe the tears from my lashes.

"Who did they take?" Mason asks, his tone low and urgent.

My chest tightens. Tucker's smell lingers on my clothes, heightening the pain of losing him. Through a haze of tears, I claw my way back to my feet. "I have to follow that ship. Get out of my way!"

Mason sidesteps me, then locks me from behind in a bear hug. "Derry! Listen to me! I need you to calm down and tell me who they took."

Sobbing, I go limp in his arms.

He turns me around to face him. "*Who?*"

"Tucker," I whisper.

I swear a flicker of relief crosses his face.

"I was afraid it was Owen." He releases me with a heavy sigh. "I've lost him."

The air exits my lungs. I blink to orient myself. "How ... you had him ..."

"He insisted I look for you before we went any farther. I left him in a grove, well-concealed." Mason's face pales. "When I went back, he was gone."

I stare at him, equal measures of rage and grief wrestling for control. "You moron! You shouldn't have left him. He's in no state to fend for himself."

My temples throb. I clamp my head between my hands, my thoughts tumbling over each other. If Owen's in trouble, there's no time to waste, even now when I'm raw with grief over losing Tucker.

"How far's the backup air vent?" I ask.

"Quarter mile or so."

"We'll spread out and comb the area. If we can't find Owen in the next hour, we'll go in through that vent. Let's round up the others."

"They're waiting for us. Where's that box I gave you in the Hovermedes?"

I rummage in my pack and shove it at him. "We need to hurry. What is it anyway?"

"It's a Faraday box. I took the radio from the Hovermedes and I need to hide it in something that will protect it from pulses. It's the only way we can communicate without the Sweepers knowing."

Mason stashes the radio in the hollowed-out tree where Tucker and I hid, then leads me through the prickly undergrowth. The afternoon air smells of wildflowers, and moss cooking in the sun. My body aches to collapse on a soft patch somewhere and sleep off the warmth of the day— but that would amount to a death sentence with Sweepers on the prowl. I grab a fistful of half-ripened raspberries from a bush in passing and stuff them in my mouth. My withered taste buds awaken as the sour juice trickles down my throat. I can't remember the last time I ate anything, but hunger pangs hit the moment I swallow the berries.

"Got any food?" I ask Mason.

He reaches into a side pocket and tosses me a hunk of deer jerky. I gnaw on it, alternating bites with small moans of pleasure.

Mason throws me a disapproving look. "If you're trying to broadcast our position, you're doing a good job."

I swallow a chunk of jerky whole and wipe the drool off my mouth. "How much farther?" I ask, stuffing the rest of it into my pocket.

"We're here." Mason places two fingers between his lips and whistles.

Big Ed answers back with a short trill.

Mason walks over to a half-buried boulder and yanks back a pile of brush from a burrow tucked flush into its base.

Big Ed pops his head out, a sprig of grass clamped between his teeth. A look of relief spreads across his leathered features.

The tension in my shoulders eases at the sight of him, but I can't bring a smile to my face. I clamber down into the burrow and glance around. There's barely room to crouch down inside, let alone stretch out. No shortage of claw marks in the dirt walls either. A shiver crosses my shoulders. Just my luck they'd find an empty bear den to hide in.

Blade and Lipsy huddle beneath the tangled web of roots, wrists bound in front of them. Lipsy's face is bleeding from several ugly scratches, but Blade looks relatively unscathed, apart from his misshapen jaw.

"We've lost Owen," I say. "He can't have gone far."

"You ain't gonna find that sucker," Blade pipes up. "Why'd you think that Hovermedes backed off? Cause they got what they came for, that's why!"

"They got Tucker," I say, fighting to control the waver in my voice.

Blade cocks an eyebrow. "Must be hard times in the Craniopolis if dog's on the menu."

I lunge in a half-crawl toward him. Big Ed grabs me by the shoulder and pulls me back.

I shake him off, and take a deep breath. I know better than to react to Blade like anything he says merits a response. I can't keep giving him that kind of power over me.

"We're not going to stop looking for Owen yet," I say. "He might still be out there. He knows a thing or two about staking out and camouflage."

Blade lets out a snort. "I ain't going back out there long as those ships are sniffing around. Right now, I'm gonna get me some jerky and bust some Zs, and if you had any sense between your ears, you'd do the same."

I stick my face up close to Blade's. In the sickly light of the burrow, the lightning bolts carved up the side of his neck make him look like some ugly hybrid badger.

"I should have left you for a wolf pack to find when you were out cold," I say, my voice oddly devoid of emotion. "But, that's the difference between you and me. I don't leave a man, even a scumbag like you, to the mercy of animals."

Blade hacks a ball of spit at the back of his throat. Instinctively, I draw back several inches. He curls his lip at me. "Them cats got your brother, I get it. But, you ain't gonna find him this side o' the fence." He throws his head back and laughs, a thin, reedy laugh that's quickly absorbed into the damp, dirt walls.

I turn to Big Ed and Mason. "Let's go. I'm done with him."

Lipsy looks up at me, startled.

"Your choice," I say to her. "You can stay with Blade or come with us."

The smile fades from Blade's face. "She ain't going *nowhere* without me, ain't that right, Lipsy?"

Lipsy picks at the sleeve of her jacket. "Th-th-that's right," she says, avoiding eye contact with me.

I stare down at her bent head in disbelief. "I don't know what you're thinking, Lipsy. Don't you get it? This is your chance to get away from the Rogues."

I reach out a hand to her, but she shrinks back, shaking her head vehemently.

I let out an exasperated sigh. "Have it your way then."

She rocks gently back and forth in response.

I turn to Mason. "Cut them loose."

Big Ed and Mason exchange a look, and then Mason pulls out his knife and slashes the ropes around their wrists.

"Have at it," I say. "You're on your own."

"Hey! Wait a minute! Give us back our bleedin' guns at least!" Blade yells after us.

I flash him a cold smile and throw Lipsy a strip of jerky.

Big Ed, Mason, and I fan out and comb the brush for the next forty-five minutes, whistling intermittently, clambering beneath root systems, checking every crevice and burrow on the off chance Owen's holed up someplace, or passed out and can't hear us. I keep thinking about how much easier this would be with Tucker's help. The sob lodged in my throat thickens.

"Maybe Blade's right," I say, when we regroup. "The Sweepers always take off when they make an extraction." I turn to Mason. "I think it's time to find that backup air vent."

A somber expression clouds his face. He moves wordlessly back into the brush. Big Ed and I exchange uncertain looks, and then fall in behind him.

Before long we're climbing a steep slope through a thick mantle of Tamarack trees. My heart weighs heavier than the pack on my back. There's a real risk this could end badly for everyone. If we don't make it inside the Craniopolis undetected, I may never see Jakob or Owen again. And I can't begin to think about what will happen to Tucker when the Sweepers realize they've snagged a dog.

Big Ed pulls up and leans his forearms on one knee, panting. "How much farther? This dang hill's steeper than a cow's face."

"It's right there." Mason points up the slope. "Beyond that burnt patch."

I stare at the charred belt of hillside above us. "We'll be fully exposed once we leave the cover of the trees."

Big Ed mops at his brow. "Sure you don't want to wait till dark?"

I hesitate. Our chances of getting inside undetected after sundown are marginally better, but we're already behind schedule. We need to rescue Jakob before something unimaginable happens to him. I shake my head. "There are lives at stake. How's the vent secured?"

"There's a metal grating that has to be unscrewed and a series of mesh discs behind it to trap smaller debris," Mason says. "Could take a while to get in."

"Then let's get on it."

Big Ed shoves his spectacles up his nose and adjusts his pack. Silently, we creep up the hill another thirty feet or so, M16s at the ready.

"Wait here." Mason motions us down to the ground and sidles forward alone. When he reaches a small outcrop, he raises his arm and flings a fistful of rocks at a clump of moss overhanging a granite slab. The clang of stone on metal reverberates in my head like an underwater sonic boom. I stiffen and grip my gun tighter, bracing for an explosion of some kind.

Mason hurries back down to us. "It's clean."

Heart racing, I scramble up to the cleverly camouflaged vent access and pull the moss overhang to one side. My heart sinks when I step behind it. Big Ed comes up behind me and whistles softly. The grating over the vent is easily four feet in diameter and securely riveted into its iron frame with mammoth metal bolts.

I look down at my feet and kick at the droppings scattered around. "Wolves. Even they can't figure out how to get in."

Big Ed kneels and examines the droppings. "Fresh. Must be a pack close by."

A shiver crosses my shoulders. "Another good reason not to be out here after dark. Let's get busy."

Mason sticks his hand beneath the moss overhang and pokes around in a crevice in the granite for a few minutes. He grunts, and I hear a scraping sound as he drags something out.

He holds up a colossal rusted wrench with an adjustable lower jaw. I'm not sure I could lift it, let alone wield it, but Mason's brandishing it in front of our faces like it's hollow. "Ramesh stashed it here in case I ever needed a way back in."

I'm warming up to this Ramesh clone. By my calculations, he's taken more than a few risks for Mason.

I watch Mason position the wrench on the first bolt and twist, the cords on the backs of his hands flinching with the effort. Even with his extraordinary strength, it could take a while to loosen these bolts.

I load my pack back on. "I'll head uphill and spot while you work on the grating."

Big Ed nods. "We'll whistle for you when we're ready."

I hike to an elevation, which gives me a vantage point to pick off anyone approaching the vent from either direction. I'm worried Blade and Lipsy might have followed us. I don't understand why Lipsy wouldn't come with us. Blade couldn't have stopped her with all of us there. It's like she thinks she's one of them now. I slip between the pines spearing their way skyward and throw my pack at my feet. A stunned field mouse darts out from beneath the leaves and scuttles off.

I pull my gun from my shoulder, adjust my scope's windage knob, and take aim, center mass on the granite slab that marks the vent entry. I've never killed a man before. Hard to say what I might do if I see Blade now. I lower my gun and run my hand along the barrel. Lipsy would finally be free.

It's the smallest of pricks when it hits. Bee sting grade. A brain-freeze jolt of pain in the temples. I fall forward, immobilized, face planting into the mosaic of shriveled pine needles looming up at me from the forest floor.

Chapter 25

I'm floating upward, but I can't figure out where to. Swaths of color bleed into grainy images that swim around me like luminescent jellyfish.

I wake with a violent start, soaked in sweat, and look into the lead-colored eyes of my captor—a barrel-chested, olive-skinned man with long, thick lashes, cleaner than anyone I've seen in years. He leans over me, a perturbed look on his face, scalp pinched tight over his smooth head.

"Do you know who I am?" His voice rumbles like a freight train.

I twist my neck to look past him, confirming the fear gnawing at me. I'm inside a Hovermedes. Harnessed in one of those egg-shaped seats. A prisoner. More lab rat status than POW. My heart sinks.

I only zoned out on the hill for a few seconds, wallowing in thoughts of revenge against Blade, but that's all it took. Owen always said it would kill me in the end. And I'm as good as dead now.

"You're a Sweeper?" My voice pitches into question mode, as if there's still a chance this could all be a horrible misunderstanding. Or, better still, a dream. Instinctively I reach up and rub the dull ache in my left temple where the tranquilizer dart went in.

The olive-skinned man opens his mouth to respond, but turns at a loud thump behind him.

A furry head squeezes into the space between us, and then, unbelievably, Tucker is straddling my chest with his paws, tail swishing contentedly behind him. I try to say his name, but there's a sob the size of a basketball stuck in my throat and all I manage is a gurgle. I pull him toward me, catching a whiff of pine and campfire in his coat. I can't believe they let him live. But maybe the Sweepers have some other sinister purpose for him.

We stay locked in our sweaty embrace until Tucker wriggles free to sniff at the jerky in my pocket. I tear my eyes away from him and glare at the Sweeper. "Why'd you take my dog?"

He cocks his head to the side. "Had to. You're inseparable."

I breathe unevenly in and out. Like he cares. He's toying with me, just like Blade does. I won't give him the satisfaction of showing my fear. I nudge Tucker aside and undo the harness that's cinched so tight it's cutting off my circulation. Surprisingly, the Sweeper doesn't react. I flick my eyes around. There's a good chance he has other options to immobilize me if I try to escape.

I run my eyes over his hulking frame. Not much chance of overpowering him. My best bet is to keep him talking and learn as much as I can. Anything he tells me could prove useful if I have a chance to escape later. "How long were you tracking us?" I ask.

He smiles, an amused intensity in his metallic eyes, as he smooths down the front of his pressed shirt. "A while. Mason was communicating with me when your ship went down. My name is Ramesh."

My head spins. I frown, trying to make sense of what he said. "You're not a Sweeper?"

"No!" His eyes glimmer with distaste. "I'm not one of them."

A sliver of hope pierces through my despair. "I don't understand. Why did you extract me then?"

"I *rescued* you. Mason sent an encrypted Mayday right before you went down."

"Did you see him down there?" I ask. "And Big Ed—the old man who was with him?"

Ramesh hesitates. "I couldn't find them on the scanners."

"They're inside the entrance to the backup air vent. They're trying to remove the grating."

Ramesh's face takes on a moss-colored tinge. "They'll never make it.

Security drones will pick them up."

"Then we have to get to them first." I bound toward the cockpit, but he bars my way.

"I can't override the extraction cameras much longer or I'll arouse suspicion." Ramesh sets his lips. "If you want to get inside the Craniopolis, you'll have to leave them behind."

I stare at him in disbelief. "How long before the extraction cameras kick back on?"

He shrugs. "Twenty minutes. If they're off for more than an hour at a time, they trigger an irregular maintenance alarm."

I twist my lips. "That's not enough time to land. But you can extract them. I know exactly where they are. Take us back to where you picked me up and I'll guide you."

Ramesh rubs a hand over his egg-shaped head. His mountainous chest rises and falls beneath his immaculate shirt as he weighs my words. He looks a little older than Mason, same build, but neat and polished-looking. He's taking a huge risk helping us, but he's a clone near the end of his life units. Maybe it's a gamble worth taking to make his life count for something.

Ramesh sighs, a resigned look on his face. "I'll make one pass. If I can't find them, I'm heading back in." He climbs into the cockpit and flicks several switches on the bank of screens. I slide into the seat beside him and secure my harness. Tucker rests his head on my knee. We glide forward, out of hover mode, and swoop around a huge granite outcrop into the canyon.

"You could still come with us, you know." I turn to Ramesh. "We can figure out some other way to get out."

He shakes his head. "They've upgraded our design since Mason left. We've been outfitted with retinal tracking sensors in the right temple that can't be removed without shutting down brain function. They send some kind of neurotoxin along the optic nerve if the sensor is tampered with."

"Why do they need to track you?"

Ramesh adjusts the altitude setting on the screen in front of him. "They only turn them on when we leave the Craniopolis. Supposedly, it's to prevent clones from falling into the hands of subversives if a Hovermedes goes down. In reality, it's to discourage us from defecting. The sensors track everything—our movements, brainwaves, temperature, organ degeneration, even mood swings. There's no way to leave the Craniopolis without authorization."

"Are they tracking you now?"

"Everything's fed into the system. But it won't trigger any alarms—I hacked into the scheduling software and logged myself out on routine surveillance."

I furrow my brow. "Mason said there's another military clone coming out with us."

Ramesh scratches the side of his neck. "Sven's been chipped too. We'll have to fake his expiration before you leave—otherwise he's a walking tracking device."

My stomach churns. "Why are the Sweepers doing such monstrous things?"

Ramesh draws his brows together, as if contemplating his answer. "They're bringing life to a dying planet through cloning regeneration."

"You can't be serious. Cloning's hardly the gift of life. An expiration date's a death sentence."

Ramesh shrugs. "If the Sweepers don't preserve what life remains, the subversives will slaughter every last survivor out there."

I shrink back in my seat, rattled by the bite in Ramesh's tone.

"Subversives are driven by primitive appetites," he continues. "There is no freedom in a world where those appetites run rampant."

A cold sensation creeps up my spine. Why is he defending the Sweepers? What if this is a set up and he's been ordered to bring us in? It's not a possibility Mason is willing to entertain, but I have no allegiance to anyone inside the Craniopolis. Without Big Ed here, there's no one's judgement I really trust. I've only my gut to guide me. "Why are you helping us then?"

He throws me a sideways glance. "Maybe I don't like being expendable." He cranes his thick neck forward to peer at the screen. "This is where I picked you up."

I scan the hilltop for any sign of movement.

Ramesh navigates closer and we drop in a tiered pattern. Tucker whimpers and presses up against my legs. Twenty feet from the ground, Ramesh adjusts the controls and we hover, silent as a suspended spider.

"They're beneath that granite overhang." I point at the curtain of moss shielding the entrance to the vent.

Ramesh taps on the screen. "I'll activate the infrared image intensifier."

I stare, fascinated, at the screen in front of me. The camera lens focuses and scans the granite with x-ray vision. Big Ed and Mason come into view, leaning into the grating, trying to turn the massive wrench.

Ramesh gestures at the gauges. "Do you want to give it a go?"

I turn to him, frowning. "What? You mean … fly?"

He shakes his head, a bemused expression on his face. "Dart them."

I stiffen. "Can't we extract them without darts?"

"Less chance of them injuring themselves if they're sedated."

"I'm not sure Big Ed's heart can handle that," I say, hesitantly. Truth is, I don't want to immobilize him. I'm still not entirely sure what Ramesh is up to, or where his allegiance lies.

Ramesh's face softens. "All right. I don't want to put him into cardiac arrest. I've never extracted someone that moth-eaten before."

I throw him an irritated look. He's as rude as Mason. Maybe clones don't know any better. It's not like there are any old ones. "So, how does an extraction work exactly?" I ask. "What do I have to do?"

"It's simple. Pull the release handle. You send down the first tube and grab Big Ed. I'll send the second one down and nab Mason."

I turn my attention back to the screen. My finger hovers momentarily over Big Ed and then switches to Mason. Why did Ramesh tell me to extract Big Ed first? What if he's really trying to take us in? The sooner Mason's on board, the safer we all are, Big Ed included. I don't even know for sure if this clone is Ramesh, but Mason will know.

I tap the screen in front of me and a familiar disembodied white head appears.

Funnel activation request. Confirm extraction.

I bite my bottom lip. I hope I'm doing the right thing in going with my gut.

"Confirm."

There's a whirring sound and the Hovermedes gives a quick shake. I stare at the screen, mesmerized by what I've unleashed. The glinting *TechnoTerra* tube shoots out from the underbelly and arcs beneath the overhang. It suctions Mason and begins an immediate ascent back to the ship. Slack-jawed, I watch Big Ed leap at it, battering it with his bare hands like a madman. My chest tightens at the look of terror plastered across his face. My only consolation is that any second now this will all be over and he'll understand. I shrink back several inches from the screen as the first tube retracts into the underside of the ship, dragging Mason behind it.

"Aren't you going to release the second tube?" I ask, glancing over my shoulder at Kamech.

His glassy eyes look past me like dried out blue bottles. He sways forward and his lips part, releasing a soft whistle of air as his body crumples to the floor.

Chapter 26

I jump up and spin around, my lungs icing over. My first thought is that Sweepers have boarded the ship and darted Ramesh. I peer down the galley, half-expecting the prick of a tranquilizer to sink into my flesh again. The ship is eerily silent, the egg-shaped seats unoccupied. Tucker lets out a mournful whine. I give him a reassuring pat on the head, and then drop to my knees at Ramesh's side to check for a pulse. My fingers recoil in horror. He's already rigid, his olive skin faded to the color of dried out bones.

A series of chimes peal out over the ship's speakers. I look around in confusion. Heart pounding, I grab Tucker by the collar and scramble behind a seat.

"Acknowledge consignment," an electronic voice booms out.

I peer around the edge of the seat I'm cowering behind. At the back of the ship, the undercarriage retracts. I watch as Mason is fed through the opening, still suctioned to the articulated tube.

"Acknowledge consignment," the electronic voice repeats in an elevated monotone.

I've no idea what I'm supposed to do or say, but if I don't try something, Mason might disappear again, and with him any hope I have of reaching the Craniopolis. "Acknowledge," I yell back.

Nothing happens. Panic surges through me. I scramble up and race down the aisle, barely avoiding tripping over Tucker who takes my mad dash to mean we're disembarking. Halfway down, the tube detaches from

Mason with a sudden flux of air and disappears back into an opening in the side of the ship. The undercarriage seals shut with a pneumatic hum.

"Mason!" I hurl myself at him. "Are you okay?"

He clamps onto my shoulders with steely fingers. "Sweepers?"

I shake my head, at a loss for words. There's no easy way to tell him Ramesh is dead.

Mason clambers to his feet, clutching his gun. His eyes settle on Ramesh's body sprawled in the aisle near the cockpit. The color drains from his face.

He treads heavily up the aisle, gripping the back of each seat as if it's a Sweeper's head he'd like to rip from his shoulders. I follow at a safe distance. When he reaches Ramesh, he kneels beside him and lifts him gently in his arms. "When ... ?" His voice breaks.

"Right before you got here."

His face sags. "He was a trusted friend."

A wave of guilt courses through me. I didn't know Ramesh long enough to trust him. He didn't despise the Sweepers the way Mason does, and that made me suspicious. They're monsters after all. But, the more I think about what Ramesh said, I realize he was right about one thing. We'll never have a free world with subversives roaming rampant either.

Mason scoops up Ramesh's rigid body and places him awkwardly in a pod chair.

"Why's he so stiff already?" I ask.

"Molecular Ossification."

I flick my eyes over Ramesh, bewildered. "What's that?"

"The nanotechnology used to create military clones manipulates the atoms in bones to enhance our strength—it's like giving us an endoskeleton within a skeleton. The downside is that the bone formation process spirals out of control once we reach adulthood, kind of like cancer cells." Mason lets out a heavy sigh. "Everything hardens like rock inside, sometimes in a matter of hours, sometimes minutes. The Sweepers can't figure out how to curb it. Kills us like clockwork every time."

I shudder. It sounds like being buried alive in concrete, only inside out.

It's creepy to know what you're going to die of ahead of time. And hopeless—knowing you'll never grow old. At least Big Ed has—*Big Ed!*

I grip Mason by the arm. "Big Ed's still down there! We have to extract him before the security drones pick him up. Ramesh said the air vent is being monitored."

Mason immediately slips into the cockpit and twists several knobs. His features harden.

"What is it?" I push Tucker aside to lean over Mason's shoulder.

He shakes his head. "He's gone!"

"What?" I peer at the screen in disbelief. "He can't be. There's no way he could have taken that grating off by himself."

Mason runs a hand across his jaw. "I'll activate a playback sequence." He flips a switch and stares at the screen as it rewinds through a series of frames. "There he is."

Mason jabs at a button on his control panel. Big Ed paces back and forth, obviously distraught. He pauses to give the grating a couple of halfhearted tugs, and then runs his hands over his craggy face. He glances around furtively, as if fearful the tube might reappear, then suddenly reaches for his pack. My heart skips a beat. I watch as he slips his arms through the straps, ducks beneath the granite and takes off running toward the tree line.

"That footage was five-and-a-half minutes ago," Mason says, his expression grim. "He's already deep in the brush by now." He leans over the screen and resets the mode to current view.

"We can't just leave him out there on his own," I say.

Mason narrows his eyes at me. "If we go after him now, we abort the mission to the Craniopolis. That's lights out for Jakob. Make a decision."

I take a step back and run my sweaty palms down the length of my braid. There are plenty of reasons why leaving Big Ed to fend for himself is a bad idea, but I know what he would tell me to do if he were here. I draw my shoulders back and take a deep breath. "Head for the Craniopolis. This may be the only chance we get."

Mason sets his jaw. He pulls a switchblade out of his pocket and tosses it to me. "Get the chip out." He gestures with his thumb at Ramesh's gnarled body, tipped forward in the seat behind me.

I meet Mason's stony-faced gaze, and know instinctively it's a test. My heart balks, but my muscles react and I spring the blade. *Right index*, I mouth silently to myself. *Slice the tip.*

Moments later, the silver chip glints up at me from the grayish crumbs of flesh in the palm of my hand. I pick it up and blow it off, avoiding looking at Ramesh's body again. I feel sick, but vindicated. I have what it takes inside me after all.

"Keep it in your pocket in case we get separated," Mason says. "You can activate any Hovermedes with it."

"No blood," I remark, handing his knife back to him.

He glances over my shoulder at Ramesh. "It's already metabolized."

I curl my lip in disgust. "Ugh! The Sweepers are insane."

"They'll never stop. The lure of being able to reengineer humanity is too strong."

"Then we have to stop them," I say. "How many clones can we count on to help?"

Mason raises his brows. "Don't get your hopes up. Most of them will side with the Sweepers, especially the Schutz Clones."

"Who are they?"

"The scientists' personal bodyguards. You'll recognize them when you see them, heavily-armed, dressed in black fatigues. We don't want to engage them if we can avoid it. They're deadly, trained in hand-to-hand combat with special knives called *Schutzmesser*." He gives a snort of disgust. "The scientists don't even trust each other."

I sit back, digesting this new information. It's hard to imagine there are clones in the Craniopolis even more intimidating than Mason. The upside is we may be able to use the Sweepers' misgivings about each other against them. The whole mission is a long shot, but we owe it to Jacob and Owen to attempt a rescue.

"Ready?" Mason asks.

I nod and settle into my seat.

The Hovermedes glides forward. Tucker brushes up against me expectantly. I scratch his head while I contemplate what lies ahead. It's a death wish of sorts. We have no real plan now that Ramesh is gone. Even if we make it safely inside the Craniopolis, we don't have any way to leave the landing dock undetected.

"One mile to go," Mason calls out.

The surround sound system crackles briefly and the lights in the cabin dim. "Craniopolis access sector," an electronic voice announces. "Molecular validation required."

Mason places his index finger in a slot on the control panel in front of him. I suck in my breath. *This is it! Almost there, Jakob.* I flinch at a sharp zapping sound coming from the speaker.

Invalid molecular readout. Invalid molecular readout. Invalid molecular readout …

"Quick! Get me Ramesh's chip." Mason's voice is ragged like I've never heard it before. I unbuckle my harness and dig deep in my pockets. "Here!" I thrust the chip at him.

He grabs it and rams it into the slot. Immediately a high-pitched two-tone chime fills the cabin. "Downlink secured. Proceed to docking."

Mason's lips form a silent "O" and his grip on the control throttle slackens. I sink back in my seat and wait for the pounding in my chest to die down.

"They deactivated my chip," Mason mutters, more to himself than me.

"Ramesh said they upgraded the chips after you left, some kind of retinal sensor," I say. "They can track everything now; brainwaves, temperature, organ degeneration—"

"What?" Mason turns his head and stares at me, a stricken look on his face.

It takes me a moment, and then it hits me. *Ramesh's sensor.* "They know Ramesh is dead, don't they?"

"Instant upload. They knew the minute it happened." A deep crease forms in the middle of Mason's forehead. "Too late to abort now. We're locked into the docking process."

My mind races. We're trapped. They're reeling us in like fish on a line. We should have ditched the Hovermedes when Ramesh expired and went in through the backup air vent like we planned all along.

My eyes widen as we begin a rapid descent. The entire top section of the hilltop below us swivels slowly off its base, revealing a giant steel-framed hanger bay housing six gleaming Hovermedes.

"Get the guns!" Mason yells.

I scurry back and grab our weapons. Tucker whimpers, an uneasy look in his eyes. I hold onto my seat as the Hovermedes drops silently into an empty slot on the concrete hanger floor. The instant we touch down, Mason slams his palm on the door activation switch and springs from his seat.

I whistle softly to Tucker. Mason sticks his head halfway through the door opening, and holds a hand up to signal me to stay put. I hunker down, my fingers looped through Tucker's collar. He waits, motionless, ears perked above his head in radar mode.

Mason motions to the supply carts lined up against the far wall alongside a couple of bridge cranes. "Over there! Go! Go!" He springs from the Hovermedes, armed with an M16 in each hand.

I shove Tucker out the door and lunge after him. Adrenalin spurts through me. I leap over a trench drain, covering the distance to the back wall in a few breakneck strides. Gasping, I plummet headfirst after Tucker into the nearest cart as an overhead steel door rolls open behind me.

Chapter 27

An odor of charred metal fills my nostrils. I must have landed on a pile of power tools or scrap parts from a downed Hovermedes. I carefully wriggle my shoulder blade off something hard as steel that's threatening to impale me. Tucker noses me to get up and I lay a restraining hand on him. He nestles his head resignedly beneath my chin. I lie motionless against him, feeling dangerously exposed and conspicuous on my jagged mattress. If the Sweepers glance over the edge of the cart, they'll be looking straight at me. Carefully, I wrap my finger around the trigger of my gun.

Seconds later, heavy footsteps approach. A bitter sludge of fear trickles down the back of my throat. I squeeze my eyes shut and think of Jakob, imprisoned somewhere in the Craniopolis, alone and terrified. I inhale softly. Whatever I do next will be for him. I slowly raise the barrel of my gun several inches and train it on the rim of the cart, struggling to hold it steady, the trigger slick with sweat.

"Mason?" a voice whispers.

My brain jams. Confused, I let the muzzle drop and then quickly raise it again.

"Mason, are you in there?" A head appears, then massive shoulders, chiseled like a load bearing beam.

I freeze in the man's colossal shadow. His thick, blond eyebrows shoot up, a startled look in his eyes. In that chilling second, I make a decision and go with my gut. I release the trigger and lower my gun, my fingers trembling.

The stranger's features slacken with relief. "Who are you?" His husky voice has a gentle quality to it. His fiery amber eyes search mine and a shiver of something unexpected goes through me.

"Derry Connolly. Who are you?"

Before he can respond, Mason appears behind him.

"Sven!" Mason exclaims.

My jaw drops. Slivers of disconnected thoughts spin around in my brain. Then it hits me. Sven's the military clone planning to flee the Craniopolis with us.

A grin opens up on Sven's rugged face. "You made it!"

I watch the two clones embrace and slap each other between the shoulder blades. It's a strangely human gesture, despite how cold and unfeeling Mason comes across most of the time.

"How'd you know it was me who docked?" Mason asks, when they pull apart.

"I intercepted Ramesh's expiration upload," Sven says. "When the docking request came through, I realized he must have picked you up before he expired." He hesitates. "I'm sorry. I know how much he meant to you."

Mason's eyes cloud over. "We had to use his chip. Mine's been deactivated."

I cast a nervous glance around the hangar. "Won't the Sweepers wonder who flew the Hovermedes back in?"

Sven turns and blinks, as if he's only just remembered I'm here. "I took care of that. I adjusted the time of Ramesh's expiration so it looks like he was already docked."

Mason nods thoughtfully, his brow pleated with concern. "So what's the plan to get us out of here?"

Sven jabs a finger in the direction of the overhead doors. "I brought the Cremat auto for Ramesh's remains. You two can hide in the back."

I glance over at the sleek, black vehicle, shaped like a beetle with multiple ridges running its length. "My dog goes too."

Sven throws Tucker a bemused look. I get the feeling he's never seen a dog before. "I need to follow procedures and take Ramesh to the Crematorium first," he says. "Then we can figure out how to get you to the biotic pods."

I jump out over the side of the cart and slap my thigh for Tucker to follow. "What are the biotic pods?"

"Our living quarters," Mason says. "They're contaminant-controlled, which keeps our immune systems boosted to maximum levels."

"You can brief her on the way." Sven gestures toward the Hovermedes. "Let's unload Ramesh."

Mason, Tucker, and I cram into the back of the Cremertauto. There are no windows and no handles on the inside—a grim reminder of the vehicle's purpose. Somewhere in the darkness, Ramesh's body lies wedged between us. "I'm sorry," I whisper to him. "I was wrong about you." I draw my knees up to my chin and hug them. Mason could be next to expire. I only hope we find Jakob and get out of here before that happens.

The Cremetauto glides effortlessly forward without a sound.

"Is it magnetically powered?" I ask Mason.

"Everything in the Craniopolis draws from the earth's magnetic fields. Free, clean energy for the masses." He lets out a snort. "The Sweepers got some things right."

I bite my lip. I wonder if Mason feels conflicted about the Sweepers' vision for the world too. Ramesh certainly thought the regeneration program had its merits. Somehow, the Sweepers convinced him that anarchy is a bigger threat to freedom than their iron-fisted regime. And most of the clones have never been outside the Craniopolis to know any better. Not me. I know what it is to fear the shadow of the Sweepers' ships, as dark as the hearts that drive them. We're in hell's laboratory now, and once I've found Jakob and Owen, I intend to shut it down.

"We're approaching the Crematorium," Sven says. "It's after hours, but there could still be an incineration in progress. Sit tight for a few minutes."

The Cremetauto slows and I hear the whoosh of doors opening. We move forward again, and then roll to a soundless stop. A leaden terror fills my chest. This is the twisted heart of the Sweepers' lair—a final resting place of sorts, for evidence of what they've spawned. In a matter of minutes, the only trace of Ramesh's existence will be the knowledge the Sweepers have gleaned from him to use in future cloning programs.

"You okay?" Mason whispers.

I give him a halfhearted thumbs-up. Tucker lets out a low growl as the door of the Crematorium seals shut behind us.

"All clear in here," Sven says. "I locked the entry doors."

Mason pulls his brows together. "Cameras?"

"I fed the security loop some dummied-up stills."

Mason grunts as he climbs out over me. I turn and look at the shape that is Ramesh's body, contorted like a draped tree limb beneath the dark cloth. Tentatively, I reach out and lay a hand on him. This can't be how things are supposed to be. I don't know how yet, but I have to find a way to stop this happening.

I clamber out and take in my surroundings. The room is long and low-ceilinged, a strange high-gloss, bluish-white hue, with two recessed bays, each of which houses a steel bed in front of what could pass for an oversized pizza oven. I stand, rooted to the spot, feeling woozy all at once. Mason jerks his thumb in the direction of my gaze. "Cremation chambers."

Heat crawls across the back of my neck. "I figured as much."

I glance up at the cameras mounted to the six-inch-steel conduit pipes running along the ceiling. The eyes of the Sweepers are everywhere. I hope Sven is as competent as he says he is when it comes to rigging this equipment. I'm half-expecting the double doors to swing open and a line of Sweepers to advance toward us, weapons pointed. The sooner we get out of here, the better.

Sven dons an apron and walks around to the back of the Crematauto. I avert my eyes and head to the double doors at the far end of the Crematorium. I've said my good-byes already; there's nothing more I can say or do, other than make good on my promise. I lean my shoulder against the wall and stare at the floor, marked off in a painted yellow grid. The Sweepers aren't invincible. I just need to find a way to bring them down.

"Those squares are linked to a software program," Mason says, coming up behind me. "Security can pinpoint movement in the Craniopolis."

"For your own protection, no doubt." I throw him a scathing look.

"It's hi-tech." He smirks. "Unlike bunker life."

"There's nothing here to be proud of."

Mason's smile fades. "Listen to me, Derry. We're going to need the Sweepers' expertise to rebuild civilization. The Craniopolis isn't just a cloning facility. Brilliant minds have been working on all sorts of invaluable research here."

I give a sarcastic laugh. "So they're monsters with obese IQs. I'd rather take my chances with the Rogues."

"*They're* Neanderthals—out of control."

"I don't want to control them. I want us all to be free."

Mason nods thoughtfully. "What if I told you the Sweepers could rehabilitate subversives?"

"What are you talking about?"

"The Sweepers can superimpose genetic codes with new segments of DNA. Think about the possibilities, Derry. They could stabilize the Rogues' violent propensities."

I take a step backward. Mason's words orbit around my brain. "You told me you hated what they're doing." My voice cracks. "Now you're defending lobotomies for the Rogues?"

Tucker sits back on his haunches, gives a low growl, and trains his eyes on Mason.

"I'm only talking about fixing what's broken. Subversives have deviant traits that turn them into criminals. Things go wrong with humans too, you know." A deep flush creeps up Mason's neck. "There are good scientists down here, men and women who can help make the future a better—"

"Now you sound as crazy as the Sweepers," I yell.

Tucker gives another, more menacing, growl, and then jumps up, barking furiously.

"Down, boy," I reach for his collar, to keep him from lunging at Mason.

He snarls at me in a way he's never done before and I realize, too late, that I've misread his warning.

With a loud whoosh the doors to the Crematorium swing open.

Chapter 28

Someone gives a feeble clap. "Magnificent! A most rousing speech to rally the heathens, Mason!"

My feet fuse to the floor at the raspy voice that wafts into the room. Tucker strains at his collar. I yank him back, my heart pounding.

A shrunken man with an unnatural stoop steps into view. My skin crawls with a new level of fear. My gun's in the Crem.auto, along with the rest of the weapons. I fumble around in my pocket and latch onto my switchblade. A trickle of sweat runs down behind my ears. The man standing in the entry looks freakishly old and frail. Tucker could take him down in a heartbeat, but my brain sounds an inner caution. He probably didn't come alone.

Before I even finish my thought, the doorway darkens and four armed men in black fatigues troop through. Big-shouldered, faces set like flint on necks thick as tree stumps. *Schutz Clones!* I tighten my grip on Tucker and command him to stay. One false move and he'll end up another carcass waiting to be incinerated. He minds me, but tension radiates through his collar.

"Welcome to the Craniopolis," the old man says. "My apologies for the modest welcoming committee, but your timing is most unfortunate. Everyone is at the unveiling of our new Hovermedes prototype." His body shakes out a shallow breath, as he shuffles toward me. "Allow me to introduce myself. I am Dr. Lyong."

I slide my gaze in Mason's direction. His face registers confusion. Then a flicker of recognition.

"What ... happened to you?" he asks, in a half-whisper.

Dr. Lyong jerks to a stop in front of me and lets out a long, trembling sigh. It's all I can do not to gag. His breath smells of decaying compost.

"Restructuring DNA proved more complex than I had hoped." Dr. Lyong runs a finger under his beaked nose and waves it dismissively in Mason's direction. The skin is stretched so tight over his hand I can see the grape-colored veins forking out beneath it. He barely looks human.

I can't repress a shudder.

He must have sensed me recoil because he tilts his head until his icy eyes are locked on me. "Do I disgust you, Miss. Connolly?"

I'm thrown off by the fact that he knows my name. I wonder who told him. *Owen?* When I open my mouth to respond, Mason cuts me off.

"You did this ... to *yourself?*"

Dr. Lyong eyes him disdainfully, and smooths a string of lank, gray hair behind a shriveled ear. "Two weeks ago I attempted to reverse the abnormal DNA structure of the aging process. I miscalculated the base pairings rules in the transcription. Regrettably, my cells retained considerable damage as a result." He curls his lip, studying Mason's reaction. "A minor setback. I've since inverted the sequencing and halted the process."

"A minor setback?" Mason growls. "Is that what you call molecular ossification too? Ramesh is dead, thanks to you."

A sterile smile flicks across the doctor's lips. "You, Mason, always were ungrateful for what I endowed you with." He pauses, his eyes radiating a chill that makes me quake. "You demonstrate a complete lack of understanding of what I am accomplishing for humankind—*every* strain of humankind." The thin skin on his brow rumples. "The galaxy is unstable. Planets are in meltdown as we speak. Our moon's volatile tidal forces will ravage the earth's crust again; it is only a matter of when. It is imperative that we humans develop alternative processes of regeneration. The science behind you, Mason, holds the key to our future."

Mason's fingers curl into a fist at his side. "You're experimenting with lives—*my life,* for what it's worth." He sways back on his heels, his eyes glowing like embers. As if on cue, the Schutz Clones train their weapons on him. For the first time, I notice the sheathed knives dangling from their belts.

Dr. Lyong waves a bony finger in the air again. "*Your* life? You forget your place. Clones were created to serve a purpose. You have no will."

Mason moves his jaw grimly side to side. I can tell he's on the verge of lunging at Dr. Lyong, but he doesn't stand a chance. There's at least ten feet between them. The fatigue-clad bodyguards will pump him full of lead before he gets within striking distance. I peer out at the doctor from under my matted hair.

But I could do it.

My eyes dart around the room and settle on Sven. I signal over my shoulder with a slight incline of my head. He blinks, slow and deliberate, as if to indicate he knows what I have in mind—which is remarkable because it's more than I've figured out. I only know the weapons are behind me, and so is he. I wish Big Ed were here right now. It's times like this I rely most on his wisdom.

Everyone's afraid, Derry. You have to find your courage and act anyway.

Slowly, I uncurl my fingers from Tucker's collar and tap a finger on his neck to command him to stay. In the same instant, I propel myself forward with a bloodcurdling yell.

I slam into the doctor, my fist connecting with his windpipe. He totters and I spin him around in a headlock to face the Schutz Clones. Their seamed faces register confusion.

"Nobody move!" I yell, pressing my switchblade to the paper-thin skin on the doctor's neck. He makes an incoherent sound that dissolves into a choking gurgle against my forearm. I keep my eyes trained on the Schutz Clones.

"Drop your weapons, or he dies," I say, hoping I still have a live hostage in my arms.

They take aim at me, their expressions a frozen cocktail of disbelief and rage. Tucker bares his teeth and snarls. There's an agonizing beat of silence, and then, behind me, I hear the door of the Cremetauto open.

A jolt of hope goes through me. If Sven can get to the weapons, there's a chance we can pull this off.

Mason's voice cracks like a whip in the space between us. "You heard her," he says, staring fixedly at the Schutz Clones. "Put down your guns. You can end this now if you'll help us."

I suck in my breath and tighten my forearm around the doctor's neck. I only hope Mason knows what he's doing. Trying to negotiate with a bunch of Schutz Clones could backfire. They're used to following orders, not thinking for themselves.

"I'm one of you," Mason continues in an even tone. "And so is Sven."

The Schutz Clones hold their positions, a blank look in their eyes. My forearm aches, but I don't dare twitch in case I trigger a volley of fire. Despite what a lightweight the doctor is, I can't hold this position for much longer. "Ten seconds," I say. "Then he dies."

I catch a glint of something in the clones' eyes and sense their triggers tightening before it happens.

A volley of fire erupts behind me. The four clones fly backward.

I dive for the floor, dragging my hostage with me. Dr. Lyong groans beneath my weight, but I don't dare shift an inch. My heart knocks against my ribs for what seems like an eternity. I'm not sure if the Schutz Clones are dead or waiting on me to make a move.

"It's over, Derry." Mason towers over me, his face drawn. "Sven took them out."

I squeeze my eyes shut and roll onto my back. Dr. Lyong smacks his gums together, sucking for air, and then lets out a gasp.

I clamber to my knees and bury my face in Tucker's neck.

"Gotta hand it to you," Mason says. "You're quick on the draw."

Not trusting myself to speak, I give him a curt nod by way of response. He stretches out a hand and pulls me to my feet. I glance over at the dead clones, and shiver. Even from where I'm standing, I can tell they've already assumed the same bloodless pallor as Ramesh.

I turn my head and spot Sven swirling his fingers over a screen at the back of the Crematorium, his forehead creased in concentration.

"What's he doing?" I ask.

"Rigging the cameras. So the Sweepers don't see the bodies." Mason reaches out a meaty fist and hauls Dr. Lyong to his feet. "Where are the Undergrounders?"

A scowl cuts across the doctor's decrepit features. "You'll never make it out of here alive."

Mason gives a wry grin. "You have that wrong. And we have your cloning expertise to thank." Mason sticks his face in close to Dr. Lyong's. "Sven can reconfigure your software faster than you can string together a new genetic code. Except, he doesn't ever screw up."

Dr. Lyong's eyes bulge in their sockets. "Mutant fool! You're turning your back on a new and improved planetary civilization, and for what? To run with a pack of subversives bent on killing each other off faster than we can replenish humankind?"

"You're nothing more than a trafficker in body parts." Mason's voice quiets to a whisper. "I'd rather take my chances with them than you."

"Done with the override!" Sven yells. "Let's hit it!"

Mason narrows his eyes and swaddles Dr. Lyong's neck with one fist. "*Where* are they?"

"I don't know who you're talking about."

I step toward him. "A boy, blue eyes, sixteen, thick blond hair, extracted a few days ago, and an eighteen-year-old dark-haired boy with a black eye, heavy bruising on his face, extracted yesterday. He's my brother."

I place my hand lightly on Mason's and, reluctantly, he releases his fist. Dr. Lyong hunches over, clutching his chest. A cold sweat breaks out along my spine.

Please don't die on me. Not yet!

After a long minute, he straightens up, waxen but alert. When he speaks, his breath hits me again, like toxic fumes from an abandoned mine. "Your brother's in Sektor Sieben."

I throw a baffled glance at Mason. The look in his widened eyes sends a rod of terror up my spine.

"What's Sektor Sieben?" I ask.

"Time to go." Mason brushes past me, grabs Dr. Lyong by the shoulder, and drags him over to the Crematauto.

"Wait!" I call out. "What about the other boy?"

The doctor twists his scrawny, loose-skinned neck around and peers at me through half-lidded eyes. "He didn't make it."

Chapter 29

Didn't make it. The room swivels. Voices ebb and flow around me as I hover on the edge of blacking out. I can almost hear my heart rupture inside my chest. For days I've pushed through hunger and exhaustion, faced every fear I've ever imagined, some I never dreamed of, clinging to the hope of finding Jakob alive and bringing him home. Now I'm deflating, adrenalin leaking from me like air from a spent tire. My voice shakes when I try to speak. "What … did you do to him?"

The doctor gives an impatient sigh. "He never made it here. He evaded the sweep."

I take a few shallow breaths, my head swimming in confusion. If Jakob's not here, then where is he? If the Sweepers didn't take him, who, or what did? I push the thought of wolf packs out of my mind. I have to believe he's safe. I can't lose hope now.

"We gotta go!" Sven's voice jolts me back to my senses. He reaches for my elbow to guide me to the Crematauto. Tucker bares his teeth and snarls at him.

I take hold of his collar and reassure him Sven's not a threat, then lead him over to the Crematauto.

Dr. Lyong's scowl deepens when I climb in. Tucker takes a quick sniff at him, and then pulls back abruptly like he's caught a hint of something rotten. Mason takes out a piece of rope from his backpack and secures the doctor's hands, even though it seems a pointless gesture. Lyong's hardly much of a threat without his Schutz Clones to back him up. In fact he looks as close to death as possible for someone who's not already in the first stages of decomposition.

I narrow my eyes at him. "If you're lying to me, you'll regret it."

Dr. Lyong lifts his bound hands and carefully wipes a dark-colored drip from his nose. My stomach trips and I almost gag a second time.

"I can assure you, your friend is not here." He lets out a heavy sigh and closes his eyes like a dying man worn out by conversation.

Sven slides behind the controls of the Cremauto and the back door seals shut.

"What's Sektor Sieben?" I ask Mason again, as we take off.

He hesitates, a moment too long for someone who has nothing to hide. "Research mainly."

Dr. Lyong lets out an extended cackle. Tucker repositions himself behind me, tail tucked beneath him, as if unnerved by the odious rasping.

"Allow me." Dr. Lyong straightens up, and gestures elaborately with his bound hands. "Mason is somewhat reticent about our greatest accomplishments. Sektor Sieben houses our Cybernetic Implant Prototypes. You see, cloning is only one approach of many we are investigating in a bid to regenerate humankind."

He dissolves into a coughing fit, and I shrink back in disgust from the spittle flying from his lips. When he catches his breath again, he wipes the back of his bony hand over his mouth and sighs. "We can now integrate many useful technologies into the human central nervous system to replace failing organs and tissues. One day very soon, we will have the capacity to live forever, and eliminate the need for cloning entirely."

I furrow my brow. What does integrating technologies into humans mean exactly? My mind races back to something Mason hinted at— *deviations* he called them. I pictured them as failed cloning experiments, but maybe they're some kind of half-human forms the Sweepers are building with technology. My pulse races. If they've even laid a finger on Owen, I won't hesitate to tear Lyong apart with my bare hands. Maybe it's time he knew that.

I grab a fistful of the doctor's lank hair, and jerk his head back. "What have you done to my brother?"

He blinks at me, his eyes bloated and watering. "Why don't you stop by Sektor Sieben and see for yourself?" He heaves a breath, his emaciated frame wracked by the effort of talking under duress. I reluctantly release him, and recoil when he slumps toward me, gasping for air.

"He's toying with you, Derry," Mason says. "Don't believe anything he says. Owen's probably still in the Intake Sektor."

I wipe a hand across my brow. "We'll check Sektor Sieben first, just in case."

A shadow passes over Mason's face, but he doesn't try to talk me out of it.

The Crematauto slows to a stop and I hear Sven exchange a few words with someone. There's a series of electronic beeps, and the sound of doors opening.

"Security guards?" I ask Mason.

He nods. "Access to Sektor Sieben is restricted to research scientists, and the Crematauto. It's a steel vault, soundproofed and windowless, no way in or out other than through these doors."

"The guards didn't ask Sven too many questions," I remark. "Just waved him on through."

Mason shifts uncomfortably. "Nobody asks questions when you're driving the Crematauto. Even the guards don't want to have to look at what you're transporting from the laboratories."

The vehicle glides to a halt and Sven climbs out, leaving the door wide open behind him. Dr. Lyong blinks and looks around furtively. He opens his mouth, but before he can say a word, Mason's hand envelops his face. "You even squeak and I'll tie your vocal cords in a knot so tight you'll never make another sound."

Instinctively, my fingers curl around the barrel of my gun. I'm not sure if Mason suspects there's someone in here, but he's not taking any chances. Tucker raises his head off his paws and looks at me expectantly. I motion for him to stay down, and carefully cock my gun.

Pop! Pop!

My heart shudders to a momentary stop. The sound, two shots in quick succession, ricochets around the room. Tucker barks sharply, scrambles to his feet. Mason locks eyes with me, and gives a curt nod. We jump out of the Crematauto together, weapons raised.

"Don't shoot!" Sven calls out from across the room. He raises his hands, holding his rifle above his head. "I fired the shots."

I follow Mason across the high-gloss floor of a spacious foyer with a large u-shaped monitoring station positioned in front of steel security doors. Sprawled on the floor between the station and the doors are two bodies, clad in white, bloodstained scrubs. I let out a gasp and sink to my knees beside them to check for a pulse. "They're dead."

"I had no choice," Sven says. "They pulled their weapons on me."

I shrink back from the blood creeping out from under the bodies. My mind flashes back to Ramesh's bloodless pallor when he expired. "They were humans, not clones," I say, my voice low and strained.

"Scientists," Mason replies, an edge to his voice.

I stare at him. "Is there a difference?"

"You tell me." He turns abruptly, and strides back to the Crematauto.

My chest tightens. I hate what the Sweepers are doing as much as Mason does, but I can't help wondering if some of them are here against their wills. Surely not all their hearts are as dark as Lyong's.

Sven sits down heavily at the monitoring station. He ploughs his fingers through his hair, and then pulls a surveillance screen on a flexible arm toward him.

Mason drags Dr. Lyong out of the Crematauto and shoves him roughly against the side of the vehicle.

"I'm only gonna give you one chance to punch in your authorization code and get us inside." Mason squeezes the doctor's throat. "After that I'm going to put you out of your misery so fast you'll be dead before you hit the floor."

I hold my breath while Dr. Lyong hobbles unsteadily over to the steel security doors. He jabs at the keypad with a skeletal finger. Seconds later, an electronic chime rings out. The steel doors slide soundlessly apart.

"After you." He gestures for me to go first, his eyes glinting.

I take a hesitant step in the direction of the doors leading to Sektor Sieben. I'm not sure what horrors lie within. Everything inside me is telling me to turn and run. But deep down I know if I falter now, I'll always falter.

I summon my courage and cross the floor. Tucker breaks into a trot, psyched by the remote possibility that he might be about to get out of here.

"Wait!"

I freeze at the foreboding note in Sven's voice. "You'd better look at this," he says, his gaze fixed on the security camera screen in front of him.

"We're too late!"

Chapter 30

"Is it Owen?" I yell, as I race across the high-gloss floor to the monitoring station. My eyes dart over the chaotic images on the surveillance screen in front of Sven. Swarms of people spilling out of a stadium of sort. Behind them, several hundred Schutz Clones in black fatigues goose step into view.

My heart pounds like a gavel in my chest. A group of scientists in lab attire, flanked by twenty or so Schutz Clones, merge into the corridor that leads to Sektor Sieben.

Sven inhales a deep breath. "Ten minutes at best before they get here." He pulls an ammunition clip from his coat and reaches for his assault rifle.

"There are too many of them." I look first at Mason and then at Sven as they ready their weapons. "We can't fight them."

My heart races as I weigh our options. We're in a vault, with no way out. Our only other choice is to hide.

"In here," I yell. I grab Tucker by the collar and make a beeline through the steel doors that lead into Sektor Sieben. Sven and Mason follow, dragging Dr. Lyong by the arms. Inside, Mason punches the automatic wall panel and the doors vacuum seal behind us with a soft whoosh. I glance around skittishly. The space we're standing in is a sixty-foot long corridor, laid out on either side like solid steel cattle stalls. Each stall has a door with a viewing monitor shaped like a giant eyeball.

A mausoleum-like silence descends. It's peaceful here, in an eerie sort of way, like the viewing room in the funeral home where they took Gramps when he died. A long time ago, before the world changed.

"What's in those rooms?" I ask.

Mason averts his eyes. "Participants."

My heart thuds. *Participants?* I can't imagine anyone volunteering for cybernetic implants.

"Is there any place to hide?" I dash to the nearest door and peer into the dome-shaped viewing monitor.

Two young men and a young woman lie stretched out peacefully in white cocoon-shaped beds, the material molded to their bodies like the seats in a Hovermedes, each sandwiched between metal frames. Tubes run from their torsos into a tower of medical equipment and feed into a series of flush-mounted wall monitors. Whatever's going on in here, at least it's not the body parts canning factory I had envisioned.

I move the 360-degree orbital eye and explore the rest of the space inside the room. "What about the cabinets?" I say. "Think we can fit inside?"

Without waiting for an answer, I reach for the handle and push the door gently open, not wanting to startle the participants. Their eyelids remain glued shut, their faces frozen.

Mason squeezes by me and wrenches on the cabinet handles. "Locked."

I stare at the upturned face on the nearest bed. The pallid features have a strange, vacated look to them. A shiver crosses my shoulders. "They must be heavily sedated. They haven't flinched since we came in."

Sven comes up beside me. His amber eyes have the look of a wounded animal. "Let's get out of here," he mutters. He turns abruptly and marches out of the room, dragging Lyong behind him.

Tucker sticks his nose under the bed, whines, and backs out hurriedly. I kneel down and ruffle his neck.

Glancing up, I catch sight of the underside of the frame. A life-sized 3D medical body chart of sorts, organs half-wired with metal valves and rubber tubing like the makings of a clock. My eyes drift to the metal axis that turns the bed frame. A jackhammer tremor goes up my spine. I lurch sideways, my body shaking uncontrollably.

"What is it?" Mason asks.

I gesture to the control panel at the bottom of the bed frame.

Mason frowns and hits the rotation icon. The young man turns from us slowly, like a carcass on a spit, revealing the underside of his body—cut away to display it's new mechanical innards.

Mason swears softly, rocks backward on the soles of his giant feet.

My breath comes in short jabs. I stare at the web of exposed arteries and blood-spattered metal parts in horror. The back of the man's head is a human fuse box, wired to control the implants. Tucker barks sharply and paws at me. Stomach heaving, I scramble to my feet and stagger out of the room. I lean back against the wall in the corridor, slide to the floor, and bury my head in my hands. I'll never forgive myself if anything's happened to Owen. I should never have trusted Mason to keep him safe.

"Derry!" Mason barks. He shakes me, and not in an anemic sort of way.

I straighten up, my shoulder pulsating with pain.

"They're coming! We're out of time!" He gestures to the far end of the long corridor. "There's a supply room back there we can hide in."

I wipe my trembling hand across my mouth. Tucker races off down the hallway after Sven and Dr. Lyong, as if there's nothing more he'd rather do than put as much distance as possible between himself and the room we just vacated. I pull myself up with Mason's assistance, and stumble after the others.

Inside the storage room, I gulp a few deep breaths of stuffy air and slump back against a rack overflowing with linens, scrubs, and boxes of medicine. I blink as I take in the vast inventory. All stuff we could have used in the bunkers a million times over. My eyes settle on Lyong, leaning against a shelf of plastic tubing and oxygen masks.

"Why are you doing this to them?" I say, through gritted teeth.

He leans toward me. "Not *to* them, *for* them."

I glare at him. "If you believe that, you're the one needs your brain rewired."

Satisfied he has my attention, he sits back. "Sektor Sieben is a pilot recycling plant for humankind. Before the meltdown, brain-dead participants were donated to cybernetics research by the world government."

"The government donated *people*?"

Dr. Lyong cocks a sparse eyebrow at me. "Left to the good will of mourning families, we would never have received enough donations. The supreme leader believed in advancing the boundaries of humankind. As a result, the government had special arrangements with reeducation centers."

"What kind of arrangements?"

Dr. Lyong shrugs. "They handled procurement. Our assignment was to work out the kinks in cybernetic implant technology."

"You're insane!" I shrink back from the doctor's foul breath that lurks like a poisonous gas in the air between us. "You're extracting Undergrounders to continue your implant research, aren't you?"

He laughs, and his eyelids drift to half-mast for a moment. "The extractions are strictly to retrieve uncontaminated DNA for cloning."

"I don't believe you. This isn't science, it's murder."

He sighs. "Murder entails malice. I, on the other hand, have sacrificed my life to provide a service to humankind."

"You're completely out of control!" I yell.

"No." He shakes his head sadly, as if to draw attention to my outburst. "I am very much *in* control now. Thanks to the strides we have made in cybernetic implant technology, some fortunate participants will have the chance to live again." He twists his lips into a sliver of a smile. "Perhaps even your brother."

My jaw trembles. I leap to my feet fully prepared to claw the rotting flesh from his face. "What have you done to him?"

Mason stomps a massive steel-toed boot in the space between us. "He doesn't even know who your brother is, Derry. He's just using the information you give him to get under your skin. You need to stay focused." He gestures at the scrubs hanging on a rail behind him. "Put these on. If we have to make a run for it, anything's less conspicuous than what we're wearing now."

I blink, reeling from Lyong's words. The possibility that Owen is in one of these cattle stalls horrifies me. But if he's not, we've got another problem on our hands—he could be anywhere in the Craniopolis. Or he could be dead.

Mason grabs a set of oversized scrubs and pulls them on.

"We can't just walk out of here and pass ourselves off as scientists," Sven says.

Mason glares at him. "Got a better idea?"

Sven shrugs and hands me a set of scrubs. Tucker sniffs at them curiously. I pull on the billowing pants and tighten the drawstring waistband. The macabre thought comes to me that these might end up being my burial clothes. Except they don't bury bodies down here, they rewire them, or cremate the botched ones. I glance around at the contents of the room in a last-ditch effort to come up with a better plan than waltzing past the Schutz Clones brandishing a scalpel.

Somewhere inside my head, a light snaps on. What we need is a diversion. I lock eyes with Dr. Lyong. "I'm guessing the stadium is the emergency muster station down here."

He narrows his eyes at me and casts a furtive glance over my shoulder, tipping me off to exactly what I'm looking for.

I turn and scan the room. Several oversized supply carts line the back wall. I scurry back and yank the carts out from the wall one by one. *Bingo!*

"There's a fire alarm back here!" I yell to the others. "It'll buy us enough time to look for Owen and get out of here."

Heart racing, I reach for the T-bar on the pull station. I grab Tucker's collar, and tug hard on the alarm. A shrill sound goes through me like a knife. The hairs in my ears vibrate. "Go!" I yell, shoving Mason in front of me. Sven grabs Dr. Lyong and we dash back out into the main corridor. "Search the left side on your way out," I yell at Mason. "I'll take the right."

I sprint to the nearest room and wrench open the door. The expressionless face in the bed has a peculiar ivory sheen to it, more like a plastic mold than skin. Light-brown hair. It can't be Owen. *Or Jakob.* I back out, and gather my wits enough to open the next door. Several ashen, half-refurbished faces with empty eye sockets, contemplate the ceiling. I beat a hasty retreat, a fresh wave of nausea surging up from my stomach.

Outside, I lean against the door and hold my hands over my ears to deaden the relentless blare of the alarm. The longer Owen's missing, the less hope I can drum up in my heart that I'll ever see him again. As for Jakob—I have to believe he's safe, somewhere far from here. Any other option would be the end of me.

"Derry!"

I jump out of my skin at the muffled sound of Mason's voice. I can tell by the way he's frantically waving me over that he's found something. I force my jellylike legs across the corridor, dreading what's coming.

He motions through the open door of the stall. I frown at a sleeping figure curled up on the bed with his back to us. The room is empty apart from the bed, no medical equipment, no monitors, not even a drip line.

Cautiously, I step toward the sleeping figure. Tucker emits a low growl that rumbles at the back of his throat like an engine about to throttle up. I plant my eyes on the man's face and freeze.

It can't be!

Chapter 31

Thin mustached lips, parted in sleep, pierced brow, cleft chin—the same sinister face I grew to dread in the short time I knew him. I reach into my pocket, flip my wrist, and ready my switchblade.

I feel as if I've wanted to kill Rummy for a very long time. Three days can morph into a heck of a hankering for revenge. My mind flits back to when I last saw him—sprawled on the lodge steps in Lewis Falls, suctioned to a Sweepers' tube, limbs flailing every which way. I tried to save him, instinct I suppose, but I didn't feel sorry for him when I couldn't. Only relieved I would never have to look at him again.

I test my thumb gently against the tip of my blade. I could slit his throat now and he wouldn't feel a thing. We'd be even for what he did to Owen and to me. My jaw still throbs when I press my fingers to it. I stare down at his still form. I'm not afraid to kill him, not after everything I've been through.

But, now that I've seen what goes on inside the Craniopolis, I can understand the fear that drove him to do what he did to us—the kind of fear that consumes a mind like a flesh-eating bacteria. The Rogues knew what was really going in the reeducation centers. No wonder they'd stop at nothing to ensure they're never taken captive again. Rummy knew someone was ratting them out to the Sweepers. Owen and I showed up in the wrong place, at the wrong time.

"What do you want to do?" Mason asks.

I pocket my knife and take a deep breath. I shake Rummy and slap him several times, but it's no use, he's too heavily drugged. "We'll have to leave him." I turn my back and whistle for Tucker. "We came here for Owen and Jakob. We can't save them all."

I march nonchalantly past Mason, but inside I've never felt more hollow. Leaving Rummy behind is a death sentence. It's a lame way to kill a man, and I know it will haunt me. Maybe I *should* slit his throat, it would be more merciful than what's in store for him.

I busy myself checking the remainder of the rooms on the right side of the corridor, half of which are unoccupied, and half of which house more wired cadavers. To my relief there's no sign of Owen.

I throw a cursory glance at the monitors, and give the dead scientists' bodies a wide berth on my way back out to the Cremateauto. Mason gives a grim shake of his head when I throw him a questioning look. "If we can get to the biotic pods, I might be able to find out from someone if he's in the Intake Sektor," he says.

I reach for Dr. Lyong by the scruff of his neck. "I should have known you were lying."

"He was as good as dead when we extracted him." Dr. Lyong flashes me a dark look. "There's only one reason he's no longer here."

Mason lays a hand on my shoulder. "Don't underestimate your brother."

I bite my bottom lip. At least Mason's optimistic Owen's still alive. I have my doubts. How long can anyone survive in a place like this?

Mason shoves Lyong toward the vehicle. "Time to go," he says. "The fire alarm will only buy us so much time. Once the Schutz Clones find the bodies in here and realize Lyong is missing, they'll put patrols in all the tunnels. We have to find Owen and get back to the docking station before that happens."

I hesitate before climbing into the Cremateauto and throw a furtive glance back down the eerie corridor. The steel doors line up on either side like nails in a giant coffin. My decision to leave Rummy behind weighs on me, my own words haunt me: *I don't leave a man, even a scumbag like you, to the mercy of animals.*

"Wait!" I say. "I've changed my mind. We'll bring Rummy with us."

Mason's eyebrows shoot upward. Without a word, he turns and hoofs it back down the corridor. A moment later, he reappears, Rummy slung over one shoulder like a kill from a hunting trip.

The tightness in my chest lets up a notch. I've reassured myself that I'm not a monster, but will I pay for this decision later? Rummy's not in any shape to handle a weapon and make himself useful. He's an added burden in an already precarious situation, and on top of that, we can't trust him.

He doesn't even twitch when we lay him down in the back of the Crematauto. Lyong wrinkles his nose in disgust, and scoots as far back from him as he can.

"Something stink?" I ask, looking pointedly at Lyong. "Other than your curdled cells."

He eyes me with an air of irritation, like a predator sizing up prey beyond its strike zone. "When the Schutz Clones apprehend you, which they will, Miss Connolly, I assure you I will take great pleasure in using *your* tissue in my regeneration."

His concrete-colored flesh contorts in a sneer. Something cannibalistic in his eyes makes my heart falter. My brain feels probed, as if he's sucking out my thoughts. He's a broken man, but the intellect inside that shell terrifies me more than all the Rogues' brutality.

I tear my gaze away and bury my face in Tucker's neck. The familiar scent rushes through me like a healing balm.

"We're pulling out," Sven calls back to us.

The Crematauto shudders briefly and glides forward.

"Stay down," Sven says. "And shut Lyong up."

Mason pulls a filthy flannel shirt from his pack and rips several strips from it. He stuffs the doctor's mouth with a fistful of fabric, and then ties the bulk of the shirt firmly around his head. The only sounds Lyong can make now are muffled grunts. Tucker flops down on his paws, apparently satisfied the doctor's no longer a threat.

"Gear up," Mason nudges me.

I pull the charging handle of my gun to the rear and lock the bolt. Tucker's ears prick up at the sound.

"Not yet, old boy." I lean over and rub his head. It's just another hunting trip as far as he's concerned. But everything's about to change for me.

I insert a loaded magazine and slap it with the palm of my hand to make sure it holds. I've never killed a human being before, let alone a clone. I slide my finger into the trigger housing and trace the metal outline. We won't get out of here without some kind of showdown, and when it comes, there won't be time to second guess myself.

The Cremateauto slows to a stop and Sven punches in the security code at the doors. "Exiting Sektor Sieben," he says. "Get ready."

I shift my position, squished between Mason and an unresponsive Rummy, and finger the safety selector on my gun. I tell myself there's nothing I won't do to save Owen.

The Cremateauto lurches forward into the tunnel. The fire alarm blares relentlessly. I raise my head a few inches and peer through the front windscreen. A cold sweat breaks out across my brow.

Two hundred feet from our vehicle, the first junction is packed with figures jostling their way in both directions. I glance at Sven. He stares straight ahead, face pinched in concentration. We slow to a crawl, hovering forward as people step off the magnetic levitation tracks to let us through. They push and elbow each other like a jittery herd, ready to bolt en masse if one of them makes a break. Few even throw us a passing glance. If anything, the sight of the Cremateauto seems to spur them on, lending credence to the threat of fire.

I gasp when I see the first misshapen form mingling with the crowd. Bulbous forehead atop an unnaturally narrow, flat face. Eye sockets punched sideways, eyeballs retracted. I twist my neck to stare after the creature as it lopes along. *A deviation.* Tucker lifts his head, as if sensing my angst.

We levitate at a painstakingly slow speed as we pull away from the intersection. More than once, someone in the crowd whacks the side of the

Cremetauto in a fit of rage as we nudge past, and once a malformed face presses up against the windscreen. My blood chills as I picture being pulled from the Cremetauto and ripped limb from limb by a mob of deviations.

"I can't get anywhere with this crowd," Sven says, his voice strained. "They're all making a beeline for the biotic pods. They know the air in there will be uncontaminated. We'll have to head for the docking station instead."

He navigates a left turn down a connecter tunnel, his features set like hardpan. The crowd thins out, and I relax my death grip on my weapon as we pick up speed.

"Where's the docking station?" I ask.

"East side of the Craniopolis." Sven swings hard left again and turns down a deserted side tunnel. "We'll take the back way."

As I sink to the floor to rest my cramped muscles, I hear a sharp intake of breath. "What is it?" I whisper.

"Checkpoint ahead. Schutz Clones," Sven says in a clipped tone. "Sit tight and let me do the talking."

I throw Mason a tense glance. He tightens the gag around Lyong's mouth.

We glide forward another twenty feet or so, and then come to an abrupt stop. I motion to Tucker to lay still, and squeeze the pistol grip on my M16. Mason gestures urgently at the door. Silently, I flip around to face the back of the vehicle. If the Schutz Clones open the back door I'll have no choice but to shoot. If Owen or Jakob are somewhere in the Craniopolis, we're their only hope.

Mason nests the stock of his gun against his shoulder, his features groomed to neutral. His calmness unsettles me. I need to see him sweat, a twitch of fear at least, to know his adrenalin's pumping. But then he was trained for this. If ever I need to trust him, it's now.

I strain my ears to listen in on what the security guard is saying to Sven.

Without warning, Lyong wriggles sideways and kicks at the side of the vehicle. I grab his leg, but he fights me with surprising strength and lands a foot below my ribs. I clutch at my stomach, momentarily winded. Before he gets another swing in, Mason rams the butt of his rifle into Lyong's kneecap. He lets out a muffled yelp and rolls over in agony.

I flatten myself back into position and refocus. Sven's voice gets louder. For our benefit no doubt. The guards must have picked up on something. "What do you mean no vehicles are authorized to run?" Sven protests. "Dr. Lyong gave express orders to evacuate Sektor Sieben and bring the participants to the medical unit in the docking station."

I press my cheek against the cold steel of my weapon and force myself to breathe. If the guards order Sven out of the vehicle, it might be only a matter of seconds before they open the back door and find us.

"Get your hands off me!" Sven yells. "I'm reporting all three of you for code violations."

Mason waves three fingers in front of my face to make sure I'm tracking. I sign *okay* back to him, and focus on my front sight post. Tucker tenses at the sound of footsteps moving toward the back of the vehicle. My breathing quickens.

The back door slider clicks. A vertical strip of light appears as the panels move apart. I ease back the trigger until there's just enough of a crack in the door to shoot through, and fire.

The sound, like rocks peppering a steel drum, ricochets around the tunnel. Mason shoots in tandem. Burnt powder fills the air. When the doors retract fully I see our kill, slumped over in a heap, chalk-white and still. My heart thuds in my throat.

Two bodies. But there were three Schutz Clones.

I slither backward into the Crematauto, and twist my head around to peek through the half-open driver's door. The third guard is kneeling behind the checkpoint, gun trained on the back of the Crematauto, waiting for us to emerge. I weigh my odds. It's an awkward shot, straining from a semi-prone position, wedged sideways between the seats. I count to three and take it anyway.

The Schutz Clone quivers for a second and then topples to the ground. I swallow hard. There wasn't a better option than to take him out, but it doesn't change how I feel inside, like I'm icing over. I exhale slowly, and then flick the switch on my gun to safety.

"Quick!" Sven reaches a hand into the Crematauto to pull me out. "He called for backup. We gotta go."

I shove Tucker out of the vehicle first, then place my hand in Sven's. A shiver runs up my arm when his huge hand closes over mine. *So different to Jakob's touch.*

"Why can't we take the Crematauto?" I ask.

"Once the Sweepers pinpoint the tracker on it, they'll implode it," Sven replies.

Mason drags Rummy out next, and tosses him over his shoulder. Sven pokes Lyong in the ribs with his M16. "Out!"

The doctor mutters something unintelligible and scoots himself forward a few inches. Sven grabs him by the scruff of the neck and hauls him out. I wish we could leave him behind, but we might need him as collateral.

"Which way?" I ask, glancing in both directions.

Sven motions in front of him with his weapon. He moves off down the corridor, hauling the disgruntled doctor after him with his free hand. Mason falls in behind, Rummy draped across his shoulders. I take up the rear, glancing behind me every few feet. At least my hands are free so one of us can get a round off quickly if we come under attack. Mason's at a huge disadvantage with Rummy's dead weight on his shoulders. Reluctantly, I send Tucker up to flank him. If nothing else, he can alert him to any ambush from a side tunnel.

Alone with my dark thoughts, I question what I've done. The stench of death is on me now, and nothing will ever be the same.

Clone killer.

The crushing words sear my conscience. I've taken a life, no matter how I define that life, or how many units that life was destined to be.

The dimly lit tunnel stretches out in front like a black hole winding its way to the earth's core. There's no sign of movement up ahead, but I'm afraid even to blink in case the Schutz Clones attack. I've been counting on Tucker to forewarn us, but I'm still not sure clones have a scent he can pick up on.

I open my mouth to ask Mason about it. It's the last thought I have before a calloused hand closes over my lips.

Chapter 32

I thrash around like a snared rabbit, but to no avail. A black fatigue-clad arm yanks me backward through a side door into a mechanical room of sorts. Tucker barks loudly as the door slams shut.

Blood pulses through me. My breathing is fast and fluttering. I feel like I'm drowning, desperate for one last chance at life before I succumb. Mustering my strength, I elbow my captor in the chest and pivot to free myself from his grasp. Balling my fist, I swing hard again and pack him square in the stomach with my elbow.

He wheezes, releases me, and staggers sideways. I fumble with my gun, frantically trying to chamber a round. I may not beat him to it, but I'd rather take a bullet than live out my days as a lab rat. Trembling, I pull the charging handle to the rear and release it.

"Derry?"

I wince as if I've been zapped. The barrel of my gun slides downward. I stare, openmouthed, at the figure doubled over in front of me, dressed in full Schutz Clone fatigues. He straightens up, clutching his stomach.

"Owen!" My jaw drops open. I hurl myself at him, wrapping my arms around him like locking pliers. Tears well and spill down my face. "I can't believe it's you!"

He stares back at me, equally dumbfounded. "I thought you were a Sweeper ... the scrubs ..."

"And I was sure you were a Schutz Clone," I say, shaking my head in disbelief. "Are you okay?"

He grunts. "That knuckle sandwich to the gut did a number on me."

I wipe my eyes with the back of my hand, laughing and shaking at the same time. "I thought you were kind of scrawny for a Schutz Clone."

A loud pounding on the door startles us. We trade bug-eyed looks, frozen to the spot. Then I hear a bark, followed by scratching. *Tucker!*

Owen pries me loose and gestures urgently at the door. "Who's the other clone?"

"Sven, he's with us."

"Can we trust him?"

I take a deep breath before I answer. It's taken a long time, and a whole lot of second guessing myself, even to trust Mason. I still haven't got my head around this whole clone thing. But I felt a connection when I first locked eyes with Sven. And he didn't turn us in when he had his chance at the checkpoint.

"Absolutely."

Owen nods and reaches for the door, but I grab his arm before he can open it. "If you go out there dressed like that, they'll pepper you with lead and ID you afterward."

I open the door a crack and whistle for Tucker. He squeezes through, whacking me with his tail as he leaps up to greet Owen.

"I'm okay! I'm with Owen," I yell to the others.

Mason throws the door wide open. His features melt into a broad grin. "Nice kit, Connolly," he says, eying Owen up and down. "And your face is healing up."

I swear his eyes mist over when Owen throws an arm around him. "It's good to see you, Mason."

I grab Owen's sleeve. "Have you seen Jakob?"

Owen shakes his head. "He's not here."

"Are you sure?"

"I've looked all over. He's not in the Intake Sektor either."

I chew on my bottom lip. So Lyong was telling the truth about that. My mind races in circles. I'm not sure if my chances of finding Jakob alive have just gone up or down, but for now I'm clinging to a sliver of hope.

"Where's Big Ed?" Owen asks.

I hesitate. The guilt of abandoning him hits me afresh. "He's out there somewhere. Our Hovermedes was shot down and a friend of Mason's rescued us. Big Ed had already disappeared into the woods."

Owen's eyes cloud over. "I wish he wasn't out there alone. He's more vulnerable than he realizes."

Owen's right. Big Ed may be a mountain man, but he's old and tired. I wish I had trusted Ramesh and extracted Big Ed first. "How did you escape?" I ask, eager to change the subject.

"The clone guarding me figured I was at death's door. When he zoned out, I saw my chance and took it. Sound familiar?"

He grins, waiting for a reaction, but I ignore the dig at my daydreaming habits. He's still acting like the wisecracking older brother, but he doesn't understand that there's nothing left of the kid I was a few short days ago. I hoist my pack onto my back. "Let's go. We have to get to the docking station before the patrols find us."

Mason slings the strap of his rifle over his shoulder. He steps out into the tunnel, stopping briefly outside the door to load Rummy back onto his shoulders.

Owen throws me an incredulous look.

I shrug. "We found him in Sektor Sieben. I thought about leaving him as a contribution to cloning, but even the Sweepers have standards. He'd have ended up on the chopping block."

Sven walks up to us, leading a limping Dr. Lyong by a makeshift leash. I cringe again at the sight of the doctor's pallid flesh stretched over his skull like a drying hide. "Who's this?" Sven asks, eying Owen suspiciously.

I turn to introduce him, and then freeze. An earsplitting boom rocks the tunnel. Over Sven's shoulder, I catch a flash of light, followed by a plume of smoke. A brilliant ball of coral and scarlet and mustard barrels toward us.

"Run!" I shout, bolting forward in a mad panic. I hear footsteps but I'm not sure they're all running in the same direction. My ears are blocked from the blast, and I can't tell if the others are behind me, or out front. The power's gone out in the tunnel and I'm running blind. I yell out Tucker's name, over and over, but I don't dare turn my head to look for him. The heat of the encroaching fireball intensifies as the tunnel fills with suffocating smoke.

Despair grips me when I realize my mistake in taking off down the main tunnel. I should have dived back into the mechanical room and slammed the steel door shut. Which is probably where the others are holed up right now.

Instead, I'm about to be barbecued underground. Desperate, I trail my hand along the wall as I run, hoping to find another door. More than once, I lose my balance and stumble, catching myself at the last minute. I briefly consider dropping to all fours and crawling beneath the smoke, but then I remember the fireball bearing down on me. I force myself to keep moving, heaving for breath with every stride.

Just when I feel I can't possibly take another step, a dark shadow bounds past me and I hear a sharp bark. Nauseous and dizzy, I lift my head and squint through the smoke. I can barely make out Tucker's profile a few feet in front of me. He barks again—muffled this time, but insistent—and then peels off down a narrow tunnel. I veer left after him, every muscle cramping, desperate to close the gap between us before he disappears again. A thunderous crackling erupts, followed by a violent rush of heat behind me, as the fireball rips down the main tunnel. I flatten my palms against the wall in front of me, legs wobbling like jelly, and wait for it to pass.

My throat itches with something caustic. I'd kill for a drop of water—anything to soothe the burning sensation. It's silent now, apart from Tucker panting somewhere ahead of me in the darkness. I close my eyes and focus.

You can hear in all directions.

Three o'clock, ten feet to the right.

I stumble forward a few feet and fall to my knees. Tucker brushes up against me and licks my face halfheartedly before deciding I've tasted better. Desperate to keep him close, I throw my arms around his neck. "Good boy!"

He pricks up his ears, hoping for a treat. I ruffle his fur and swing my pack off my shoulders. Maybe I can salvage something from it to give him. I rummage in the side pocket for my last piece of jerky. It's covered with fuzz—and a smaller scrap than I remember. I'm tempted to break it in two anyway, but Tucker's earned the right to our last morsel. If he hadn't led me down here, I'd be toast by now. I toss it up in the darkness, and he snatches it out of the air and gulps it down. He sits back on his haunches, smacking his lips on the off chance the jerky was just the appetizer.

"Sorry, old boy. That's all I've got." I pull out my water canteen and give it a quick shake to confirm it hasn't spontaneously refilled itself. The hardened skin on my lips feels like flaking concrete. I pull out my flashlight and slide the switch to ON. A scant finger of tawny light appears. Barely enough to keep me from tripping over my own two feet. I pat Tucker and push him forward. "Go find Owen!"

He bounds off in the direction of the main tunnel and I chase after him, still breathing heavily. My flashlight dies completely after about three steps. I shake it vigorously and manage to coax a dot of light back behind the lens. The air is thick and smoky, and my burning eyes are streaming. I focus on Tucker's murky shadow up ahead. His nose is the only thing navigating the darkness now.

I yell for Owen and Mason intermittently, my scorched throat stinging like an open wound. To my relief, I finally hear a muted voice up ahead.

"Over here!" I scream, dropping my flashlight and waving my arms up and down as if I'm somehow visible in the pitch-black tunnel. A moment later a shallow beam picks me out. I whistle for Tucker and run toward the light. I'm halfway there before it occurs to me that I have no idea who I'm running toward.

Chapter 33

I stop dead in my tracks, blinded more by terror than by the yellow halo twenty feet in front of me. It's too late now to turn and run.

Stupid! Stupid! Stupid! I ignored everything Mason taught me.

Slowly, I raise my hands, feigning surrender to buy myself some time. If it's Schutz Clones, I won't let them take me alive. Not after what I've seen here. An unexpected wave of sadness washes over me for everything that will never be. For a future with Jakob I will never know.

My rifle dangles like a dead weight from my shoulder. Tantalizingly out of reach. The blinding beam gets closer, searches out my face. Tucker lays his ears flat, gives a menacing growl. My mind races, scratching to come up with some last ditch punch that will take out as many of them as possible before they kill me.

I shield my eyes with the back of my hand, then peer tentatively around in the darkness. Am I surrounded? Panicked, I drop and roll, fumble for the safety on my gun, half-deafened by the dogged fire alarm.

A guttural voice mumbles something unintelligible. I hear a clop, like steel on stone, followed by a swish. The blood in my veins turns to ice water. It's now or never. I scramble to my feet and run toward the light, aiming dead center.

Clop, swish. Clop, swish.

A hunched figure limps into view, clutching a flashlight.

Finger on the trigger, I squint through the smoke and shadows.

Before I can take the shot, Tucker blitzes past me and leaps up, knocking the feet out from under the stranger.

I stumble forward, and stare in shock at the distorted form pinned beneath Tucker's paws.

A deviation.

Her eyes—one blood red and bulging—appraise me from deep within a bald, mottled skull. Spidery fingers clutch the flashlight in her right hand. The other arm is a shrunken fingerless, stump. She lifts her head, attempts to speak. The noises she makes sound like she's being strangled.

I swallow back the bile creeping up the back of my throat. "Down, boy." I push Tucker to one side.

I keep my gun on the deviation for good measure, and blurt out the first thing that comes to mind. "What's your name?"

More gibberish as she gestures frantically behind me with the flashlight. I reach out a hand to help her up. Our eyes lock, and I sense her gratitude. A strangely human connection. I shudder as her rough fingers close over mine, hating myself for being repulsed by the sight of her. She's not the monster—monsters did this to her.

I pull her to her feet, and she immediately begins clop-swishing her way back down the tunnel. She turns and motions for me to follow. I grab Tucker by the collar and fall in behind her. It's not like we have a better option.

She comes to an abrupt halt at an intersection and jabs with her flashlight down the tunnel on our left.

I frown. "What is it?"

She shoves me forward and gestures for me to keep going. "Dhur, dhur, dhur."

I take a few steps forward, disoriented by the alarm still blaring in my ears. And then I see it. The door to the mechanical room. I throw the deviation a look of uncertainty. How did she know we were hiding in there? She jabs me with her spidery claw.

"Thank you," I say, running my hand briefly over hers. I race toward the door, Tucker at my heels. When I reach it, I turn to wave, but the deviation has vanished.

I pound on the door with both fists. "It's me, Derry! Open up!"

My knees almost buckle beneath me when the door swings open and Owen steps out. I stumble forward into his arms. Relief floods his face. "Where have you been?"

"I panicked. I took off down the tunnel." I pause to catch my breath. I'm still reeling from what just happened. *A deviation saved me*! I tuck away a seed of hope. Maybe we can rally the deviations to help us overthrow the Sweepers.

"You're not hurt?" Owen appraises me anxiously. He gives Tucker a cursory pat on the head as he squeezes past us and disappears inside in search of water.

"I'm fine. That fireball came out of nowhere though. I thought Sven said the Cremautauto would implode, not explode."

Owen grimaces. "That wasn't the Cremautauto. Someone tried to blow up the tunnel."

I stare at him stupidly. "Why would they do that?"

"I'm not sure. Let's get inside before someone spots us." He pulls me in and slams the door shut.

Mason gives a tight nod when I step back into the mechanical room. He looks relieved to see me, but I realize right away that something's wrong. I glance around the room.

Someone's missing.

My eyes meet Sven's and the expression on his face confirms my fear.

"Where's Lyong?" I ask, half-hoping Sven will tell me the fireball reduced him to a pile of ashes. Something tells me that's wishful thinking.

He throws a harrowed glance at Mason and then looks back at me. "He got away."

Dread simmers up inside. "How?"

Mason motions over his shoulder with the pencil thin beam of his flashlight at an open trapdoor in the floor. "It's some kind of maintenance shaft. It was pitch black in here, smoke everywhere. Shyster saw his chance and he took it."

Sven grimaces. "He'll send every last Schutz Clone in the Craniopolis after us."

"You shouldn't have waited for me," I say, grabbing Tucker's collar. "Let's go."

"Not so fast," Mason says.

I whirl around, honing in on a peculiar note in his voice.

"What?"

But, it's not me he's addressing. He's sizing up Sven like he's about to take a swing at him. I tighten my grip on Tucker's collar. Surely he doesn't think Sven deliberately let Lyong escape?

"You can't come with us, Sven," Mason says, quietly. "Lyong knows who you are now. He'll turn on your tracker. We don't have a hope of making it to the docking station unless you lead them away from us."

Sven's powerful chest heaves up and down. For a stony moment, the two clones face off. Some emotion ripples across Sven's face, but he suppresses it before I can be sure what I saw. Fear, disappointment? Slowly, he raises the barrel of his gun. I try to say something, but my throat's dry as sandpaper.

It takes me a moment to realize what's unfolding. Sven's aiming his gun at *Owen*.

I let out a gasp. Tucker growls menacingly, the fur on his spine raised like a ridge of thistles. He'll die defending us if he has to.

"Sven! What are you doing?" Mason's voice rings tinny in my ears. I can tell he's as stunned as I am. Cautiously, Owen reaches for his gun.

"Don't touch it!" Sven says. Owen straightens up, his face bleached of color.

My eyes dart to Mason. Other than Sven, he's the only one of us holding a weapon.

"Take it easy, Sven," Mason says.

"You can't just ditch me now that you've found Owen. The deal was if I helped you, we'd leave together."

"I know what the deal was. That was before you let Lyong get away."

Sven's face darkens. "How was I supposed to know there was another exit?"

"You were *supposed* to be guarding him. I had the Rogue."

Sven waves the barrel of his M16 at Owen. "I risked my life to help you find him. Either we all leave together, or none of us leave."

Mason shakes his head. "No one's getting out of the Craniopolis alive if you come with us now. You know that."

Sven takes a step toward Mason. "Put down your gun."

My mind races. I could give the command and have Tucker charge Sven, but I can't be sure he'd make it before Sven fires.

Mason's shoulders sink in resignation. "All right. Take it easy." He crouches down, then carefully lays his M16 on the ground in front of him.

I grit my teeth in frustration. Disarming Mason puts us in an even more precarious position than before. But I can't fault Sven for being desperate to escape this place. I have to go with what my heart tells me, and believe that's all he wants.

Out of the corner of my eye, I catch Mason slip a hand inside his coat. Instinctively, I know what he's going to do before he pulls out the Glock.

"No!" I scream, flinging myself at him. Tucker barks and leaps on him.

Caught off balance, Mason swivels sideways, and the Glock skids across the floor.

I turn to Sven and gamble everything on what I hope I see in his eyes.

"Sven's coming with us," I say. "If we leave now, we can still make it to the docking station. Lyong's injured, dying. Even if he does find his way back through the maintenance shaft, it will take him some time to activate Sven's sensor and round up the Schutz Clones."

"You're making a big mistake," Mason says. He rubs the back of his hand slowly across his jaw, eyes locked on Sven.

I grab Mason by the shirt and force him to look at me. "I undervalued the life of a clone once already, remember? I won't make that mistake again."

For a moment his lips tremble. A deep flush creeps up from his neck and spreads over his face. He takes a sudden, deep breath as if coming up for air, and then snaps back to pokerface. "Lucky for Sven you're the one calling the shots."

I slide my gaze in Sven's direction. His clenched lips soften into a grateful smile.

An unexpected tingle goes through me. I tear my eyes away, whistle for Tucker, and slip out into the scorched tunnel with Owen. I'm not sure why I fought so hard to bring Sven with us after the stunt he pulled. I barely know him, but something I saw in his eyes drove me to stick my neck out for him. He emerges through the door, Rummy slung over his shoulders like a trussed up goat. I'd like to think it's a gesture of goodwill that he's offered to lug Rummy the rest of the way, but something tells me Mason insisted on it after that showdown.

We tread quietly along the smoky tunnel. Tucker pads steadily at my side. As much as I hated the sight of Lyong, I can't help thinking it would be better if he were still with us. He was the only bargaining chip we had if we run into trouble.

After a few minutes, the fire alarm cuts out and I stop dead in my tracks. The sudden silence deadens my brain. My nerves, moments earlier jangling from the blare of the alarm, are now taut with a cold fear of the damp hush that's descended. It's illogical, but my brain's choking like an engine flooded one too many times.

"Keep moving!" Owen hisses in my ear. I put one leg in front of the other and focus on the sliver of light up ahead from Mason's flashlight.

Behind me, Tucker gives a warning growl. The unmistakable strain of voices drifts through the tunnel. A moment later, the overhead lights flicker back on. Shouts ring out.

My brain erases every rational thought not aligned with survival. I break into the panicked run of the prey. My burning muscles no longer feel anything but adrenalin swamping my system. I throw a glance behind at Sven. Head down, he charges past me in a few powerful strides, Rummy flapping around on his shoulders. "This way," he shouts.

A hail of bullets zings overhead. I increase my speed, my lungs gasping for a fresh breath in the acrid tunnel. In some distant place in my head, I hear Mason roar, "Left!"

Tucker veers off the main tunnel, and I follow him, taking the corner blind, and slam straight into Mason's rigid frame. He grabs me by the arm to steady me. "They've cut us off. They're closing in—likely have an armed detail up ahead."

Owen rushes up to us and bends over wheezing. Sven lets Rummy slide to the floor and rests his hands on his thighs. "Now what? The main tunnel's our most direct route to the docking station."

I peer down the narrow feeder tunnel we're grouped in. "Can't we get out this way?"

"The Craniopolis is designed like a web," Mason explains. "Everything leads back to the stadium, but they've probably sealed—"

A snapping sound overhead cuts him off. Owen and I exchange baffled glances. *A loudspeaker?* A string of crackling erupts, and then a familiar rasping laugh bounces off the tunnel walls.

Chapter 34

A fist of fear squeezes the air from my lungs. I force my brain to engage. Lyong must have made it out through the maintenance shaft and reached the Schutz Clones already. If he's switched on Sven's sensor, he knows exactly where we are.

He might even be watching us on a camera somewhere. The thought sends a cold chill through me.

The intercom static resumes, and then Lyong's scratchy voice fills the tunnel. "Regrettably, our short time together was not very profitable. But, you can still remedy that. I am willing to release the Undergrounders in exchange for the safe return of my clones. If you refuse, you will leave me no choice but—" He breaks off into a coughing fit that sounds as if his insides are coming up his throat.

I tense, glance around, half-expecting an army of Schutz Clones to materialize around us.

"You made your point with your little explosives stunt," Lyong continues, his voice wavering and thin. "I am willing to negotiate."

Our little stunt? I glance at Owen and see the same confusion swirling in his eyes.

If the Sweepers didn't blow up the tunnel, who did? My pulse races. Unless that deviation had something to do with it?

"We don't surrender," I whisper to the others. "No matter what. If this ends in death, it's better than ending up in a petri dish."

"I'm with you," Sven says. "I'd rather die on my own terms than on an expiration date."

"All right." Mason rubs at the stubble on his jaw, snapping back into tactical mode. "We can't go back into the main tunnel and fight them on two fronts. We'll have to draw them in."

"How?" I ask.

"We'll retreat as far into the tunnel as we can. Look for cover, a storage room, even an alcove or something."

Sven bends down and reaches for Rummy.

I place a hand on his shoulder. "You don't have to lug him with you anymore. You can't fight with his dead weight."

He contemplates it for a moment, and then grabs Rummy by the collar. "He might come in useful as a shield. I reckon he'd rather die in a hail of gunfire than go back to Sektor Sieben anyway."

I decide against trying to talk him out of it. I suspect he's only doing it because I persuaded Mason to let him come with us. I can't fault him for feeling obligated to return the favor, even if it is for a Rogue.

Sven adjusts Rummy's limp frame across his shoulders, and then follows Mason and Owen down the narrow tunnel that leads to the center of the Craniopolis. I fall in behind, Tucker close by my side.

Our footsteps ring heavy in my ears, like a bell tolling time we're running out of. There's a possibility the Schutz Clones have already infiltrated this tunnel, and we're walking into an ambush. But with the main duct to the docking station impenetrable, it's the only option left.

A few minutes later, Mason's voice rings out. "There's a door here to my right. I'm gonna blow the lock and see if it leads anywhere."

I ease up and glance nervously over my shoulder, but there's no sign of anyone in pursuit. Maybe they're waiting us out in the main tunnel. Or, maybe Lyong has a worse surprise in store.

I flinch when Mason's gunshot echoes through the tunnel—confirming our position. He motions us forward and then quickly disappears through the doorway. Owen and Sven follow, weapons poised. I'm still unnerved each time I glimpse Owen's fatigues. It's impossible to tell it's him from behind, and that could be disastrous.

Tucker bounds after the others and I hurry after him, reluctant to be the last one standing, alone and vulnerable, in the dark tunnel. My jaw drops when I stumble into the dimly lit room.

"What is this place?" I look around in bewilderment at what appears to be a series of robotic assembly lines.

"It's an underground factory." Mason kicks aside a bin of drip lines. "This must be where they make the medical equipment."

"Parts for the Hovermedes too." Owen points at an overhead pulley system, strung with matrix cushions in a familiar egg-shaped design.

I run my hand along the conveyer belt closest to me. "It's still warm. They must have shut down operations when the fire alarm went off."

Sven lays Rummy down behind a metal supply cabinet and then strides across the room to the vacuum double doors in the back wall. He keys something into the entry panel with a few practiced strokes. "That should reset the code and give us a few extra minutes."

"What about the side door we came in by?" Owen asks.

"We'll pick them off as they come through." Mason counts his cartridges. "I'll take the left side. Owen, you back me up on the right. Sven and Derry, you're on the main entry double doors once the clones start coming through there. Until then, cover us."

Owen embraces me without a word and then follows Mason over to the side door.

I send Tucker to a back corner of the room with a command to lay still. He's not thrilled, but he trots off and settles in the shadows anyway, eyes watchful in case I change my mind. My arms feel like lead when I load a round into my gun. I wonder if I'll have the courage to put a bullet in Tucker if the clones break through and overpower us. I could never forgive myself if I went to my death knowing I'd left him in the Sweepers' hands.

I crouch behind a conveyer belt and train my gun on the doorway. Minutes tick by. Globs of sweat push through my pores. I probe my leathered lips with the tip of my tongue. I'd give anything for some fresh, cold, spring water right now. I rub my face vigorously. I need to stay focused on Mason's instructions. I adjust the sight on my weapon and take a few deep breaths.

Every few minutes I alter my position to make sure I don't zone out. There are no second chances any more. I blink back sudden tears. Not even with Jakob. My biggest regret is that I didn't find him. I'm not even sure he's alive. Maybe that's why I'm going all in.

Shots ring out in quick succession.

Startled, I lurch forward into position like I've crash-landed. I steady the barrel of my M16 on the conveyer belt and ease back the trigger. Mason and Owen release a steady spray of gunfire at a group of Schutz Clones trying to force their way into the room. When the first one bursts through, I fire a round at his head. His body twitches and flips to the floor. I narrow my eyes and refocus through the sweat pouring from my forehead. My skin's on fire, my pulse pounding in my temples like a war drum. I chance a glance back at Tucker. He raises his head expectantly, but I motion him back down.

In the few seconds I'm distracted, one of the Schutz Clones gets past Mason and Owen and dives behind a metal tool cart to my right. I grit my teeth and train my weapon on the cart, my thoughts unraveling in a flood of panic. I've let them break the line. I've compromised our position.

I steady the stock of my weapon and survey the area, contemplating my options. I have no shot. There's nothing I can do but wait the sucker out. I signal to Sven to back up Mason and Owen, and he gives me a thumbs up. I hunker down, with my back to the entry, and squint into the far corner, searching for even the slightest movement.

More shots ring out by the entry. Seconds later, an agonized scream pierces through the shelling. *Owen!* A strangled cry comes from my own throat in response. I jerk around in time to see him fall backward, clutching his left thigh. I fire randomly at the clones who pour through the entry. No longer counting kills.

Lost in the horror of the carnage, I become aware too late of a dark shadow hovering on my right. Before I can swing my gun around to take aim, the giant Schutz Clone drops like a stone, shot in the head by Sven.

The clone's weapon skids across the floor in front of me. Panting, I scoot backward from the lifeless body and reposition myself to cover Owen. Another Schutz Clone rushes past, seemingly unaware Owen's not one of them. The fatigues are working in his favor.

I watch Mason's upper body shudder like a machine gun as he unleashes a hail of gunfire on the advancing Clones. Without Owen's fire to back him up, several more Schutz Clones force their way through. I blast them, backed up by Sven, who's now crouched behind the assembly line next to me. Mason retreats behind a wall of metal cabinets. From our vantage points, we quickly take down the clones that make it inside, but more pour through the doorway every second. Several hunker down and form a shield, allowing dozens more to stream freely through.

The room is a cauldron of fire and smoke, shadows and shouting. My mind blurs, transforming me into an untamed savage. I let loose round after round, my last cartridge tucked safely in my side pocket. For every Schutz Clone that falls, five more appear like specters. We can't fend them off much longer.

"Hold your fire!" Mason yells hoarsely.

I freeze and look over at him in confusion. My eyes dilate with fear. A group of Schutz Clones circle Owen like a pack of vultures. One of them kicks his M16 aside. They've recognized him. Trembling, I pull back, choking on a mixture of bile and adrenalin, my thoughts an incoherent scramble.

We agreed not to surrender, but I thought that meant we'd all go down together. I can't let them kill me but take Owen back to Lyong alive.

Chapter 35

Fear forks through every fiber of my body. Trembling, I toy with the trigger, torn between going out in a blaze of glory or dropping to my knees to beg for my brother's life—but what kind of life would that be? I hold my gun in a death grip, my eyes sweeping the room for some way out of the situation.

Something glints at me from the ceiling. I sneak a glance upward, then squint at the vent for a moment longer, perplexed. Is that a muzzle nesting behind it?

A fresh wave of despair grips me. They must have penetrated the air ducts as well. We're finished. My grip on my M-16 slackens. I glance over at Sven, and frown, mystified, when he gives me a sly nod. Some instinct tells me not to lay down my weapon just yet

A moment later, the intercom sputters to life and Lyong's voice bleeds into the charged air. "Regretfully, you elected to ignore my directive. Here are my new terms. Surrender peacefully, and you may yet live at the pleasure of the Craniopolis."

From behind the next assembly line, Sven mouths something at me, but I can't make out what he's saying. I shrug in response, and he motions up at the vents. I nod to indicate I've already seen them. What difference does it make? We're surrounded.

The lingering smoke in the air itches my nostrils. I try desperately not to sneeze, afraid I'll trigger a volley of gunfire before I've even had a chance to respond to Lyong's terms. I breathe slowly in and out, my lungs moving like compressed bellows.

I trace the trigger housing on my gun and count the remaining clones congregated around the room. We're grossly outnumbered. And Owen is weaponless. This can't end well if we don't comply.

"You have thirty seconds to accept my terms," Lyong says, a nettled edge to his voice.

I shiver, picturing his one-eyed tic appraising me in a monitor somewhere as he talks, his papery skin rippling with the effort of speech. I can't see a way out of the situation that gives me any chance of saving Owen, other than to negotiate. Hesitantly, I raise my arms and step forward.

"My brother's injured," I yell. "If you give us your word you'll help him, we'll turn over our weapons."

My heart strains in my chest. I'm counting on Mason and Sven to hold their fire. I wait for what seems like forever, steeling myself for Lyong's response.

The intercom crackles to life, but Lyong's words are drowned out in a barrage of gunfire. I pitch sideways beneath a conveyer belt and huddle in a ball, shaking. Debris pelts me from every angle; chunks of seat cushions, shredded medical tubing, shards of glass from exploding computer screens. A pungent chemical smell fills the air.

All over the room, disoriented Schutz Clones fly backward. I stare in disbelief as they writhe in death throes, ossifying before my eyes. Mason bolts across the floor and rolls under the belt beside me. His eyes gleam like cat's eyes in the dim light. "It's the Council," he yells, between breaths. "They've penetrated the Craniopolis!"

I blink as I digest what he's saying, my ears roaring.

Mason slams a fresh cartridge into his gun, his knuckles bleeding profusely. "They must have triggered the explosion. They've been planning an attack for months."

My brain slowly wraps itself around the information. There's still a chance we can make it out of here alive. I unload my pack and roll over into sniper position. "Then let's finish this." I lock eyes with Mason. "For Owen."

Mason wipes a bloody hand across his brow and steadies the barrel of his gun on a metal support bar beneath the assembly line. The freshly daubed blood on his forehead glistens like a symbol of war. My courage soars.

I search the wreckage for a target and quickly take out a Schutz Clone crouched behind a lathe. He topples forward without a sound. Cautiously, I edge forward on my hips and scan the blood-spattered zone around the entry door. There's no sign of Owen anywhere. I gesture over my shoulder to Mason to cover me, and wriggle out from under the conveyer belt. I sprint in a half-crouch to the next assembly line, and then drop back down onto my belly. Two feet from me, a spread-eagled Schutz Clone stares up at the vent, eyes protruding like golf balls. From beneath his torso a rust colored, lava-like flow creeps in my direction. I scoot backward and take aim, but before I take the shot, he expires. I lower my weapon and stare, appalled, as his body stiffens and his features fade to gray.

There's no sign of movement in the area where Owen fell. He could be dead, or the clones might have taken him hostage, but I tell myself he managed to crawl to cover.

"Owen?" I scream, not caring anymore who hears me.

"Over here!"

A giant swell of relief swoops me up and carries me the last ten feet to where he lies curled up behind a stack of supply bins. I dive down and inch painfully forward on my elbows through a soup of metal shavings to reach him. A tremor goes through his body when he sees me.

"How bad is it?" I ask, glancing down at his blood-soaked pant leg. I've helped Jakob dress enough wounds in the bunkers to know it doesn't look good. I wish he were here right now. The Septites know about this kind of stuff.

"I'm fine," Owen lies, his eyes flickering with pain. "Just finish them off." Another tremor passes through him. He looks like he's about to pass out.

I shake my arms out of my jacket and yank an extra shirt from my pack.

"Don't waste your time." Owen stares at me with a gauzy look in his eyes that terrifies me.

"Listen to me! You're gonna be okay." My voice cracks as an image of Da slipping away in my arms flashes to mind. I swallow back a gut-wrenching sob and hurriedly tie my flannel shirt around the entry wound in Owen's thigh. "This is all the combat care you get for now." I force a tight smile through my tears as I cover him with my jacket. "Hang tough."

He leans back, his eyelids fluttering.

I heave a few deep breaths and then pull myself into position with renewed vigor. I've done what I can to stem the bleeding. The only way Owen's getting out of here alive is to finish them off like he said.

Most of the lights have been shot out, but I can still make out the basic layout of the room. The air is thick with dust and my eyes water as I struggle to line up my gun's sight in the dimly lit space. I spot an injured clone crawling for cover beneath a conveyer belt, and quickly put a bullet in his head.

The shot echoes and I realize with a start that the gunfire has broken off. A jolt of hope goes through me. Judging by the fatigue-clad shadows heaped around the room, the Schutz Clones were as blindsided by the attack as I was.

I maneuver forward a few feet on my elbows and signal to Mason by forming an "O' and a thumbs up that Owen's alive. Mason holds up two meaty fingers and points to a badly damaged computer rack, leaning precariously to the left. The loose wiring in front sways ever so slightly back and forth, a good indication someone bumped the rack when taking cover. I make a sweeping gesture with my hand to tell Mason to flank it from his side. He nods and begins worming his way forward beneath the conveyer belts. I approach from the other side, catching my breath when I wriggle into an ossified corpse. It's all I can do not to gag. After a moment, I slither forward again, careful not to look down this time.

Ten feet from the rack, I pull myself up into a crouch. Mason follows my lead. I ready my weapon and slice through the air with my hand.

We circle in like wolves, blasting round after round as we run to the back of the unit. I pull up short when I see the Schutz Clones, one half-ossified, the other bleeding profusely, head hinged back, staring up at the vents as though that's where he expected the shots to come from. Mason finishes him off and I turn aside, not wanting to watch another one of them crumble into powder.

"Good work," Mason says. "They were the last two."

I glance around to be sure, and then dart back through the wreckage to check on Owen.

His head is flopped to one side, eyelids fastened shut. His chest moves slowly up and down, so I know he's still alive, for now. We'll have to move quickly or he won't be for much longer. I hunker down beside him and whistle for Tucker, holding my breath until I hear him bounding across the room toward me. Weak with relief, I gather him in my arms and squeeze him until he squirms free.

Sven pokes his head around the supply bins and looks at me questioningly.

"Owen's alive, barely," I mumble.

Sven grimaces. "Rummy's still breathing, for what it's worth. Slept through the whole show."

Tucker contemplates Owen for a moment before gently licking his fingers. Owen's eyes pop open and pivot uncertainly.

I lean over him, willing him to focus. "We did it, Owen! We finished them off."

He smiles past me through clenched lips.

"Let's go!" Mason slaps the side of a supply bin. "I'll take Owen."

I look up in time to see a long, rope ladder tumbling down from an opening in the air duct closest to us. Mason drops to one knee at Owen's side. He slides an arm beneath his head and another under his legs, and then slowly gets to his feet. I'm hit with a fresh pang of guilt when I think of how abominably I've treated Mason. Without him, I'd never get Owen out of here alive.

With Sven's assistance, Mason drapes Owen carefully over his left shoulder, and then kicks at his pack with his boot. "Bring my gear, Derry. Sven can take Tucker."

"What about Rummy?"

Mason narrows his eyes. "Charity case stays here. We did what we could."

The rope ladder sways precariously when Mason steps onto it. Owen moans softly. I grab the ladder and hold it taut while Mason climbs. He pulls himself effortlessly up one rung at a time. When he reaches the top, several pairs of arms reach down and lift Owen from his shoulders and out through the vent. I nod to Sven and he loads his pack on, and then leans over and scoops Tucker up by the belly. I keep my eyes fixed on Tucker to reassure him it's all part of the plan, but halfway up he whines, ears aloft, and wriggles to get free of Sven's grip.

"Stay!" I raise the palm of my hand and he reluctantly settles back down, his eyes willing me to follow him.

Moments later Sven hands him through the vent and climbs out after him. I swing Mason's pack over my shoulder and place one foot on the bottom rung. It's an awkward load, with my own pack already strapped to my back, and I'm forced to adjust my stance several times before I'm comfortable attempting the thirty-foot climb.

I reach for the rope, and then hesitate, not sure where the sharp rush of fear that hit me came from. I throw a hasty glance around but no ghosts float up from the ossified remains.

I shake off the foreboding feeling and haul myself onto the next rung of the ladder.

An unsteady footfall. Six o'clock.

The hair on the back of my neck electrifies. I twist my head around, my neck crawling with fear, but I can't see a thing over the packs. I jump back down off the ladder and pivot.

My breath lodges like icicles in my throat.

Rummy edges toward me, eyes feverish and dilated, a serrated knife in his hand. *A Schutzmesser.* Laced with blood. He must have taken it from a dead clone, *or killed one.*

"You left me to die," he hisses, stabbing at the air like a man possessed.

"No! We rescued you, Rummy! Lyong took you to Sektor Sieben."

"Left one of those bloodsuckers alive to finish me off, didn't you? But guess who ain't dead yet!" Rummy raises his blade a few inches, and jabs it again in my direction. I look in his eyes, and I know he's considering it.

Suddenly, the blood on the blade fades to ivory and wafts to the ground like crumbling plaster. Rummy's eyes bulge. He stares at me for a long moment and then carefully wipes the knife clean on his pants.

I stretch out my hand to him. "You can come with us, but give me the knife first."

He takes an unsteady step backward and runs the tips of his fingers menacingly over the blade. I groan inwardly. My gun is stashed in my pack and I can't reach it without unloading Mason's gear first.

"We need to go, now, Rummy. This place will be crawling with Schutz Clones any second."

"What you waitin' for, Butterface?" He hikes the corner of his bottom lip up into a threatening grin. "I'll be right behind you." His eyes flash deliriously and I think better of challenging him again.

I turn and reach for the ladder. I have no choice but to start climbing. I tense the muscles in my back, fully expecting the Schutzmesser to sink between my shoulder blades at any minute.

Rummy clambers onto the bottom rung when I'm ten or so feet off the ground. Fueled by a new rush of adrenaline, I pull myself up from one rung to the next. The ladder sways precariously with both of our weight and the loaded packs. I climb furiously, but the vent is a long way off. Anything can happen between here and there. I throw a glance back down at the floor and flirt with the idea of kicking Rummy off the ladder when we get up a little higher. If I clock him just right on the head with my boot, it might work. But it's the kind of thing that could go horribly wrong. I might end up being the one tail spinning thirty odd feet to my death.

The packs weigh me down like boulders. My neck screams with pain as I push my muscles to work harder. If I can stay far enough ahead of Rummy, Mason could possibly take a shot. He must have seen Rummy by now, seen the knife too, so at least he knows he's armed.

I push my body harder. I won't die on this ladder at the hands of a Rogue. Not after surviving an attack by Schutz Clones. Legs buckling, I finally reach the top of the ladder and grasp at the firm hands reaching through the vent to help me. A jolt of electricity shoots through me when the familiar fingers close over mine.

Chapter 36

Jakob's hands!

Tears well up at the cruel trick my frazzled mind is playing on me. I peer up into the dark air duct, blinking furiously, and for half a heartbeat, I think I see his blurred face. I teeter precariously on the edge of a rung, confused and disoriented.

My head snaps backward. The loaded packs pull on me, heavy as drowning men, wrenching my arms from their sockets. My fingers begin to slip when, suddenly, I'm grabbed by the armpits and yanked up through the vent opening.

I lay on the floor, beetle-like and helpless—Tucker furiously licking my face in some kind of canine resuscitation ritual—until I'm unceremoniously flipped over and the packs pulled from my back. Tucker gives a short bark and nudges me for a response, but my mouth is so dry my lips have set like concrete. Someone helps me into a sitting position and holds a canteen of water to my lips. I gulp, greedily, my mind slowly clearing as the liquid floods my cells.

"Derry! Are you okay?"

Jakob leans over me, his face creased with concern.

My chest convulses like I've just been shocked back to life. I stretch out trembling fingers to touch him, praying he doesn't disappear like a mirage.

He folds his arms around me and laughs. "You look like you've seen a ghost."

I breathe in the sawdust-and-leather scent of him. My safe place. For a long moment I cling to him, gripped by the irrational fear that he'll disappear again. "You're alive," I whisper into his chest.

"The Council rescued me from that Sweeper attack on the trail," he says. "I wasn't sure you got away."

"How did you know we were here?"

"I was on the plane that attacked your Hovermedes. We thought it was Sweepers." He pauses, blinking back tears. "We saw the second Hovermedes extract you and Mason. I persuaded the Council to attempt a rescue."

"Time to move out!" Mason barks. "I'll take Owen and lead the way to the docking station."

"Why aren't we going back out the way the Council came in?" I ask.

"Security's swarming all over the vent access now," Jakob says. "There's no way we can get by them."

I peer over Jakob's shoulder at several unfamiliar faces gathering up their packs. I'm surprised to see that none of them look much older than me. It's not an encouraging visual. I was banking on the Council being a force to be reckoned with.

I suddenly become aware of Sven staring unabashedly at me. I pull apart from Jakob, unsettled by Sven's attention. I'm not sure what it is I feel when his eyes are on me. Surely there can't be that kind of chemistry between a clone and a human? Or can there?

I get to my feet, relieved to see that Rummy's hands are secured behind his back. Given the choice, he must have decided to cooperate.

One of the strangers grabs Mason's pack. I reach for my own, my shoulders screaming in protest. Without a word, Jakob takes it from me. I can't help but notice the brooding look he gives Sven.

"Thanks," I say, somewhat embarrassed, but relieved I won't have to lug my supplies any farther on my aching shoulders. I fall in behind Mason and Jakob.

"How's Owen doing?" I call up to Mason.

"Breathing," he replies, without breaking his stride. "We need to get that bullet out."

"Jakob can do it," I say.

Mason gives a curt nod. "Soon as we're safely out of here."

We move, single file, along the air duct, bending at the waist to avoid bumping our heads at occasional low spots. Tucker lopes at my side, his faith in me renewed now that I've rescued him from Sven the Dog Catcher. Jakob walks directly in front of me. Sven and the remaining Council members take up the rear.

"How many are in the Council?" I ask Jakob.

He shrugs. "There's thirty or so of us."

I press my parched lips together. It's not what I wanted to hear. So far, the Council in the flesh is dashing any real hope I had of eliminating the Sweepers.

"Thirty of *us*." I give a hollow laugh. "Sounds like you're a shoe in."

"I *am* in," Jakob replies.

I frown. "What do you mean?"

"I'm staying with the Council." He turns around and stares at me. "Blood was spilled today, and I initiated the attack. The Septites might have forgiven me for chasing after you, but not for what happened here."

My jaw hinges open and closed, but before I can string together a response, Mason hisses at us over his shoulder.

"Zip it you two! Let's not make it any more obvious which direction we're headed in."

I take a deep breath, watching Jakob's easy stride as he moves. There's nothing to go back to our bunker for now anyway, but he doesn't know that. I keep telling myself that the rest of the Undergrounders, Jakob's parents included, are still part of our reality. The likelihood is they're all dead.

Mason slows to a halt, and Jakob motions at me to stop.

"Are we at the docking station?" I ask, relieved to see Owen's eyes flutter open at the sound of my voice.

Mason gives a tight nod and lays Owen down in an alcove. "With any luck, there's no one down there. The tunnel access is blocked, so it should be clear, unless someone was in there before the explosion happened."

"Not likely," I say. "Lyong said everyone was at the unveiling."

"Do we have a clear view of the docking station?" one of the Council members calls out.

"Affirmative," Mason replies. "I'll assess the situation on the ground."

He gets down on his belly and creeps, reptile-like, toward the grille. When he reaches the edge, he lies in position for a long time, his head barely moving, before inching backward toward us.

"See anything?" I ask when he's within earshot of a whisper.

"No." He frowns, then shakes his head as if to convince himself of it. "I thought I glimpsed a shadow flit behind the Hovermedes at the far end of the station. Must have been one of the lights flickering."

A slight, dark-haired Council member pulls out a pair of bolt cutters from her pack. She cuts out the mesh grille with a few swift snips, and tosses it behind her.

Jakob uncoils the rope ladder and hands it to her.

I turn to Sven.

"I got your dog," he says, reading my mind.

I smile up at him, my cheeks burning under his molten eyes. He's so dang distracting when he looks at me like that it's hard to think straight.

Once we're safely on the floor of the docking station, Jakob and the other Council members spread out and begin sweeping the area. I peer around, half-expecting the Schutz Clones to materialize out of nowhere and begin shooting at us again.

Rummy curls his lip when I catch his eye. I turn away, shivering when I think of how close I came to ending up as a human pumpkin—or worse. He'll have to be dealt with once we're out of here.

I turn my attention to Owen. His skin is mottled and I don't like the gurgling sound I hear in his throat when he tries to speak. I lean over him and hold a canteen to his mouth. He sucks at it like a baby, but the water trickles back out through his cracked lips. Tucker licks it up appreciatively.

"Sorry," Owen gasps, as if fists are crushing his lungs.

"It's okay. Don't try to talk." Ever so carefully, I pull down a corner of the shirt wrapped around his thigh and peek at his wound. Still bleeding. I bite my lip and tighten the shoddy bandage. It's so dirty it'll lead to infection if we don't replace it soon. I'm kicking myself I didn't grab some antibiotics from the supply room in Sektor Sieben.

One by one, the Council members rejoin us. "All clear," the slight, dark-eyed girl says, sliding the selector switch on her rifle to safety.

"How much time do we have before they clear the tunnel?" Jakob asks.

"Let's find out," Sven replies. He strides over to a row of transparent screens. I fiddle with my rifle, trying desperately to curb my impatience. We have to get out of here soon. Owen's running out of time.

Sven moves his fingers deftly over the thermoplastic surfaces, then stops and rubs the back of his neck. I blow out a breath and look away. If I'm reading his body language right, this isn't going well. But, what do I really know about clones?

He starts up again, tapping furiously on one of the screens. A few minutes in, his shoulders tighten and the clicking stops. He stares intently at the monitor in front of him.

"What's wrong?" Mason asks.

"Lyong's blocked my authorization code. I can't log in. Can't access any of the cameras—nothing." He slams his fist down on the desk. "Not even the launch process for the Hovermedes."

"Can you use Ramesh's chip?" I ask.

He shakes his head. "They've already deactivated his account."

My stomach does a series of sickening flips. "What about hacking in?"

Sven moves his jaw grimly side to side. "It could take hours. The security protocol for the upgraded authorization software is complex." He leans back and blows out a breath. "There's a slim chance I could reactivate Mason's old account long enough for us to fly out of here. Give me a couple of minutes." He leans over the desk and begins sketching rapidly over the screens with both hands.

I rub my clammy palms on my jacket. Every minute we waste, Owen's life is ebbing away in front of me. I wish I didn't feel so helpless, but, for once, even Mason's running idle, a glazed look in his eyes.

Jakob comes up behind me and lays a hand on my shoulder. "How is he?"

I shrink under his touch, afraid the sob I keep stuffing back down my throat will explode like a geyser. "I don't know if he's gonna make it. He's breathing like he's swallowed a hacksaw."

"He needs you to stay strong. You've come too far to lose hope now."

I shake my head despondently. "It's my fault he took a bullet. I turned around to check on Tucker."

"You can't blame yourself."

I let out a long, shuddering breath. "I zoned out—Owen always said it would kill me in the end. I just never dreamed it would kill him."

Jakob gently turns my face toward him. "A good soldier looks out for everyone in his unit. That's all you were doing."

I give him a rueful grin. "Tucker's a dog, Jakob."

"Canine unit," he retorts.

"Looks like we're in!" Mason gestures toward the computers.

Sven gets up and walks heavily toward us.

"I managed to reactivate Mason's old account temporarily, but there's a hitch." His eyes dart around and settle on the Hovermedes nearest us.

I frown. "What?"

"The old system Mason was chipped under requires onsite departure authorization."

"What does that mean exactly?" I throw an anxious glance at Owen who's struggling to sit up.

"It means," Mason says, folding his arms across his chest and staring at Sven. "That someone has to stay behind."

Chapter 37

The words snap like a whip in the static air. Unease ripples across the faces of the young men and women standing around. The two clones face off, hulking figures in our undersized midst, their features unflinching.

One of the Council members signals Jakob with a furtive look as he slips his fingers into the trigger housing of his gun. I steal a glance around and realize they're all triggering their weapons. My brain sounds a silent alarm. They have no allegiance to either clone. My pulse thuds in my temples. Do I?

Mason draws his heavy brows together, eyes still glued to Sven. "If you come out with us your sensor will lead Lyong straight to the Council's camp."

The Undergrounders shift nervously. Sven stares Mason down. I can tell by the deep flush slowly seeping down his neck that he has no intention of letting us leave without him.

It's my fault for leading him along. I acted on instinct—telling him he could come—knowing there was no way to circumvent the sensor and bring him out without endangering all of our lives. Maybe it was a selfish desire on my part to keep him with me. It's up to me now to resolve this before we all end up dead.

Eyes planted on Sven, I somehow manage to wiggle the safety selector on my gun to the fire position. I'll shoot him if I have to. But it won't change the fact that someone will have to stay behind. And if Sven dies, that person will be me. I can't ask Mason to make that kind of sacrifice now that he's tasted freedom.

I steal a glance in Jakob's direction. His gun is slung casually over his shoulder, but his finger is locked tight around the trigger. Guilt grips me when I realize he'd sear his conscience to save me. I don't see a good way out of this for anyone.

"De … Derry."

I spin around at Owen's quivering voice. His upper body shudders as he tries to raise himself on his elbows. Tucker hovers anxiously at his side.

I drop to my knees. "Don't get up!"

His eyes roll around in his head before he locks onto my face. I'm shocked by the sunken craters beneath his heavy-lidded eyes—now glistening with an unhealthy sheen. He grabs the collar of my jacket and pulls me to him. When he opens his mouth, he makes that unnerving gurgling sound again. The unmistakable stench of urine fills my nostrils.

Panic floods my brain at the realization that his body is shutting down. I put my hand on his forehead and gasp. He's burning up. I suppress a moan and cradle his head to my chest. He opens his mouth, but then flops unnaturally sideways. His body shudders once more, and then his eyelids flutter closed.

For a long, tortured moment, I think he's gone. Then he twitches in my arms. "Quick!" I gasp. "We have to get him out of here, *now!*" I plead silently with the faces cinched around me.

"What's it gonna be, Sven?" Mason demands.

Sven's eyes dart around the group, and then, ever so slowly, he reaches his right hand into the cargo pocket of his fatigue pants and pulls out a gleaming Schutzmesser. My heart lurches in my chest. He must have taken it from Rummy.

One by one, the Council members train their guns on him.

Sven studies the knife, turning it over several times and testing the tip on his thumb. He steals a glance around, as if contemplating who to take out before someone puts a bullet in him. He slowly curls his left fist into a crunch.

I tense and line up my sight to take a shot. My hand shakes when he raises the steel blade to his right temple. An eerie hush falls over us. Trancelike, he presses the honed tip into his skin in a suicidal salute.

"Nooooooo!" I yell. Tucker springs to his feet, barking in solidarity. I grab him by the collar and hold him back. One slash from a Schutzmesser would silence him forever.

Sven draws a heavy breath, his thick fingers wrapped around the handle of the knife. "Lyong deactivated my authorization code—maybe the retinal sensor is down too."

My jaw goes slack. He can't be serious. I'm trying to remember what Ramesh told me about retinal sensors—something about a neurotoxin being released into the brain if the sensor is tampered with.

"You don't have to do this!" Mason takes a half step toward Sven, gun held high above his head in a good faith gesture. "You can tell Lyong we forced you to help us. You're the best programmer the Craniopolis has. He can't afford to terminate you."

"I want to be free of this place," Sven says, looking straight at me. "With the tracker out, I won't be a liability anymore." He gives Mason a rueful grin. "Then we can draw straws to see who stays."

Mason lunges at him, but before he lands a tackle, Sven lets out a savage roar and twists the blade into his temple. I stare in horror at the dark blood spurting out the side of his head. His eyes flash briefly and then close. The knife slips from his hand and clatters onto the floor.

I wait for what seems like an eternity for him to keel over and erode like a crumbling statue. His massive chest rises and falls a couple of times, but then he sighs and reaches his fingers into the wound in his head. With a deep groan, he pulls something out and drops it into the palm of his left hand.

No one moves. My heart thunders in my chest.

After a few minutes, Sven opens his eyes and slowly stretches out his upturned hand. Jakob and the other Council members exchange uncertain glances, before closing in to take a look. When I catch his eye, Sven breaks away and walks over to me. I stare incredulously at the bloody capsule cradled in his enormous hand.

"You were right," I say, my voice shaking. "The tracker must have been immobilized when they deactivated your code."

Sven presses the sleeve of his shirt against his bleeding temple. "Either that, or the neurotoxin was just a ploy to keep us compliant."

"So now what?" Jakob asks.

Sven levels his eyes at Mason. A satisfied smile flicks across his lips. "Now we find out who stays."

Owen grabs at my arm, his breath rattling in his throat. He strains to lift himself up, and this time I help him into a sitting position, hoping it will ease his breathing.

"Leave *me*." He blinks at me sharply.

"What are you—"

"I'm bleeding out." He cuts me off with a dismissive wave. "Not … gonna make it. I can launch the ship if you … go … now." He falls back against my chest, his lungs wheezing like deflating balloons.

"No!" I shake my head firmly, the tang of tears in my nose. "I won't leave you!"

"Let me … do this." His eyelids hover somewhere between open and closed. "I won't … die in vain."

"One of the clones should stay, this is their world."

"They've earned their freedom."

"Then we'll leave Rummy."

Owen makes an incoherent sound. "He won't … launch you."

"Then *I'll* stay."

Owen's feverish eyes latch onto mine. He grips my face in his hand and squeezes my cheeks in his sweaty fingers. "The Council needs you. Promise me … you'll leave and find a way to shut this hell down."

I forward Jakob a helpless look. He hunkers down beside me and places an arm protectively on mine. "How far is the Council's camp?" I ask, desperation creeping into my voice.

He rubs a hand across his brow. "Once we land the Hovermedes on the other side of the river, it's a day's hike into the mountains."

Owen convulses a couple of times, and I know in my heart the end is near for him. I look up at the circle of eyes looking down at me. My heart screams at me not to give up—to cling to the irrational hope that Owen's going to be all right—that I can still find some way out of this nightmare. I lay his head gently against my pack and drag myself to my feet, the terrifying weight of my decision bearing down on me. My legs tremble beneath me, but I focus on Owen's words: *the Council needs you.*

One by one, the frightened Council members drop their gaze. Somebody has to stay behind, and somebody has to make the decision who that's going to be. Owen grasps the tips of my fingers and gives a feeble squeeze. I flinch, my brain screaming at me to do what my heart won't let me.

"You heard him," I hear myself say through the din inside my skull.

Mason approaches me, his footsteps thudding like a funeral march I set in motion. His eyes bore into mine. "Are you sure about this?"

I glance around again at the scared, young faces of the Council members. I'm sure if I don't do this, everyone here will die in the docking station along with Owen. I look back at my brother, my heart heavy as lead.

Owen's eyes pop open and rest on me. He says nothing, but I can feel him pleading with me through his pain.

I nod grimly at Mason. "Bring him across to the computer station."

Silently, Sven picks the bloody Schutzmesser up off the floor and wipes it on his pants, avoiding eye contact with me.

My brain feels like a freezing fog has moved in and taken over every neural cranny. We finally have a way out of the Craniopolis, but it's not the victory I envisioned. I feel gutted. Like an organ donor's next-of-kin, except Owen isn't even dead, yet.

"Which Hovermedes are we taking?" I ask Sven, brusquely. I wanted him to come, but not in Owen's place. There's nothing about this that feels right.

"Alpha dock. It's flight ready." He motions to the ship nearest us.

I turn to Jakob. "Can you have the Council load up the packs?" I gesture with my thumb at Rummy. "And him."

Jakob nods and then closes a fist around Owen's fingers and squeezes good-bye. Mason scoops Owen up and I hear a faint animal-in-distress howl that cuts off abruptly. The nauseous feeling in my stomach returns. I turn away and busy myself with Owen's pack.

When I've tightened the straps to breaking point, I hand the grimy orange pack off to one of the Council members and watch her disappear inside the Hovermedes with the only piece of my brother I'll take from this place. A sob catches in my throat. When he's gone—I'll be all that's left of the Connollys.

I take a few deep breaths, and then make my way over to the computer terminal.

Owen is slumped in front of the screen, his head awkwardly supported by a rolled up shirt. I watch as Mason ties him loosely to the chair so he doesn't slip to the floor. His eyelids flicker when he hears me approach. I falter, then swallow hard. "It's not too late to change your mind."

He lies motionless, hunched to one side. His skin resembles a purplish moonscape—a sure sign of internal bleeding. I know he can't possibly survive much longer.

I ram my knuckles against my forehead. This isn't right. I can't leave my brother here to die alone. I should just overrule his decision to stay—he's not in his right mind after all. I pace back and forth behind his chair. "He doesn't even have the strength to press the button," I say, turning to Mason.

He frowns. "The man says he can do it—he can do it."

"Owen?" I lean over him. "Can you hear me?"

There's a muffled, high-pitched sound of air being forced between his parted lips. "Tell Nikki …"

I lean in closer so he doesn't have to strain his voice. "What?"

"Tell … Nikki … to love her is to live forever." He presses her crumpled photo into the palm of my hand.

I blink, too late to stop a tear tracking down my cheek.

Owen's frame contorts like he's being pulled by invisible strings.

A sob lodges in my throat. I slip the photo into my pocket and grab his free hand. "Owen, I can't do this. I won't leave you here—"

Suddenly, his chair begins to vibrate and his clammy hand jiggles in mine. At first, I think he's going into cardiac arrest, but then a pneumatic drilling sound fills the room.

Chapter 38

I look across at Mason. *They're coming,* he mouths.

My scalp electrifies. Owen's eyes zigzag past me as he scrapes together another breath. "Go!"

A giant shove from behind sends me flying forward. Panic hits. My legs pump like pistons beneath me, oddly disconnected from my body. Every cell inside me charges, but my brain's not in the loop—I've no idea where I'm going.

Half-blinded by stabbing tears, I slow my pace to get my bearings, and trip over someone's pack. Before I can regain my footing, burly hands lift me off the ground and toss me through an opening in the side of a Hovermedes. I lay blinking in the dim light like a discombobulated sack of cargo while Tucker licks my salty face. A moment later, the metal door of the Hovermedes slides shut with a sickening whoosh.

Somewhere in the midst of my confusion, my instincts trigger.

Owen!

I scramble to my feet and lurch across the ship. With a scream that comes from somewhere deep inside, I fling myself at the sealed door and claw at the solid steel. Jakob tugs repeatedly on my shoulders, but I batter the door undaunted. Faces press in around me, their jaws moving up and down, but I can't make sense of what's being said. Only the pain in my hands feels real. I lift my head and catch the fleeting look of regret in Mason's eyes as his fist swings toward me and everything explodes.

A soft buzzing, like a distant swarm of insects. I swat mindlessly until my brain clears. The murmur of voices washes over me. I turn my head toward the sound and flinch. The entire left side of my skull feels like a cracked leather punching bag. I crinkle my eyes and try to remember what happened, and where I am.

Jakob comes into view and contemplates me for a moment. He edges tentatively closer. "Are you okay?" He tweaks a smile, but his lips sag.

I hesitate before responding. I can tell by the heavy tone of his voice that something terrible has happened, but I can't remember what. I massage my brow gingerly. "My head aches."

A stricken look flits across Jakob's face before he masks it.

"What is it?" I ask, clutching Tucker's fur. A vague feeling of paralyzing anxiety awakens inside me.

"Don't you remember?"

I frown, but before I have a chance to pick through my muddled brain, Tucker jumps up and growls, peering intently at something down the aisle. Mason slams a cartridge into his gun and vaults out of his seat. I pull myself up to get a better look, and realize I'm in a Hovermedes. But we're not moving. I don't understand.

Tucker takes off to the back of the ship, and then pulls up short, barking madly at a section of the undercarriage. Mason drops to a knee beside him and trains his gun on the spot.

There's a scraping sound, then banging.

Without warning, a panel in the floor flips open. Two thin, brown arms rise through the opening like antennae. Sven grabs both wrists in one hand and yanks out a small-framed man in a lab coat. My eyes bulge.

Mason jabs the barrel of his gun in the man's chest. "Who are you?"

The man gives a deep bow, and then pokes his wire-rimmed glasses back up the bridge of his nose. "I am Dr. Won, Chief of Cybernetics. Please, I don't intend to harm. I hide into access compartment."

My head throbs as fragmented bits of information fly through my brain and reassemble themselves.

We escaped the Craniopolis.

The stabbing realization hits my brain like an icepick. I turn and grab hold of Jakob. "Owen?" I whisper, as it all comes rushing back. *The sound of drilling, someone shoving me forward, the door of the Hovermedes closing.*

Jakob clutches me tighter, as if he expects me to bolt for the door.

Instead, I fold into his arms, empty and spent, and stare blankly at the stowaway.

Mason grabs Won by the throat. "I knew I saw a shadow in the docking station. Trying to sabotage our departure I bet."

"No! No! I help! I launch you."

Mason lets out a snort. "We already launched, moron. We've just landed on the other side of the river."

Won's words swim in my brain for a moment. I narrow my eyes at him. "You mean *you launched us*?"

He nods passionately, his miniature spectacles sliding back down his nose. "Yes! Yes! I launch you."

I unwind myself from Jakob and make a beeline across the aisle until I'm standing directly in front of him. "You're lying! My brother launched this ship."

Won shakes his head. "No! He no launch you."

I take a step back, my heartbeat careening out of control. "What are you talking about?"

Won gives an apologetic shrug. "He fall off chair."

My blood chills. I steal a glance at Mason.

He clears his throat. "It's true. I thought we were done for when he toppled over, but then the Hovermedes took off so I figured he'd managed to hit the authorization button before he … died."

My heart races. I stare at Won suspiciously. "How could you have launched us if you were stowed away on the ship?"

Won pats his lab coat pocket. "Remote launch device." Beaming, he reaches into his bulging pocket and pulls out a sleek, black controller.

Sven's eyes grow wide. He snatches it from Won's hands and examines it. "I didn't know this existed."

Won flashes a row of yellow, uneven teeth at him. "Lyong not know either. Private project. Remote device overrides onsite authorization requirement." He beams at us, his eyes wide with expectation. The smile fades from his face when no one speaks.

I use what strength I have left to grab him. My hands tighten like a vice around his scrawny neck. "You stupid idiot! My brother would be here with us now if you'd shown your stinking face in the docking station."

"Let him go, Derry," Mason says. "He's no good to us dead."

I sink down in a nearby seat and bury my head in my hands, reeling from the shocking revelation. I left Owen to die alone for nothing.

Jakob places a hand on my shoulder and squeezes gently. "It's time to go."

I look up and knit my brows together in confusion. "Where to?"

"The Council's camp. We have to hike from here."

Reluctantly, I straighten up, an empty feeling in the pit of my stomach. I don't want to go any farther. I thought I wanted to be a player in the Council, but now I'm not so sure. I'm shaken by the cost of freedom.

Sven strides up into the cockpit and presses a couple of buttons. The side of the Hovermedes eases open, exposing a familiar pine-studded backdrop.

The Council members jump out and set to work unloading the packs. I stick my head out through the door and snatch a breath of the freshest air I've smelled in days. Tucker bounds out past me and rolls around excitedly in a drift of half-mulched pine cones. Despite the throbbing pain in my head, and the hole in my heart, I smile sadly as I climb out after him. I have to keep going. If I give up now, Owen's death will have served no purpose, and the Sweepers will have won.

We waste no time camouflaging the Hovermedes under a tangle of brush and branches. When we're done, we cover our tracks and load up our gear. It's almost light out. Shafts of yellow ooze through the rocky crags of the horizon, a risky time to hike, but, under the circumstances, we're left with no choice.

"What about him?" Sven flicks his chin in Won's direction.

I eye the tiny Chief of Cybernetics with disdain. If he's telling the truth about launching us, we owe him our lives. But, he could also be a monster without a conscience. I don't know why he's really fleeing the Craniopolis.

"Bring him," I say, after a long moment's hesitation. "If nothing else, we might be able to extract some useful information from him."

Sven binds Won's hands and ties him with a line to Rummy's waist. "We have the makings of a chain gang here," he says, with a smirk.

Rummy scowls. I question whether we should take *him* with us any farther. But, it's not like we can release him back into the wild—he's far too dangerous.

In a compromise of sorts with my better judgment, I fall in line directly behind him, so I can have the satisfaction of being the first to shoot if he tries to pull a fast one. Jakob comes up beside me and reaches for my hand. "How are you doing?"

I kick at a pinecone in my path. "It doesn't seem real. I guess it hasn't sunk in yet. I should have stayed with him."

Jakob adjusts the brim of his cap. "It wouldn't have changed anything. And you'd be dead now too, or worse."

I let the impact of his words settle for a moment. The good thing about Jakob is that he never shoves the truth of what he's saying down your throat.

"I wonder why Won left the Craniopolis," I say, eying him from behind.

"My hunch is he's not too fond of Lyong. Rivals, perhaps? Maybe there are more dissenters in the Craniopolis than we realized."

"The deviations—"

Bam! Bam! The crack of a rifle rings out behind us. I tighten my grip on Jakob's hand and we bolt forward like greyhounds out of the starting gate. Together, we dive for cover beneath the heavy brush to the left of the trail. Tucker follows suit and flattens himself beside us. The Council members scatter into the undergrowth and return fire. My mind races feverishly. How did the Sweepers get here so quickly?

Multiple shots follow in rapid succession. I cock my gun and shoot blindly down the trail. Surely Lyong couldn't have penetrated the docking station and tracked us down already. The sickening thought hits me that we might be shooting at Undergrounders. With a Rogue, a Sweeper, and two clones in tow, we probably look like a dangerous alliance bearing down on the Council's camp.

It's chaos for several minutes, and then the volley of gunfire dies away as unexpectedly as it began. Tentatively, I stand and peer out over the brush. My heart trips in my chest.

A few feet down the trail, Mason sinks to his knees and sways forward, a trickle of dark blood seeping from his trembling lips.

"Nooooo!" I vault to my feet and run to him, Tucker barking madly at my side. Mason clutches wildly at the air as if he can't see me. I reach under his arms in a vain attempt to lift him to his feet. Jakob runs up behind me, but even between the two of us, we can't budge him.

"Find Sven," I say, my voice low and urgent.

Jakob hurries off without a word.

Mason gags, and I drop to the ground beside him, my hands slick with the blood oozing from his chest and back. He stretches his right index finger toward me, his eyes commanding an unspoken order.

"No!" I shake my head vehemently. "We don't need it now. We can use Won's remote."

He inhales a choppy breath. "Don't … trust him. Take it." He jabs his finger in my chest.

The color in his face mutes before my eyes. He grabs me by my collar and topples toward me. "*You* have to lead them." The words sputter out like jagged shards of glass.

I stifle a scream. This can't be happening. Not now, not after losing Owen. How can I go on without either of them?

"I need you, Mason. I'm afraid."

"They're all afraid." He clutches his chest with his left hand, and waves his finger at me again. "They need … someone to believe in."

His voice trails off and I hear his breath whistling at the back of his throat.

Shaking, I reach into my pocket and pull out my hunting knife. I grasp his thick finger in my left hand and slice off the tip in one swift movement. Blood sprays the sleeve of my jacket.

Swallowing back the bile in my throat, I extract the metal chip just as Mason collapses on the grassy trail.

"You okay?" A gangly Council member grabs me by the shoulder in passing, throwing a frightened glance at Mason's body.

I nod, distractedly, and swallow the lump in my throat.

"Let's go," she urges.

I stare after her retreating figure. She doesn't care that Mason's dead. But then, why would she? He's just another clone to her. An inferior life form. She's watched dozens of them expire in the past few hours.

I close my fist over the chip and a flurry of white powder trickles through my fingers.

Chapter 39

I glance down at the rigid form at my feet, eyes screwed tight in shrunken sockets, and swallow back a sob. The life recedes from Mason's graying face, faster than sand into a sinkhole. I press my fist to my lips, feel my warm breath grind in and out, knowing that Mason's lungs will never fill with air again.

"He's dead," I whisper woodenly, when Sven comes running up with Jakob.

Sven falls to his knees by Mason's side and rams his hands into his hair. He breathes unevenly, an empty look in his eyes that I fathom only too well. I lay a hand on his shoulder and a powerful tremor goes through him. He turns and crushes me to his chest with one hand, his whole body shaking. I close my eyes and listen to the steady boom of his heartbeat. How can a heart this powerful ever expire?

Tucker gives a forlorn yelp and wedges his way in between us. I lean down and ruffle his neck. "It's all right, boy."

Sven releases me, wipes a sleeve over his eyes.

"He shouldn't have died like this," Jakob says, frowning.

"*No one* should die like this." I kick at a fungi-enameled stump and startle a field mouse out of the rotting wood inside. Mason was a better man than most, and it was only in the last unit of his life that I acknowledged it.

Despite the crushing loss I feel, a strange sense of calm comes over me, as if Mason has somehow reached out and given me a parting gift of his indomitable grit. I won't burrow back down beneath the earth and hide from the Sweepers. I will avenge him. With Sven's help, I'll find a way to free the clones and deviations.

The thudding of running feet catapults me back into action.

"We gotta go," insists the gangly girl who ran by earlier. She twists her lips as if the sight of Mason's body repels her.

Sven stands, his eyes bloodshot. "I'll get the prisoners," he mumbles, before walking off.

I kneel and gather a fistful of powdery ashes from Mason's shrunken corpse, stashing them in a side pouch on my pack. Big Ed says everyone comes into the world with a soul and nobody's proved him wrong yet. When the time is right, I'll give Mason a proper funeral. I only wish I could do the same for Owen.

I dust my hands off on my pants, and then jam my fists guiltily into my pockets. It feels too casual a gesture under the circumstances. "Did you find the shooters?" I ask the girl.

She nods. "One of them's dead. The other one got away."

"Schutz Clones?"

She shakes her head. "All tatted up like that Rogue you dragged out of the Craniopolis."

My brows shoot up. I hadn't even considered the possibility that someone other than Lyong was after us. Unless—

I swallow hard. "Where's the body?"

The girl gestures behind her. "In the brush."

"Come on!" I grab Jakob's hand and make a beeline back down the trail. My legs weave, as if I'm sleepwalking through the trampled undergrowth. But I can't be, because there's an awful buzzing in my head that's getting worse as we approach the body.

Two Council members are already at work piling brush on the remains.

"Wait!" I croak.

They look up, startled.

I grab the branches on top of the body and toss them aside. Tucker jumps in and starts digging—like it's some kind of game.

Jakob yanks on my arm. "Derry! What are you doing?"

I ignore him, scrabbling to clear the leaves and debris from the shooter's face. My breathing quickens when I see the tattoos. My hunch was right.

Sort of.

It's Lipsy.

I stare down at her. Silent and still in her final resting place. Tears prick at my eyes. I never even knew her real name. I wish things could have ended differently for her. She shouldn't be here.

Tucker stops burrowing and sits down quietly on his haunches, as if sensing from my mood that the game has ended.

"You seen her before?" asks one of the Council members.

"Yus." My voice comes out thick, slurred like Da's when he'd been drinking. My thoughts run together in a jumble of rationalizations. It's a good thing Lipsy's dead, isn't it? If she killed Mason, she deserved to die.

Truth is, I wish it were Blade lying here. I know he must have masterminded the attack. Lipsy didn't have enough between her ears to pull it off.

I look up at the sound of someone thrashing through the brush. Sven stomps over to us, Won and Rummy in tow.

Sven stares down at Mason's killer, his face unreadable. "A woman," he says. "Hard to tell at first with all those tattoos."

I bite my lip and throw a glance in Rummy's direction. His eyes bore into me. He shoves Won aside, and peers around Sven at Lipsy's body. A sinister shadow crosses his face. "Where's Blade?" he asks.

Sven frowns. "Who's Blade?"

Rummy wheels around and throws his bound fists in an uppercut punch into Sven's jaw. "Blade's my little brother, you overgrown freak."

My eyes widen. *Brother?*

Sven grabs Rummy's wrists in one hand and raises him several inches off the ground. "I've got news for you, sleazebag. The only freaks here are you and your cohort in the dirt."

I rub my brow, trying to piece it together. It makes sense. The unspoken bond, yet constant rivalry, between them. Blade's desperation to rescue Rummy from the Sweepers. Tattoos aside, they even look similar.

A dreadful thought comes to mind. I turn to Rummy, still dangling from Sven's fist. "Did you know Blade was following us?" I yell at him.

A smile splits his face like I've told a joke. My skin turns clammy and cold. The fleabag could have warned us Blade and Lipsy were tracking us. Mason would still be alive. Rummy owed us as much. We saved his life— but that doesn't mean squat to him. I scrub my hand over my face in desperation. I was a fool to bring him along. I should have left him to his fate in the Craniopolis. A shiver runs down my back. Now I'm going to have to find a way to get rid of him.

"We need to go," Jakob says.

Sven drops Rummy back to the ground and shoves him forward. Won stumbles, half-running after him to keep from falling.

I grab some branches and help the others cover Lipsy's body back up. "Did you get her gun?" I ask, turning to one of the Council members.

He gestures to the rifle propped up against a tree behind us. I glance at it, and then spin back around for another look. A sickening feeling rises up inside me. I trudge over to the tree, my stomach knotting tighter with every step.

I pick the gun up and turn it over—custom stock with a silver stag inlay. I run my fingers slowly over the antique ornament to make sure.

"What is it?" Jakob leans over my arm.

I stare at him, my breath coming in ragged spikes.

His eyes flicker in comprehension.

I hunch forward, bracing myself against a wave of unbearable pain. Blade and Lipsy must have killed Big Ed for this—*with* this.

I force a breath in and out. All this time I had clung to the delirious hope that Big Ed could take care of himself. But, he was an old man after all. Skilled in mountain ways, but no match for desperate Rogues—Blade's been harboring revenge ever since Big Ed ambushed him on the trail to Lewis Falls.

"Sweet piece, isn't it?" the gangly girl says, holding out her hand for the gun. "It came with the Rogue."

I fix her with an accusatory stare. "It belonged to an Undergrounder from our camp."

She looks decidedly uncomfortable. "I guess you can keep it."

"You guess?" I stare at her coldly until she gives a one-shouldered shrug and walks off.

"It doesn't mean he's dead," Jakob says. "If anyone can survive out there, it's Big Ed."

I look away. He's right, only this time I stacked the odds against Big Ed by leaving that dirtbag Blade alive in the bear den. Rage swells inside me. Every time I show the Rogues mercy, it comes back to bite me. Not this time. I call Tucker to heel and swing my pack over my shoulder. "Someone's going to pay for this."

"Wait!" Jakob wrinkles his brow, but before he can stop me, I take off running through the undergrowth. My heart beats wildly, anger rapidly displacing my grief. I'm not sure how, or when, I'm going to avenge Mason's death, but I can start by exacting retribution for Big Ed's.

Chapter 40

I crash through the brush, all my fury focused on the only person I can touch now.

My breath comes in loud rasps, as if someone's kneeling on my ribs. I sniff back tears, nightmarish images flashing through my head—Owen's battered, swollen face in the tent, Rummy's sluggish eyes watching me like a puff adder, Schutzmesser in hand, deliberating. I wish I'd let the Sweepers have him. Written him off as a donation to science—his rightful penance.

I finally spot him up ahead, skulking along behind the others, still tethered to Won. I charge him from behind and tackle him to the ground, battering him in the face with my fists until Sven drags me off him. Rummy rolls around, bloodied and moaning. Won scrambles up to his hands and knees, shaken and disoriented, like a dog confused by its leash.

"What was that for, you little vixen?" Rummy yells, struggling to sit up.

I rub my stinging fists. "Your sleazebag brother killed Big Ed and took his gun."

"I ain't buyin' that," Rummy scowls.

I narrow my eyes at him. "You let Blade kill Mason too, didn't you?"

"I didn't see nuthin'." Rummy feels his way around his jaw gingerly and then gestures to Sven. "How could I? This ape's got me and Buddha-head tied on a four-foot rope like circus animals."

"Right where you belong!" I say, shrugging off Sven's restraining hand. Maybe it was the ape reference, but this time he doesn't try to stop me when I knee Rummy hard in the chest. He recoils and falls backward with a muffled oomph. I kick him in the ribs one more time for good measure and then turn around to the dumbstruck Council members. "What are you looking at?"

The sun's already a dying glow nesting in the distant granite peaks when we finally reach the vicinity of the Council's camp, exhausted, and eager to get below ground before darkness settles over the canyon.

"There's our final marker." Jakob points to an upright arrow carved into a nearby tree trunk. "The Council scouts will pick us up now."

Right on cue, several young men and women slip out from the cover of the forest to guide us to the bunker entrance, expertly concealed beneath a gnarled root system. We exchange a few terse greetings as they open the hatch. I instruct the watch to keep an eye out for Blade and to shoot any Rogues on sight. Under my direction, the Council takes the two prisoners, Won and Rummy, down first.

"Don't untie them, no matter what," I say, Mason's voice echoing in my head.

Jakob ducks beneath the fibrous fingers of the root system next, and Sven follows, wedging his way through with a disgruntled Tucker in his arms. My worn out legs move like concrete posts—I'm hugely relieved we've made it, but sick inside at the horrific losses I haven't fully acknowledged as real. I descend the bunker ladder unsteadily, and freeze when a choked voice wafts up to me.

"Like I said, no better woman for the job."

Woozy and weak, I cling to the ladder and peer down the shaft, swaying precariously. There's only a wink of light to see by. *Am I hearing a ghost?*

I stumble the rest of the way down the ladder and jump off, colliding in the process with a wide flannel chest that smells of wood fire and pine and jerky. I lift my head, scarcely breathing, and look up into Big Ed's rheumy eyes smiling down at me from beneath an unfamiliar hat. He chuckles softly at my flabbergasted expression. Shaking all over, I grasp him in a bear hug. "I thought you were dead!"

He pulls away and gives me a rueful grin. "Might have been, if the Council hadn't found me. I set my pack and gun down by the river after I cut my hand cleaning out a squirrel. Dang knife slipped. Bled like a Billy goat. Next thing I know my gear's gone. Figured it had to be those bozos Blade and Lipsy. Must have been tracking me the whole time. I underestimated them."

"Lipsy's dead," I say.

Big Ed hefts a shaggy brow upward. "What happened?"

"They attacked us on the trail—they killed Mason with your rifle before we took Lipsy out."

He furrows his brow, crinkling the puckered skin around his eyes. "What about Blade?" he asks, his voice hardening.

"He got away."

Big Ed raises the rim of his hat and scratches his forehead, eyes brimming with remorse like he blames himself for Mason's death. I know how he feels.

I brush my sleeve across my moist lashes. "Owen's ... dead too," I say, my lip wobbling uncontrollably.

The lines branching across Big Ed's face deepen into dark crevasses. He stares down at me, his dove-gray eyes widening like search beacons. Only the slight quiver of his sprawling beard betrays his grief.

Wordlessly, he wraps me back up in his arms and crushes me to his chest for the longest time. I close my eyes and lean into the comforting canyon smells clinging to him—even the fish guts are an oddly calming reminder of happier times a few short days ago. I'm grateful not to have to recount the whole excruciating story to him yet.

Inside the main bunker, the Council serves us the first decent meal we've eaten in a week. I devour the rabbit and potato stew, not caring that I'm dripping juice all over myself.

When I've finally eaten my fill, my sanity returns. I glance across the bunker to where Jakob is already curled up on a mat. I need to rest too, but my mind won't let me. I wipe my sleeve across my mouth and take a good look at the faces gathered around. Young, pimply skinned, around my age. Some a few years older. All casting curious glances my way, maybe because I brought the freak show with me.

A short, stocky guy around Owen's age walks over and sits down beside me. "I'm real sorry about your brother. I'm Trout, by the way. It's my last name, but it's what everyone calls me." He sticks out his right hand and I shake it. It's calloused and missing part of a finger. There's any number of ways he could have lost it in this unforgiving existence of ours. Best not to know.

"Who's in charge of the Council?" I ask, by way of conversation.

He raises his brows at me, disconcerted.

"*You?*" I shrug, after an uncomfortable pause.

Trout throws an uncertain glance at Big Ed sitting on the other side of me. "Um, guess you weren't clued in." He hesitates, rubs his jaw distractedly. "Your brother led the Council. He recruited all of us."

I press my lips tight together to seal in my shock. *Of course!* It makes perfect sense. All those overnight trips he went on. *Hunting* trips.

"Owen didn't want you involved." Big Ed's voice is distant, like it's drifting to me in a fog.

"I'm involved now," I say, sharply. "And Owen's gone. So fill me in."

Big Ed gestures for Trout to continue.

"We're all from different bunkers. We set up base here once we discovered the location of the Craniopolis. We've been working for months on a plan to cripple the Sweepers' operation. The idea was to collapse the tunnels in the Craniopolis through a series of timed explosions and force the survivors out." Trout twists his lips in a grimace. "Kind of blew our cover when we went in to rescue you, but your boyfriend wouldn't take no for an answer."

I look over at Jakob, but he's fast asleep and it's Sven I end up trading flushed glances with. I bite my bottom lip and turn my attention back to Trout.

"How did you penetrate the air duct system?" I ask. "I'm guessing you've got someone on the inside."

Trout jerks his chin at Won, staring intently at us from across the room. "He shouldn't be listening to this. We can talk later. I've called a meeting for tonight."

I nod. "You're right. I have a few questions for him now anyway."

Trout signals for me to go ahead.

I get up and walk over to Won who's busy shoveling down food, his plate held tight to his chin.

"We haven't established that you're worth feeding yet," I say, grabbing the plate from him. "Around here you earn your keep."

Trout comes up beside me and folds his arms across his chest. Won's eyes flick to the one-knuckled finger, and then to the floor.

"I help you," he wheedles.

"Tell us about the research you worked on," I say.

Won glances around uneasily. "Is the sovereign leader's brainchild."

"Hogwash!" Trout cuts in.

Won gives an apologetic shrug. "The world government supply brain dead participants. The Craniopolis develop cloning and cybernetics technology."

I think back to the wired cadavers in Sektor Sieben—stock-still like a clip from a silent horror show. An icy shiver cuts down my spine. "The sovereign leader would never have authorized that kind of technology."

Won gives a yellow-toothed grin. "Sovereign leader embrace all technology to neutralize or optimize life. Is necessary for population control."

I gape at him, the bottom dropping out of my stomach. He has to be lying.

Won stares back at me, pupils black and huge in his glistening yellow face.

I blink uncertainly. "How did the government come up with brain-dead participants?"

He looks past me, shifty-eyed. "Come from reeducation centers. Lot of people die there."

"How?" Trout asks.

Won studies him through narrowed slits. "Maybe no food, too many beating, maybe hammer blow on neck." He thumps his fist on the back of his head by way of demonstration.

A horrified look flits across Trout's face. "I thought the subversives were being reeducated in the camps."

Won blinks. "I go many times to select participants. He sniffs and rubs a sleeve across his nose. "Cloning and cybernetics save humankind."

A wave of revulsion washes over me. "I saw what you're doing in Sektor Sieben." I prod Won so hard he's forced to take a steadying step backward. "You're not saving people, you're destroying them."

"You are wrong about that." Won's beady eyes bore into me. "I save your brother."

Chapter 41

A creeping numbness travels up my spine. I hold Won's gaze, repulsed by the thin, sneering lips slick with grease from the meat he was gnawing on a moment earlier. He's twisting the knife, trifling with my pain. *Like he has the power to resurrect Owen.* I jerk back a few steps, my muscles locking. "You're a sick madman!"

Before he can respond Trout takes aim, and lands a punch square in Won's jaw. He folds like an accordion at my feet. A thin ribbon of blood trickles from his left nostril. Trout rubs his knuckles with satisfaction. "Been itching to do that. I'm only sorry he crumpled so quickly."

"Tie him up and get him out of here," I say.

Trout signals to a couple of Council members watching from the sidelines. They whisk Won up by the armpits and drag him out of the bunker.

"What do you think he meant about saving Owen?" Trout looks at me curiously. "I thought he was dead."

"He is," I say, too sharply.

The room falls silent. My brain screams a million thoughts at me. I clench my trembling fingers into fists. It all seems unreal—the kind of heart-stopping nightmare you wake up from, gasping for air, soaked in sweat.

After what Won said, I'm questioning everything. What if I've made a terrible mistake? What if Owen's still breathing when Lyong finds him?

What if they take him to Sektor Sieben and hardwire some kind of circuit board into his brain? I jam my hands into my hair and blow a few listless puffs of air over my face. I'm suddenly burning up in the bunker. I turn around and walk unevenly back to my seat, legs bending like reeds.

Big Ed scratches the back of his neck, throws me an uneasy look. The Council members look at me expectantly, but I avert my gaze and sink back in my chair, undone and disconnecting. I have nothing to offer them. All I ever wanted was the chance to step up and be somebody, but my dream's become my burden. Do they think I can just take over where Owen left off? Lead a teenage flash mob to take on the Schutz Clones.

And now that the Sweepers know we have some kind of resistance movement going, they'll be ready for us when we go back. I groan and bury my face in my hands. *When* we go back. It's like I have a subliminal death wish.

I save your brother. Won's words sear my brain. Even more agonizing because the lie preys on my tattered emotions. There's nothing Won can do that will bring Owen back, but I can't stop speculating about what he meant. I know what Won's idea of saving brain-dead participants entails, and the thought of Owen being subjected to anything like that makes me want to put Won's head on a spike.

I rub my hands vigorously over my face as if to scrub the grisly images of Sektor Sieben from my mind. It may be too late to save Owen, but there are others. I owe it to Maron to try and free the rest of the clones. And then there's the deviations—I felt their silent pleas. The Sweepers have to be stopped.

But how?

I look across the room and catch Rummy's eye. He stares at me, long and hard, before getting up and shuffling toward me, hands bound in front of him.

"What you gonna do, Butterface?" he says, winking at me. "They think you're the alpha dog now your brother's gone." He makes a short, explosive choking sound.

My knuckles sting from the last time I slugged him, but I'm still tempted to take another swing.

I get up and squint into Rummy's inked face. "What exactly do you want from me?" I ask, in a tone designed to convey he's wasting my time. Inwardly, I'm fighting to silence Mason's words that rush back like a call to arms. *They need someone to believe in.*

He sniffs, wipes his nose on his sleeve. "You should go back and rescue your brother."

"My brother's dead."

He drives his dark brows into a harsh 'V.' "You only know what the clone told you."

"Mason had more integrity in one cloned cell than you'll ever have in your ugly skull."

Rummy brushes a finger across the piercing in his chin. "He lied. To protect you, I'll give him that, but he lied all the same."

I eye him skeptically. "What do you mean?"

He leans toward me, spittle vibrating on his bottom lip. "Your brother weren't dead. That sucker tried to inch his way back into the chair after he fell."

I let out a gasp before I catch myself. "You're lying!"

I throw a helpless glance in Big Ed's direction. He bows his head and rubs his hand slowly over his matted hair.

"Why'd you think your clone crony couldn't look you in the eye when you asked him about it?" Rummy asks. "He watched your brother clawing at the chair to get back up, but there weren't nothing he could do about it. Doc Won had already activated the ship."

My mouth goes dry. My mind reaches back, trying to recall Mason's exact words. *He keeled over ... I thought ... I figured ...* A twitch of unease shadows the memory. It's more what he didn't say.

Pain hammers in my eye sockets. "Why are you telling me this now?"

Rummy lowers his voice. "If you're going back to the Craniopolis, you'll need help." He gestures around the room with his bound hands. "These fairies ain't gonna cut it. I'm talking heavies who can take out the Sweepers—men who can slit them devils' throats quicker than they can take a drag on a smoke." He grins at me, as if some unspoken contract has just been signed between us. "You need subversives. And there are plenty of us." He leans in close. "Holed up in the Wilderness of No Return."

I stare at him, incredulous. Does he really think, after everything that's happened between us, I would consider an alliance with subversives, with *him*? I thrust my hands deep in my pockets. "We don't need your type to help. The Council infiltrated the Craniopolis once, we can do it again."

"Is he bothering you?" Sven asks, appearing at my side.

I shake my head, my heart racing.

Rummy scratches at his jaw for a moment. "I don't know what you think our type is, but some of us got a bum rap from the get go. Maybe we're looking for another chance too. But there ain't nobody getting a second shot at nothin' long as them mad scientists are on the planet." He jerks his chin at Sven. "Them freaks want out too. They could help us."

Big Ed glances up, his white brows tenting his eyes like a layer of frost. For some reason, I think of the axe incident. Maybe Rummy's got a point about second chances. Who am I to judge who gets to start over in this balled-up mess?

"The Rogues was thinkin' all along it was Undergrounders selling them out to the Sweepers." Rummy cracks his jaw. "I can set 'em straight."

"So what are you proposing?" Sven interjects.

Rummy straightens up and begins talking rapidly. "Way I see it, we got ourselves a common enemy." He fixes me with a piercing stare. "I know how much you hate them Sweepers. I can see it in your eyes."

My cheeks flush. I don't like that a dirt bag like him sees straight through to the darkness inside my own heart. I'm no better than him, full of anger and hungry for revenge. I look away, uncomfortable beneath his penetrating gaze. The room ripples with static murmuring. Council members shift in their seats, watching me for some reaction.

Sweat beads across my forehead. If we join forces with the Rogues, and the rest of the subversives, we may have a fighting chance of defeating Lyong and ending the Sweepers' reign of terror. I only wish there were a better option than throwing in our lot with a pack of thugs.

Big Ed gets up and peers at me over his glasses. "It's your brother back there. This is your decision to make."

I shake my head. "The Rogues will massacre everyone in the Craniopolis, even the innocent." I rub my skinned knuckles distractedly. "I can't okay that kind of killing. No one can."

"And if we do nothing?" Sven asks. His amber eyes search out mine. "What does that say about the lives we leave behind?"

In the silence that follows, I realize that to turn back now would be unconscionable—to sanction a worse kind of killing, the systematic annihilation of everything it means to be human. Fear grips me when I think of the fight that lies ahead, a fight I know deep down I have to finish. "You're right," I say. "We owe it to Owen and Mason to stop the Sweepers, or die trying." I look Rummy in the eyes. "We'll take whoever wants to fight with us."

Dusk falls and tempers flare as the Council kicks around Rummy's offer to recruit the subversives. Trout favors the idea, but not all the Council members agree. What's worse, Jakob's dead set against it.

"I don't trust them," he says, "and we don't need them."

"We can't destroy the Sweepers without their help," I say.

Jakob takes my hands in his, his eyes wide and pleading. "It could be a trap. You know Rummy wants revenge."

I blink unhappily. "It's a chance we'll have to take. I have to believe he wants to stop the Sweepers as much we do."

Jakob lets out an exasperated sigh. "He's a subversive from a reeducation center, not your new best friend. You can't trust him."

He looks at me, rattled—heaving breaths in and out. "Even if Trout's too stupid to listen to reason, I won't let you lead the rest of the Council into a trap."

"It's their decision to vote on."

He stiffens, eyes glittering like lights on dark, unsettled water. "Yes, it is." The look he gives me is unmistakable: *if you leave, you leave without me.*

By the time the vote gets underway, it's clear Jakob's not alone. Half the Council's convinced Rummy's out for revenge and looking for an easy way to pick us off. The other half, including Sven, is keen to strike at the Craniopolis before the Sweepers can regroup—not bothered what scum they enlist to help.

Big Ed abstains from voting, mainly because we've agreed he'll stay behind to manage the base. I don't tell him Trout isn't willing to drag an old man along, or that my reason for leaving him behind is utterly selfish. I want him to keep an eye on Jakob. I know Jakob won't change his mind about coming, and it's probably for the best. I can't trust him to pull the trigger if it comes down to it.

When the votes are in, it's so close we do a recount to be sure. Seventeen against the alliance, eighteen in favor. We glance around the room at each other warily, weighing the evidence in each other's faces.

Jakob hunches inside himself, like a muted still life portrait. Sven stares fixedly at a spot on the floor in front of him, arms locked across his chest. There's a strange air in the room, a division of brothers, the hint of a serpent among us. I wonder if it would have been better for all of them if I'd never come here.

"Pack up your gear if you're coming," I say. "Only those who voted *yes* are bound to go."

Big Ed rises heavily to his feet. "That's it, then. Will you be leaving the dog?"

My chest tightens like he's hit me with a sledgehammer.

The crepe-like skin around his eyes fans into a smile. "Let me guess. He voted *yes.*"

I steal a glance at Tucker curled up asleep against Sven's chest—dogcatcher turned nap snatcher overnight. "Yeah, he's discovered he has a thing for clones after all." *Maybe we both do.*

Big Ed chuckles. "Guess they really do have a scent then."

I lay a hand on his arm. "Jakob—" I begin, telepathically willing him to understand what I'm about to ask.

He turns back to me, a bemused look in his eyes. "You're taking the dog and leaving the boy?"

"Not by choice. You heard him."

Big Ed pulls at his beard. "You have my word nothing will happen to him, just like I have Sven's word that nothing will happen to you."

I give him a nod of thanks. My head's spinning so fast it feels like it might gyrate right off my body. Maybe this isn't really happening. None of it—the stupid vote—the decision to throw down the gauntlet that's divided the Council and driven a cosmic-sized wedge between Jakob and me—left me in the protective custody of a clone who stirs up something inside me I've yet to unravel.

Big Ed grips my shoulders and stares into my eyes like he's searching for something. "Godspeed," he says, his voice husky with emotion.

I give him an awkward grin. How fast would that be exactly? Speed of light? Right now, I'd rather make time stand still. So I never have to return to the Craniopolis and face my demons.

Big Ed claps me on the back, then turns away, his eyes moist beneath the rim of his hat.

I watch him ruffle the fur on Tucker's neck with his stocky fingers and then lumber over to the ladder that leads to the main tunnel.

My heart beats in short, ragged bursts. We leave tomorrow night at midnight. Only half the Council is with us—but I can hope for Godspeed. After all, the sun still rises.

END OF BOOK ONE

If you enjoyed the book I would REALLY appreciate a short review. Your help in spreading the word is invaluable. Your review makes a BIG difference in helping new readers find the series, and that makes it possible for me to keep writing stories. **THANK YOU!**

Join my **VIP READER CLUB** and be the first to know about new releases, exclusive pro-motions, behind the scenes and giveaways!

http://eepurl.com/bGSLlb

Visit below to download a free map of the underground bunker system Derry shares with the other Undergrounders.

http://normahinkens.com/downloadable-bunker-pdf/

Connect with me on Facebook, and LIKE my page for giveaways, cool stuff & more!

https://www.facebook.com/NormaHinkensAuthor/

<<<<>>>>